The City of Yes

THE CITY OF YES

PETER OLIVA

M&S

CANADIAN CATALOGUING IN PUBLICATION DATA

Oliva, Peter, 1964-
The city of Yes

ISBN 0-7710-6861-1

I. Title.

PS8579.L325C57   1999   C813'.54   C98-933012-5
PR9199.3.O44C57 1999

We acknowledge the financial support of the Government of Canada
through the Book Publishing Industry Development Program for our
publishing activities. We further acknowledge the support
of the Canada Council for the Arts and the Ontario Arts
Council for our publishing program.

Typeset in Aldus by M&S, Toronto
Printed and bound in Canada

McClelland & Stewart Inc.
The Canadian Publishers
481 University Avenue
Toronto, Ontario
M5G 2E9

2 3 4 5   03 02 01 00 99

for N.O., with love

Lunar moths who know there are 28 ways
to enter the ancient battlefield of night.
Why is the night female? Because orchids are dying.
And because, my love, their strange flight . . .

— John Minczeski, "Orchid Flight"

It was a city at the end of its tether.

— Bruce Chatwin, *Utz*

Prologue to flight

When crows become too old, or too fat and lazy to fly away from soybean fields, they are fashioned into lacquer brushes. The lucky ones are ground into charcoal cakes, mixed with water, then brushed into written words. The ink is silent, low in static, and distilled to resemble a pool of black cormorant feathers. But if these birds are to glimpse immortality, they will become dark streams of calligraphy, tributaries of words that pour down paper scrolls, opaque screens, and mulberry walls. They are happiest when they splash through windowpanes, for the glass in this place is also made from paper.

A book's pages are usually doubled – all the better to support a bird's flight – and each sheet is made by screening a cloth-covered frame through milk, rice, straw, bits of bone, roots, and water. A common sight in Japan: cormorants, spread out across a paper sky, leaning into the fibres as though bracing for wind.

And the words themselves? The stories that follow?

When narrative begins, a story takes to the air in a cataclysm of winged intent. Whatever the tale, meaning chases the birds' flight, as though the crows and cormorants have just glimpsed a haiku's trajectory. A story unravels, or pours, or drifts toward one outcome or another. And the birds try to outwit the ending – that moment of death, sudden closure.

You see, on the page, stories are frivolous collisions that place image just before idea. As if to compose a thought, the poet must first build a city. A context is given: the day, a shaft of light that gouges the earth. A hole in the ground that soon widens into a subway. And by the third line, an idea emerges like a tired salaryman. To fully understand this place the salaryman must piece the city's architecture together one journey at a time, commuting from one stop to the next, until he finally contains the whole city in his head. Like a novel.

Each day the salaryman steps into the gush of streetcar steam and momentum, letting the crowd pull him out, toward the city and toward the light of day. A fistful of paper flutters in his hand.

Wild geese

Balloons from Japan

Fade to black

He was busy falling into the sea. His head fell back. His eyes – unhinged by the sea's movement, by the moving pendulum beneath his boat – searched the sky for some solid anchor, something steady to consider. And as his boat was overturning the sailor noticed – in the detached way that someone in immediate danger can notice such a detail – that the sky was perfectly clear.

Above him, a brown fleck appeared from the west. A colour that soon spread into three, then five, then seven dull smudges. *The bellies of wild geese*. He looked at the birds and suddenly imagined the sea's reflection against the sky. The world seemed newly tied together, sky and sea, each one a mirror image of the other. And in that long (impossibly long) moment, as his feet and knees and stomach submerged into the dark strait, he looked up at the sky – at the geese – and watched the bottom of his boat overturning in broad daylight.

The current was cold. It dragged through the sailor's clothes and made him shiver. He seemed to wake to the moment, recognizing his own body's shocked imperative. He scissored his feet, struggling to stay both warm and close to his fallen boat. Felt a surge of blood in his limbs. His fingers spread wide, grasping for something as tangible as hope.

He remembered the whaler. Perched in the rigging, he once watched Japan fifty miles in the distance. Now, moving against the slosh of waves and his own boat's path, the country seemed to have sailed her own course and clean disappeared. From the sea his horizon was a mere mile away. He rolled across waves and open water, imagining the height that he would need to see the country in its proper size. One hundred feet, he thought. With one hundred feet and a spyglass he'd be looking down at breakfast . . .

And in the next second he remembered similar journeys, groaning passages through winters of unexampled severity. The flash of horizontal snow and the speed of wind that had always carried him forward. Ironic that through those dead winters he had always imagined a spring flood, his canoe's sharp passage through dallies, rapids, chutes, and cataracts on the Columbia River. Maelstrom eddies. The chronic hostility of weather that could sometimes pick him up and buoy him through the worst of it. Was it impossible that he had imagined water to carry himself through snow?

Inside dozens of notebooks he spoke barely to the conditions of the moment. A hurried hand bounded ahead of a storm that was always at its worst, just a page behind. Written wholly in pencil, three-fourths of his entries were usually written outdoors, without the extravagance of liquid ink. Yet within two thousand miles of winter (and imagined water), he had never sketched a likeness of fear. He kept to comings and goings, the stories of old painters who met young porcupines. A mail route that was slower than laying newsprint.

His pencilled travels were not precise, but they were dream-inspired. He might list a train of conjectures about wandering freedom or the wild strain of blood that drove his imaginings. Campfire idleness and daguerreotype decisions coloured the world either black or white in his mind. Then he would return to matters of more import. We arrived in Fort Calgary, he wrote, and found nothing but Viking bones littering the riverbeds. Smashed a dinosaur pelvis digging the new well. What a howler that the scientists were digging into the wrong spot.

Later, time blurred these thoughts into shades of grey, until they became remembrances that were neither good nor bad, but simply past.

Walking to Fort Edmonton, in the knot of winter, he used to focus on the closing pages of his imagined journals. The trip seemed shorter if he could conceive the ending. If he could read the final pages by squinting his eyes into that biting white. He saw himself enter some lofty palisade, a log stockade that promised flannel sheets and the warmth of all safe places. He imagined the dream that approached, like a letter that bore good news. Like a gelding moth that pranced above his head.

The wind would die and the snow would furl without sound. Thin shapes might appear beside him, not to surprise but to choreograph his steps through some warm, discernible dream. They helped him to walk through this cold and through the more difficult, hurried part of his journal. He could imagine his escape from the storm and he could tell himself this story, over and over, until it rang true.

Near the ragged edge of Japan he scissored his feet to stay above water. He walked through the cold Tsugaru Straits, imagining the end of his travels. In the waves he met blue sailors – velella jellyfish – that sailed past him with their small, triangular sails. When he tired, he climbed into his own boat, shook the water from his joints. Waited for the next wave to scupper his thoughts. And then, to begin his story – and a fresh notebook – he capsized again.

In the winter of 1993 – while employed by a local gym to erase squash-ball marks from the corners of four square walls, day after day – I decided to put my English degree to better use and find some kind of work abroad. I told myself that I'd grown tired of editing squash players with big white erasers. The yen was riding high and Japan seemed like a logical place to look for a job, perhaps teaching English.

This was about the same time that Canada had finally acknowledged its horrible treatment of prisoners of war and Japan was investigating its own shameful wont for Korean comfort-women. An embarrassment of wartime acknowledgements, declassified secrets, and official disinformation seemed to be running naked through the media. And among all the scraps of belated governmental news reports, I read that twenty Japanese balloons had passed over our house, in 1945, on their way east through the Crowsnest Pass.

The balloons measured five metres in diameter and were made of coated mulberry paper and silk. Each one carried forty-five kilograms of explosives. As slow as Degas ballerinas, they whirled across the Pacific Ocean on high-altitude air currents, dropping small bags of sand if their internal barometers indicated that they were drifting too low. In all, ten thousand pastel balloons were fashioned between 1944 and 1945. The weight of the atmosphere pushed them up, through the clouds, and the balloons pirouetted toward America.

When I first read this article, I imagined a warehouse full of Japanese women urging miles of silk through black sewing machines. An assembly line in some nondescript building, a factory that carefully boxed the empty gowns and then railed them to the coast. The balloons were then unpacked, unscrolled, and carefully filled with hydrogen. The women would have released them like pigeons when the wind was blowing east, waited out those days when the wind was ill-fated toward China. Perhaps they watched the balloons until they disappeared into the sky. The Pacific winds carried them so far east that they finally landed in the Far West.

Cloud-weary, the balloons fell to the ground and the fires began.

Whatever my own romantic conjectures, the scientists and factory workers had no idea that most of their balloons actually fell into the ocean. As for the other balloons that made it to America, I already knew that they discharged grains of sand over the Canadian Rockies. My father told me that the chinook winds were their high-altitude conduits, swinging them up along the

Pacific Coast, into Oregon, north over Washington then east into Alberta. He said that one balloon dropped as it was intended – on a beach in Florence, Oregon – killing a woman and five children when they bent down to touch it. Another exploded a sheep herder's hut southwest of Medicine Hat in March 1945. Another drifted over Lethbridge and was shot down between Enchant and Vauxhall by some overeager duck hunters. And a farmer who lived southeast of Pincher Creek found one tripping his cattle. Thinking it was a weather balloon, he put the odd device in the back of his truck and brought it to the RCMP two weeks later. The police bought his silence with a stern warning from the American Department of National Defense and the discovery was officially suppressed, then officially forgotten by anyone who mattered.

This farmer, however, was concerned about other people stumbling on the bombs.

So, on the weekend that the RCMP confiscated his "official weather balloon" he wondered – aloud – whether some warning could be given to people who made a habit of being outdoors.

"Maybe we should let the posties know about the balloons," he said.

"You might as well tell the whole world," said the police. "Once those gossipmongers learn the truth, everyone in the Crowsnest Pass will know about the Japanese."

And Japan – a secret that prattles through a small town, talking to everyone – entered my father's vocabulary. The entire country, a hometown whisper. In 1945 my father was nine and the world seemed large enough without Japan in his vocabulary.

Suddenly there was a new reason to watch the sky, a new place to fear, and a new country that seemed dangerously close.

To my ear, Japan was an entirely different word. I wanted to leave Canada, to break out of my cramped status quo, and the Orient seemed like the farthest place on earth that I could imagine. They needed English teachers, I'd heard. They paid well. So I wrote to thirty schools and heard back from two. Their postmarks were illegible, but the stamps were in English and celebrated International Letter Writing Week and the Bear's plain: the province – or prefecture – of Saitama.

"Our Deer Colleague!" began one letter. I took the typo and the exclamation mark to be good signs and tore open the other letter. "We are sorry distinguished English Instructor. And we are very sorry to hear from you . . ."

My decision seemed easy. A one-year appointment, a fixed salary, travel and housing arrangements provided: it all sounded a bit too good. From researching job advertisements at the university I knew that there were other places than Saitama to look for work. One newspaper listed a remote village in Chibu – faced with a dwindling population – that was offering free cattle and fishing boats to new residents. I didn't know whether this invitation was open to foreigners (without work visas), but I imagined that their boats were little more than rafts. And I wanted to be as far away from cattle as I could possibly get.

Every other job listing in Japan seemed tied to a major city, swarming with neon promises and fast-food English. Cities where English reigned in McDonald's and Taco Bell, and where computer guidebook translation could be termed the Foreigner's Only Art. Cities where – I'd heard – foreigners were a general source of disdain for other foreigners.

It seemed a popular conception. The traveller desires, above all else, the chance to see and hoard Japan for himself, as if he could wrap the Orient up inside a *bento* lunch box and bring it home to eat in small, exotic portions. Of course, this is the mythical Asian Discovery, and the reason I was ready to avert my eyes whenever I caught sight of another *gaijin* – foreigner – in a crowded subway. I believed in the unwritten code of behaviour never to betray another traveller's fantasy.

And I must have subscribed to my own set of traveller's delusions because I decided to skip the politics of sight and being seen or unseen, and chose Saitama prefecture as my best escape route from the modern world. I was thrilled that no map listed my town's name. In fact, the largest city was a half-hour away, by bus. I was to live in a nondescript suburb of Kumagaya city, completely surrounded by ricefields. Tokyo was a day trip away. The blue mountains of Chichibu were within sight, and at least one school presumably needed English teachers in an area that was famous for its mushrooms, its bone-dry riverbeds, and its distant, mountainside retreats.

In one guidebook I read that Chichibu's only blemish was a partial mountain that hovered above the town. Next to an article on Buddhist pilgrimages, listing temples 26 through 34, I found a photograph: one side of Chichibu's mountain was pared down to the shape of an upright apple core. In another book I learned that concrete was Japan's only natural resource,

Chichibu being one of two places in Japan that could (and did) cement the entire country. From what I could see in the photographs of Tokyo, and the rest of Japan, this national project was already close to completion.

My ticket was round-trip to Japan, by way of England. I had planned a short holiday before my work contract began. I'd found a cheap London flight and a bucket-seat sale that freighted passengers to Japan on Russian cargo planes.

Aeroflot: I'd heard the stories but booked a ticket anyway. Walking to my seat, in the dim, energy-deficient cabin, I saw no space-saving aluminum shelving units, no plastic cups. It was all wooden crates and bulletproof-glass bottles of orange juice and vodka. Most of the bottles were empties, destined for a Kremlin refund. These Russians were cost-conscious. I could see them – the attendants, their sexless shadows – lumbering down the aisle swinging wooden crates from one shoulder down to the floor, arms so long they managed this feat without bending over.

Our passenger seats began to rattle as soon as the pilot opened the plane's hydraulic wing flaps. *Tock, tock, tock*, the metal flaps strained against their casings and I assumed he was testing the plane, but it was as if his elbow had fallen asleep on the controls of his rear-view mirror.

Something wet slapped the hand I had resting on my stomach. I reached up for the chair light and I could see – quite clearly – a strip of eggplant hanging off my forefinger. And despite the chaos, despite the chicken crates and the eggplant, I couldn't help staring across the aisle at a large man, already asleep, his huge face yawning, threatening to swallow the whole cabin as he sucked in the air in great slurps, spittle running out at the side of his mouth. I could see a gill, just under the third fold of his neck. I wiped my hand on the back of the seat in front of me and watched this man for the entire length of the tarmac. The only other possible villain was my neighbour, in the seat next to mine: a surprisingly thin man with beady eyes and long, thin fingers.

I contemplated these fingers. I contemplated their length and the advantage he clearly possessed for flinging eggplants or whole vegetable gardens impossible distances. Then the plane stopped and we were back, at Heathrow, ten minutes into our journey. After one false start the bunch of us were waiting for an air-traffic controller to give us the go-ahead.

The man with the fingers introduced himself. He was an Italian director. His name was Claudio Crespi and his next film was to be called *Escape from Ascoli*. Almost immediately Crespi reached for the briefcase between his legs. The fingers emerged with a folder and the storyboards for the first seven minutes of his film.

"A storm enters," said Crespi, waving the folder across the plane's cabin. "The film – it is a mystery – begins with a ghost! *Un fantasma.*"

I looked at the storyboards. Each page held nine boxed comics. I saw a flourish of pencilled swirls, an exaggerated arrow that signified a close-up, and a character's grimace of surprise. A storm raged for several pages, then the shadows began to take form, and finally . . .

I dropped the storyboards to my lap when Crespi began describing the film's story, what was real and what was not. His film seemed only slightly more fantastic than flying Aeroflot.

We were, at that moment, still grounded at Heathrow. The plane's side door was open for an intolerably long time. And a thick Russian accent informed us that there were "small problems with aerodyne front-tire rotation, but is no problem. Aeroflot technicians are fixing your flight for safe and pleasurable journey."

I was determined not to worry about the wheels but I was a little concerned about the fat man sleeping next to me. A medium-sized oyster was threatening to slide down the corner of his gaping mouth.

Then the cabin door closed and the evening disappeared. I opened *Escape from Ascoli* and began to read . . .

A fizzing noise made Crespi jump. He wagged his head and looked out every nearby window. Behind him, a stewardess appeared with a bottle of mineral water. When she offered Crespi and me a drink, he relaxed back into his seat.

"I don't think I'd go to Japan," he said, suddenly wistful. "This is a well-known fact: the ghosts in Japan have no feet. I'd spend half my time in the editing rooms airbrushing toes or looking at my horror scenes on the cutting-room floor."

Crespi stared at his storyboards, still in my hands, so I went back to them. For some minutes this image of ghosts without feet, this bizarre fork in his story, stayed with me long after I turned the page and, finally, looked up.

After a series of false starts we were moving fast down the tarmac. The plane seemed to find every bump in the runway, veering slightly from side to side. The wings bounced up and down as though the plane was hitting shovels of wind. Crosscurrents slapped the plane's steel wings, denting our progress.

That's when I looked back from the window and focused on the inside of the plane. I looked to my left to see Crespi, beside me. A nervous grin on his face. To my right, the fat man wrapping his large lips around the seat in front of him. Crespi's thin fingers, sharpening themselves around a long, whetted thumb. And finally I noticed the butterfly.

Still at Heathrow, the plane was attempting to rattle down the tarmac and already the cabin pressure began to change, in part because the fat man was sucking out the cabin's air. I could tell that we were still on the tarmac by the roar under my feet.

Against this momentum a butterfly was whirling above some children four rows ahead of me. The children tried to catch the insect with wild, cruel hands but – thankfully – they were belted in their seats, too far away from the butterfly's path. I was bolted in, too, but felt the insect's pull. It was small, with yellow and brown pools (owl's eyes) centred on its hind wings. The forewings rose as sharp as ears, so that the whole effect – the eyes, the ears, the dark outer margins of the wings – made the butterfly look like a bird's head or a cat in the dim light. A nocturnal camouflage that was more convincing than reality.

A woman up front stretched for the butterfly, without success. The butterfly was too erratic and the movement of the plane, struggling for flight, jostled the woman's arm. As the butterfly moved up and down the aisle searching for light, a few passengers managed a swing, missed by inches, and lost the insect as it fluttered behind their seats, tempting new passengers.

Crespi, wide-eyed with fear, put his hands together and began to pray for the butterfly.

"*Madonna mia,*" he said to himself, "don't let them catch it."
Then to me, "Butterflies are lucky, aren't they? The Lady Maria
protects butterflies and ladybugs. *Tutto due.* Butterflies are like
dolphins – they must be – and if it is bad luck for a sailor to kill
a dolphin, it must be just as bad to kill butterflies in airplanes!"

"Don't worry," I said. "This can't be the first time they've
harboured stowaway insects."

"You're right," he said, "maybe they all go down. Maybe
every plane that confines a butterfly goes down. Do you know
how many butterflies are in Bermuda? The triangle is *full* of
them!"

"But we are in London."

I tried to convince Crespi that the insect was actually following its natural migratory path, but I had no idea how a
butterfly could make the journey to Moscow, then touch down
and refuel in Japan. Against all the laws of physics our medieval
plane was struggling for speed, for air, for flight, and Crespi was
determined to link us to the butterfly's own fated existence.

"Butterflies are dolphins!" he called out, his voice rising
above the clatter of bottles and warped steel.

The plane seemed to be rattling toward something monu-
mental or turning itself into a squeaky mattress on wheels.
Crespi's voice was lost as the sound of our chair hinges rose from
our feet to our ears. Three oxygen cups fell from the bulkhead
and whirred a high-pitched complaint. Crespi grabbed for a laminated card in the pocket in front of him and read the top line
from Aeroflot's Emergency Procedures: "If you cannot read this
card please inform flight attendant."

I almost laughed but these words had a calming effect on him. Resigned to his future, Crespi finally sat back in his seat. "Everything is fate," he said, shaking his head. "Nothing happens in this world without a reason. You'll see. History is a wheel. History is our front-tire rotation."

I nodded and looked down at his storyboards to see the words "Down, Pan right." I looked to my right and down. The window was busy proving the world was falling away. Up again, I saw the butterfly disappearing near the cabin lights above our heads. Beside me, across the aisle, the fat man was still snoring through increasing levels of altitude, the cabin regaining air pressure so the man sucked still more air into his throat and lungs, into his heaving chest. And then I saw the butterfly again, hovering for a second above this man's huge, swollen face. The air currents rushing into the man's throat seemed to bring the butterfly closer – just slightly – to his mouth.

High above London, the yellow butterfly moved close to a gaping chasm within a metal-alloy airplane. To stall the inevitable, I looked down at the earth that was disappearing under my feet. I felt the tail of the plane slide back and forth, as if we were settling into an enormous armchair. We passed through a thin carpet of English cloud and then I lost the ground completely. The plane levelled out in the sky. And when I looked back at the fat man, I was surprised to see that he was suddenly awake – breathing regularly and rubbing his thick eyes. He swallowed – as anyone might have done before a morning stretch. Then he cleared his throat, swallowed again, and looked at Crespi with a suspicious eye.

I shut my eyes then, the words "Fade to Black" written in the margins of my sight. Resigned to our collective fate, I pushed my seat back and felt the plane's forward momentum begin to wane. Gravity returned to normal. And the butterfly, I told myself, escaped.

Salaryman & salt

Elevator ascent

Handkerchief, moon, weep

Alien Registration procedures

My plane was thirty minutes late arriving in Japan. Butterflies, Russians, and all, we touched down – unscathed – on a windswept morning in late November 1993.

I was pleased with the bad weather – happy to be out of the plane and closer to the outside world. So I followed the other passengers through the airport and glanced at the airport's windows, at the sky, for seven revolutions of our bags. I was watching a series of grey, fist-like clouds that threatened snow. The clouds were large and bruised, as if drawn from the storyboards of Crespi's next feature film.

My own baggage was late, then pronounced missing by the airport officials, so I cleared customs and looked for the school's driver (who was scheduled to meet me). I was relieved to find him standing in the airport lobby. I noticed him immediately because he was quite tall and because my name was written on the cardboard sign that dangled from his left hand.

I coughed and pointed to the sign. He smiled. My job was waiting for me, he said, "and already there is teaching tomorrow."

The road to Saitama – I barely remember it – simply blurred me from the airport, through Niigata, Tokyo, and past Kumagaya. There were no visible breaks between cities or towns, only perpetual "outskirts," a relentless suburb that throbbed on and on toward a town that was just on the edge of nowhere. For two or three hours I watched the buildings, gas stations, and sexy, incomprehensible billboards hug our path. And then – as the clouds had promised – a light snow lit the sky just as we arrived.

My driver's name was Hideo Endo. He looked about fifty years old. He was so tall that his head touched the roof of the car. He was also painfully thin, with a long, smiling face that supported a pair of black-rimmed, bottle-thick glasses. His cheeks were scarred with pocks and slightly indented, making him look all the more malnourished.

He told me that he was the English grammar teacher at our school. His job was to augment my lessons in Conversational English, he said, and explain the structure of the language to our students in Japanese. I would be teaching alone for these private-school classes, but three days a week I would be "rented out" to the public schools, for "native teaching exercises."

There was one other foreign teacher at our school. She was scheduled to arrive sometime after Christmas. As for the other staff, Mr. Endo kept referring to someone named *Shacho*. And though I didn't know the direct translation of this word I slowly realized that it applied to our Japanese boss: the president of our "five-salaryman company."

"Sa-ra-ri-man," Hideo Endo said, "is from the word *salt*." He'd looked it up. "We are paid in sodium chloride, then jarred and pickled for the company's winter season." He shrugged, as if to say, *What else can be done?* At least I think he shrugged. His gestures were so tightly controlled that it occurred to me that he might have shivered or flinched, just a little. Then he said that Shacho was to be addressed formally at all times. This was rule number one. He said there was a sign, written in English, on the outside of Shacho's office that simply and succinctly defined this invisible man as "The President."

Endo smiled. He seemed to sense the mood in the car had somehow changed, and that the dark clouds outside had worked their way into our conversation. He compensated for this lull by raising his voice and shouting out the window.

"But we are salarymen," he said, "from the salt!"

Hideo Endo was born in Hakodate, a city in northern Japan that was built on a slim Hokkaido peninsula. The city actually pointed toward the main island, Honshu, like a toenail snagged on the sea. Because the city was held by water on three sides it often flooded, and fish could be seen in the gutters, wildly flapping from one coast to the other. The mountains of ancient Yesso were farther north and capped with snow most of the year. Civilization and the provincial capital of Sapporo (with its subterranean shopping malls) were just far enough away that Hakodate remained something more private than a seaside resort.

It was also a city that escaped most of the war, being too far from the railroads or major industrialization to be considered a suitable target. A city that had always kept a healthy show of dignity for visitors, a pleasant façade that was like a mask or mirror, while some flash of life swam beneath the surface.

Just before his father went to war, on September 25, 1942,

Hideo tumbled into this city, as if over a cliff. Hideo's mother was dizzy with pain and the boy was as blue as a carp. His father clapped his hands and Hideo fell into his arms gripping the umbilical cord with both tiny fists. The doctor – a man with terribly long nails – said that he'd never seen such a small trawl. But Hideo held on to the rope and the doctor had to uncoil the boy's small fists, one blue finger at a time.

"He's a strong one," said the doctor. "But I can't decide if he's trying to return or if he's fighting the line that's pulling him back in." It was unclear if the doctor meant a fishing line or a genealogical line, but Hideo's father didn't respond. He'd hardly heard the joke. Instead, he watched the doctor use his nails to pry open Hideo's fingers. And as the doctor worked, some flush of life seemed to glow within the boy's skin; blood circulated to his limbs, filling his blue fingers with colour, until they looked like mandarin orange segments in the doctor's large, fastidious claws.

Mister Endo saw Hideo only once during the war, and he missed seeing his son grow from the fish he remembered into the serious little boy he would become. His station, in Saitama, was nowhere near the sea and even farther away from their home in Hokkaido. Saitama prefecture was also known as *dai-Saitama*, a big-city slur that connotes "the sticks" or "the boondocks" to the Tokyo ear. The word made Mister Endo wince, even after the war ended. For him, the province was populated with *beddo* towns, each one a long two-hour commute from Tokyo. Saitama was simply a place to sleep and to house a family. It was also a factory-ridden prefecture; Saitama's uninspiring plains were the natural choice for Japan to manufacture and test its first airplanes.

Here, in 1894, an inventor named Chuhachi Ninomiya had experimented with a flying machine almost a decade before the Wright brothers pioneered their first motor-powered flight in 1903. While the rest of the world realized flight and while Elisha Graves Otis watched his vertical railcar go up and down (three storeys in less than a minute), Ninomiya's plane hung motionless in a display case, as if waiting for wind. Finally, in 1913, a gust of wind coincided with the arrival of two men, named Tokugawa and Hino, and flight became possible. And so it was that Tokugawa and Hino, seated in a borrowed French biplane, made their first successful flight into Japanese skies. From this recycled beginning, the Japanese bought and remodelled more French biplanes using the popular Maurice and Henri Farman designs.

There were two photographs of these planes, both in a museum in Kumagaya. The first showed a Japanese Imperial Army lieutenant standing up in the cockpit of a Maurice Farman biplane during a training exercise in March 1913. The photo was cropped, so the plane resembled a mishmash of lines and crossbeams, centred on a high washbasin with tricycle wheels. Lieutenant Tokugawa stood fully dressed in flight gear, wearing goggles and a white scarf that stretched all the way to his knees. His arms were outstretched like wings – they were impossibly straight – and he was looking off to the right at the small crowd of people who had gathered to watch him. Hino, his friend and co-pilot, made some last-minute adjustments to the wheels. Perhaps he was posing, showing off the wrench in his hand, the raw tool that would help their tin bucket to lift, to roll, and to glide.

Japan's fleet of biplanes metamorphosed into Farman-inspired impersonations. By 1919, they had constructed flying tubs with single propellers, elevator-wire cabling, silk-covered wings and tail-skids. And from two wings, they soon graduated to three (for better manoeuvrability), then to four, then to twenty, until they seemed to be aviating entire bathrooms instead of airplanes – twenty sets of narrow wings hid each pilot like a venetian blind. After that last experiment, Japan's airplane designers went back to two wings and began to move slightly away from the French, as if searching for more congenial bathing partners.

The second photograph was actually a war poster and showed an old Nakajima Type 5 airplane, the pilot leaning back against the side of the plane, and in the background a series of shack-like hangars could be seen, as if through fog. These buildings formed the first unit of Saitama's Tokorozawa airfield – today a magnificent tennis club – where the Imperial Army first tested the Nakajima in 1919. A total of 118 units were built before the Tokugawa-type biplanes fell out of favour, and, after that, flight spread from Saitama to other prefectures. But there was Hino, much older, standing off to the side. Posing again, with a fish flapping in his left hand. He was giving the fish to a young boy, who stared up at the man in awe. At the bottom of the poster, a wartime pledge: "Launched from the sea, a Maurice Farman hydroplane can leave the coast of Oihama and land in Saitama before a hand-held fish drowns in oxygen."

Hideo grappled for the fish and felt the sting of salt water in one eye. He was fascinated by flight and by the foreign principles that made it possible. When the war ended, his father wrote the family in Hokkaido, asking them to join him in Saitama. His letter described a Ginza department store that paid well. A small house in a *beddo* town was waiting for them. And they would not miss the sea so very much.

He'd become a salaryman, he said. From the salt.

Mister Endo arrived at work and asked his entire staff of sales clerks, bookbinders, and advertisers to stand on both sides of the store's entranceway and bow – like falling dominoes – to the first customers who opened the door.

It was quarter past nine, December 24, 1948. Ginza's shopping district awoke at the same time each day. Swept and washed, the street's cobbles gleamed like wet turtles. The shop entranceway was scrubbed with bath water. The American doorknobs were polished. And while the street lanterns were crushed into accordions their wicks were checked and topped with fresh whale fat. The merchants performed these tasks silently.

Hideo sat on a short yellow stool and watched the day unfold as it should. Each morning was a solemn ritual that he watched only occasionally, out of a profound ambivalence to the present, until that moment when his father needed him for the daily opening ceremony, and then they all took their places.

Half past nine arrived. A breeze left then entered with the first pull of the door. Near the door his shoe salesmen began to bow, then the clothiers, the shirt makers, the button men, the hat fitters, then the cashiers, on and on, until at last his mother – the accountant – bowed just a whisper longer than the rest. And as their blue uniforms doubled over, one by one, a long blue kite seemed to unravel, peopled with employee respect.

Mister Endo stood at the end of his kite next to the store's only steam-powered elevator. He was a tall man with bright eyes, and he believed in the aphorism that "the customer is God." In those days he managed the *depaato* – an American-style department store – and he was usually bursting with new-found enthusiasm for the future. He had already acquired three coats with tails and had the habit of carrying a foreign cigar in his breast pocket. He used these props to inspire everyone he met. With a flourish, he pulled out the cigar, cut the tip with a pocket guillotine, then held a match at bay, delaying the inevitable.

Freshly lit, the cigar's ember flared then settled. A pillow of smoke rose above Mister Endo's head. Then a tired strawberry appeared at the end of his cigar, which he liked to sand on the sole of his shoe. If he began a conversation he quickly choked the cigar and put it aside. And while he listened his eyes would come alight; they would sparkle so sharply that all his props – his fantastic suit, the tails, a cherry-wood cane, the dying cigar, every foreign object near him – would seem to disappear while he focused entirely on the speaker.

Whoever they were, Hideo was usually jealous of the genuine interest his father gave them. There was the sparkle, but there was also something else: the way he stopped everything to hear them speak. Hideo had never seen his father's eyes catch fire when he spoke. He faded to the edge of his father's sight, ate a stick of sun-dried squid, and watched his father listen to one story then another.

Later, when his father took the stage and began to speak, all the props came out and the fires truly began. Hideo watched him grow, watched him become that man whom others called

"Mister Endo." With the benefit of a hand-held cane, Mister Endo pointed at his mountainous sales charts. The brass tip of his cane followed a chart's path, scaling projected sales, then doubled back to show a better incline. His cigar punctuated each effort, each success, and he usually smoked during rest stops. It was as if he wanted to take them places, toward Western ideas they'd never before imagined.

So each week Mister Endo assembled his staff, and his family, and urged them all to follow him, as if to say: *Over here! Can't you see? It's just a little farther.* Then he pointed to his charts. The cane moved ever higher, imagining their future and a safe, careful ascent. His employees looked at the cane's flight of fancy and tried to forget that a family (young Hideo, especially) depended on their collective efforts. The boy was six, and just old enough to recognize obligation in their eyes.

His mother used to say that everything had a colour, and that obligation was the same as resentment or jealousy, without the yellow. It was a mix of emotions, she said, that depended on "an innocent coax of blue."

Only once (that Hideo could remember) did his father slip in some beguiling family reference to bring this colour out in his eyes. It was three months before Christmas – in the month of long nights – when Hideo heard something new in his father's voice. Something brighter, or sharper, or something far beyond their cloudless destiny had snagged his father's imagination. He was talking about embracing Western business techniques when suddenly an idea formed in front of him, a gleaming bone of a thought that gave him, and all his staff, pause. His eyes glazed over, turning soft.

"Santa Claus," he said, savouring the moment. "This year Santa Claus will visit Japan."

Then Mister Endo sent for a dictionary. He fixed the cigar in his mouth to signal the end of the meeting, his last word on the subject. And in the weeks that followed his staff researched each entry for Christmas and the holy Santa-san. The original English sources were checked and compared with the library's archival records. Old books suddenly appeared in their house. Hideo watched accordion volumes stretch from one end of the kitchen to the other. Spineless flutter books – with concertina pages – struggled for flight whenever a window was left open. *Detchōsō* (butterfly) books lay in sombre, piled stacks in every habitable room.

Hideo was mesmerized by the bound books because each one was pasted or tied together, and if opened the spines seemed to crack. He could hear the sound, just faintly. Left on the floor, a book's doubled pages spread like two wings, then wavered with the room's movement or the unseen passage of air. Like a butterfly on a branch, each book seemed to contemplate the world and Hideo within it.

During those weeks Mister Endo's eyes were as bright and as black as hot coals. Instead of telling Hideo bedtime stories, he read aloud from his broken books. He read Chinese Tang books that were stitched together with bright silk thread or woven hemp. Best of all, he read pouch-bound dictionaries that followed the scattered testimonials of shipwrecked sailors. Mister Endo wanted to research everything the Occidentals had said on the subject of Christmas, and inside each envelope he found more clues about the strange man they called Santa.

While Hideo struggled to stay awake, his father continued reading into the night. His father's voice – a thread in dark mountains – droned through Hideo's imaginings, and sometimes he heard his father leave the room just before day approached. Most nights he was only dimly aware of his father's voice, even and melodic. If he didn't sense the moment of his father's departure, at least he felt his absence, which seemed to loom large in his mind, all while his voice diminished.

At the shop, most mornings, Hideo watched him revise his sales charts and directives with a swat of his cane. And out of the dictionaries a plan seemed to form (*to bloom!* Father said), as if the seeds for his new Christmas display had been left behind (*planted!*) by patient lexicographers who had a gift for reading tea leaves instead of books.

Despite his own enthusiasm to rush toward a goal, time slowed for Mister Endo. He grew restless and took to pacing through the shop and through his house. Hideo's bedtime stories continued. He had the impression that the ending of the tale was very far away. So he listened to his father walking through rooms, then out, into the night. He dreamed that the first of December approached, reluctantly, then darted past his father like a mutt on the street. After that, the days dutifully plodded toward the end of the year.

Still the researchers conferred, argued in bathhouses, bribed librarians, and avoided his father's questions. Hideo listened to them fight over the repetition of the word *ho*. On its own the word meant nothing in Japanese, except to qualify some direction of sorts. But *ho, ho, ho!* – put together, with exclamation – were words that only *rikisha* jockeys understood: "Turn left, here, here, *here!*" Words, they believed, that were meant for Santa's reindeer. These words, in fact all the words in the English language, were entirely new to them.

Only a few years into Japan's sudden "openness," the world seemed so far away, so distant from their untranslatable present, that they had trouble imagining a coherent Western history that could mingle with their own.

A tent next to the elevator hid all their plans. Between the wall and their curtained ambitions Hideo saw that the elevator's car-guide rails were tastefully hidden behind three bales of hay. Part of the wall was painted brown to look like a barn door. Under the tent's skirt he saw several four-legged animals, what looked like a ceramic sheep and a two ceramic goats. Their silhouettes grazed on plastic sweet grass that sprouted from the wooden floorboards. He recognized the green sprigs, clipped from the inside of a sushi *bento*-box.

Each day Hideo watched the men go in and out of their tent, carrying long shafts of wood and bright boxes with ribbons. He heard them hammering and sawing. He watched them quarter off the elevator area while they built their mysterious Christmas display. The days seemed to stretch out, until they were as long as his father imagined them to be. It was the only moment in his childhood when he knew that his father's sense of time had slowed to the same pace as his own.

Finally, one day before Christmas, the *depaato* researchers announced that the first Christmas display was ready.

So there he was, Hideo's father, wearing a new coat (*with tails!*), a discernible smile on his face, his bright eyes ready to leap toward the first customers who arrived at half past nine.

———

As the door opened, and as his staff adjusted their blue uniforms, he took his place at the end of his living kite. The shoe salesmen began to bow just as Mister Endo stepped onto a stool and reached up. The clothiers were next, and Mister Endo's hand found a silk tassel that hung from the ceiling. The silk tassel bounced two pulleys into action; the movement strained a tent beside him. A ruffled, blue streak approached, snapping the hat fitters like the lick of a blue flame. Under the tent, the inaugural Christmas display twitched in excitement. With one brave tug, Mister Endo unveiled a large, white-bearded mannequin wearing red and white clothes. The mannequin was huge; he filled his bright costume admirably. An explosion of colour, the mannequin was like a red sumo wrestler with great knobs of fat on the backs of his knees – but he was pinned to a twenty-foot-tall crucifix.

The sheep and goats ignored Santa's pierced boots, his outstretched arms. They were also oblivious to the sound that came from the wall. The wall, solid and moss-filled, which seemed designed for the sole purpose of propping up the large man and his belly.

Behind this wall the elevator whirred and groaned as its counterweights shifted up and down. Despite Mister Endo's attention to detail, the man on the crucifix looked uncomfortable. Steam emanated from the edges of the elevator shaft and did nothing to help the crowd's general opinion that the large man had a very bad case of gas. Santa-san was positively audible. His stomach turned, it percolated through floors of uneasiness. The steam-driven pulleys behind him scrolled through the elevator's intestinal ropes. Up then down, the car wrenched to another start, then complained to a full stop.

Beside Santa's black boots, a brass sign promised safe passage and three storeys in less than a minute. An incredible feat, Hideo thought, for a storyteller. But the promise was certified by Elisha Graves Otis, who proved the Vertical Railcar and his Patented Braking System at the Crystal Palace Exhibition in New York City, 1853. The first steam-powered passenger elevator had appeared in the Haughwout Department Store in 1857. Electric elevators in 1880. The first transparent elevator on the Eiffel Tower in 1889. Push-button controls in 1894, and a new hoisting device, in England, in 1895. Elisha Graves Otis was responsible for everything, said the sign. He was the inventor of this marvellous transportation device that carried a maximum of eight people or 1,360 pounds, whichever came first. There were several brass buttons below the sign, next to the door. And Hideo pushed the brass button controls, anxious to hear the secret sounds of Santa's breakfast swimming through his enormous belly.

More children squeezed past their parents and joined him. All ears were listening to the future. It was as if they could hear the gurgle of a gearless drive sheave that had not yet arrived in Japan. Connected to the armature of an electric motor, this new invention would make speed limitless, all this, and only six years away.

Near his father, the advertisers flipped through their dictionaries and sales charts and deemed their research an Eiffel success. That was the word they used – *Eiffel* – because the chronology of the country seemed newly fixed to a foreigner's measurements for height and greatness. And in that morning's heady altitude, high above the crowd, his father seemed to notice him completely. Hideo knew that this day was one worth remembering, or that it was one of those few moments in life that could not be forgotten. His father was across the room – fifty people separated them – and it was as if all those nights when he'd heard his father leave the bedroom led up to this morning, in the *depaato*. The Christmas display his father had laboured over was complete, and he had finally flashed his famous eyes on his son.

Mister Endo: a tall man in a suit with tails. He seemed larger than Hideo had ever known him to be. A living apogee, he looked down from his great height and watched the children strike their fists at the elevator's gleaming buttons. He allowed himself one broad smile. Hideo's heart jumped, as if over a puddle.

His father watched them punch the elevator buttons and he saw Santa wheeze and churn with twentieth-century, steam-powered zest. Santa inflated with each wheeze and then sputtered like a spent candle. In sync with their fists, he wheezed, ballooned, and wheezed again, as if their efforts actually kept the crucified man up, high above the crowd.

And in the next moment, when Hideo expected his father to huff and puff the joys of group efforts, or company victory rah-rah-rah, or Great Western such-and-such, his father took the opposite route. He did not take the credit he deserved for bringing Santa to Ginza. He did not thank his researchers. Instead, he broke the gaze that he shared with his son – broke that moment in two – when he reached into his pocket and fumbled through his English dictionary.

He was searching through the dictionary, turning pages, looking for some self-deprecating phrase to explain the arrival of Father Christmas. Hunting for some Far Western idiom to mark the occasion, some English aphorism to describe (in modest terms) how proud he felt, how puffed with gratitude and optimism he was.

The lines in his face suddenly relaxed. He pulled the cigar from his lips and said, in English, "I smoke . . ." He let the seconds pass. "I smoke like a fish!"

The dictionary in his father's hands was an old one. But what a book it was – words and phrases in every state of undress. From S to T, sons of sea cooks mixed freely with lifelong teetotallers. Under the S, brothel salutations and sword guards were discarded next to top hats. And in the Ts there were earnest attempts to describe how English neckties once doubled as mouth swathes.

In the evenings, Mister Endo read Hideo these strange words as if they were stories. Hideo slept through most of them but they would, years later, turn him into an English teacher. He listened to his father for as long as his ears and consciousness would let him. He would fall asleep to the sound of his father's voice, a dull and safe metronome in the night.

The words and stories marched on. Santa Claus lumbered toward a barn with his sack of presents. Hideo watched him climb up and down from one thatched house to the next. Later, he saw the men who spoke those English words, all the ship-wrecked foreigners who had come to Japan with their heavy books and their dark beards.

His father, ever anxious for the future – for all things foreign – read the English words and Western customs that, since the end of the war, were now deemed legal in Japan. Words like *building* and *taxi* could be spoken aloud instead of using the old Chinese equivalents. A general enthusiasm for Western knowledge had sparked Japan and lit the country afresh.

And a dictionary (more than a steam-powered elevator, said Mister Endo) gave the country rise. He told Hideo that the first English teachers in Japan helped compile dictionaries inside Hokkaido prisons. Some of these teachers arrived as far back as 1848. They were shipwrecked sailors who had washed ashore – illegally – and were allowed to live. They spent their prison sentences speaking English to visiting scholars, and the words they assembled were so minutely written that they filled twenty-four small pages in six scribblers labelled Johnson's Progress Company. The guards transcribed these notations and created flutter books and accordion volumes which mashed English phrases against the Dutch, Portuguese, and Japanese equivalents. Mister Endo, searching for the word *Santa*, read these books night after night.

His father had a singular gift for bringing a page to life, an ability to imagine the water that still swirled in antique *washi*-paper. In Hideo's hands the pages were stiff and unwieldy. Little more than brittle cardboard, each one seemed ready to break in his hands. Each page seemed burnished, if not by his own fingers then by time.

In the middle of one notebook he found an ink drawing of a Japanese woman serving two men. Despite the simple brush lines that shaped her figure, the woman's kimono was plainly visible. Hideo was secretly thrilled by her presence, and by the way that her neckline – at the back – drooped low enough for him to imagine the colour of her skin. In the sketch, the two men sat on either side of a low table – they were looking at her within that moment that a cup of tea needs to settle – then the dictionary resumed.

In all, Hideo counted 1,453 translated words, not including the small glossaries of phrases at the back. The glossary re-enacted the sincerity of a prisoner's lessons: "You may be sure of it," one notebook began. "Do not doubt it," said another, "I assure you." If the students – the guards, who learned these like-minded phrases – remained sceptical or unmoved, a prisoner then added the next line: "You can believe it."

Other entries begged credibility for the lessons they recounted: "Take patience, Sir. Upon my honour. It is the very truth." The last line read, "Do you believe me?" Turning the page, the tone of this glossary quickly changed to more ship-worthy subjects. "The wind has turned, man. Where is the Dutch ship? At your service, Sir. I am in health." Then, after con-jugating dozens of dishes, cups, and people – *one people, two peoples, three peoples* – Hideo listened to the pronouns for *aunt, uncle, niece,* and *nephew.*

The list was intolerably long. Hideo was about to fall asleep in the soft midpoint of someone's great-great-grandfather when he heard his father turn the page and breathe something new into the story. The words: *laugh, angry, strike, dagger, sword, sham, lie, under, earthquake, thunder, asleep, awake, weep.*

When his father strung those single-word entries together, he seemed to assemble a fresh conversation. Hideo imagined how the prisoners taught this early English vocabulary to their Japanese hosts. The order of these words seemed to catch a linear conversation with the guards, as if Hideo and his father were on the other side of the wall, listening to every other word the prisoners spoke.

The earliest entries were easiest to decipher because they were arranged by subjects. "Stab" was written beside the words "to fight with both hands." Then there were similarly inspired directives: "to cut the belly, to bleed, to give the last gasp, to run away." Later entries included dinner etiquette, cutlery terms, and names of holidays. But between these sections a prisoner sometimes wrote a string of words that woke Hideo away from the dictionary's confinement: *love, adultery, pleasure, beginning, end, Asian, different, again, same, handkerchief, moon.*

Mister Endo told Hideo that these were the words and lessons that were used to open the gates of Japan after two centuries of isolation: *handkerchief, moon, weep.* Armed with this vocabulary, the first Japanese students will meet Commodore Perry on the docks at Uraga Bay in 1853. One hundred years after Perry, Hideo and his father will chase the Western prisoners through libraries and prisons, from Hokkaido to Nagasaki, assembling their lessons, their odd conversations, and imagining that moment when the Commodore stepped off his ship and was greeted by a battery of perfect English: "How do you do, Sir? Yamaguchi and Tokojiro at your service. We wish you a Merry Christmas."

It was actually July, but what could they say?

"There's the rub," said Mister Endo, nudging Hideo awake with an English aphorism.

He flipped through yet another notebook and said that an English prisoner would have called it a *howler*. To be utterly forgotten by history. The Commodore: a man who arrived with cannons and commandments. A man who opened Japan – forcibly – with all the world in attendance. A man with a foreigner's licence and a brass-buttoned uniform, he persuaded everyone that his moment in time would be remembered.

"But history," said Mister Endo, "can still be found inside a dictionary."

Hideo mumbled his agreement and tugged a blanket over one shoulder.

"A dictionary is memory's ultimate lexicon!" said Mister Endo, turning the page. "Listen to history's debris . . ."

The lessons continued. In the dim light of his bedroom Hideo half listened to foreigners who were held captive ten years before the Commodore arrived. Officially, these men and their dictionaries didn't exist. They were castaways, wet rags of official embarrassment. They washed up on Hokkaido and were hidden by prison documents that simply catalogued the exchange of men.

At first Hideo listened to these stories, their strange words, waiting for his father to tire. As Mister Endo talked and talked and finally droned the story into the next day, the men came to live in Hideo's thoughts and dark imaginings, and he looked forward to seeing his foreign sailors grow larger and more hairy with each night's telling.

My contract specified that I should work thirty-five hours, of which twenty hours may be teaching time. I was to teach both adults and children. The modest pay included some housing support, but our president, Shacho, was also the owner of a new apartment building that I was to inhabit. A mysterious government program to help foreigners gave him some funding, which he listed on my Alien Registration application, then he deducted this amount directly from my salary. His unique method of accounting may have rivalled the oldest Venetian double-entry bookkeeping techniques, but I was unaware of this practice when I first moved in.

I should have known something was wrong. I'd watched a team of men in red jumpsuits build a steel fence between our apartment building and the school. After they had finished laying the sod on either side of the fence, a government official arrived to authenticate the mandatory barrier. Then he departed.

Ten minutes later, the five jumpsuits returned, dug out the fence, rolled up the sod, and paved a driveway between the two buildings. Though I cheered the fact that I lived so close to the school, it was clear that the separation between work and play had disappeared.

I watched all of this from my bedroom window – a window that faced the open balcony that serviced all our apartments. When the officials and the fence workers were finished, I decided to search for more privacy and shift my futon away from the view.

Hideo Endo walked by and quickly advised against it.

"That is the southern end," he said.

He stood silent, as if waiting for something more to be said. His arms fell straight and seemed to dangle off his shoulders. There was an unmistakable confusion in his silence, and I had no idea that he was considering my bleak southern future.

"Only the dead face that direction," he said, "when they sleep."

I repaired my fate immediately, and put the bed back near the window, facing north.

"I am sorry," he said, "it's just a superstition."

I nodded.

"After I leave, you can point the bed in any direction you please."

"No," I replied, "thanks for the tip. Really."

Unconvinced, he shook his head, sadly, and walked away.

As Endo – as I now called him – promised, three days out of six I was leased to three different junior-high schools on the Kanto plains. These were usually less labour-intensive classes to manage, since they were meant to be joint lessons for me to share with a Japanese teacher.

On my first day in school I was quickly called to the principal's office. Across a low maple table and a high, insurmountable language barrier, we sipped green tea and nodded to each other. We grinned and glanced at the floor. I noticed that the principal had white socks with Playboy emblems jutting from his ankles. We nodded again. The mayor arrived and presented me with a bouquet of flowers and we bowed awkwardly (I was unsure of the depth needed to satisfy both thanks and respect). He bowed again. I bowed. And, thankfully, the principal led us both out of his office to an assembly meeting that coincided with my official "unveiling."

While I sat on a small steel chair in the middle of an empty stage, the class leaders from each grade made their way to a podium to greet me with a welcoming speech. They gave me three more bouquets, of roses, carnations, and irises. Then the school band played an exit song, the students filed out, and the principal escorted me to my first classroom.

I found English on every desk. Each student had a pencil case with a phrase that seemed to approximate some Japanese sentiment, or fascination, in happy Western terms:

- Speed fiend. Dart adventure spirit. And for this the people will pile up the days and days of vigorous practice.
- Good Stationary Tortoise Club. It's good. Tasteful. We feel happiness to be in not hurry. Necessaries of your life. He has a portable house.

- Boutique Little Popeli. Happy and cheer. The little popeli is good fragrance and lovely. I like the smell of the little popeli.
- Gimmie Five. Winners go from failure to failure until they finally achieve victory.
- Tuxedo Sam. Flags. Often mark important spots like ice cream stands. Refreshments need a place to rest. Sailing can taste a little salty. I feel baked. Like a pizza? A beach umbrella is a good thing to have.
- I perfected a snowman. PATAPATA! Oh! No – you're a monster.
- In The North of England My dad is a bull dog. My Mom is a white terrier. I was born in the early 19th century in a mining district in the North of England. I am stronger than you might think.
- Be a Man. I can recommend it with confidence like a most intelligent stationary of basic design.
- A Solitary Chap. Young snufkin.
- Pinny's member. Please be aware of the argyle style for a new Autumn collection. Provided to fans.
- On the Earth. This planet is not only for human.
- With meaning. Flower dancing team.
- Shoppers pencase. We give you an answer to everything. You've always wanted to know about LOVE and HAPPI-NESS.

My team-teaching plan was similarly optimistic. It called for the Japanese English Teacher (the JET) to greet the students joyfully, followed by the American English Teacher (AET) to greet the students joyfully. Despite all of this scheduled happiness, I was surprised to see a less-than-joyful group of faces in front of me. Sixty students, standing beside six rows of desks, said "Herro, Mistar Teacher-san," and then sat down.

Without prompting, the entire class opened their *Utter English* books and launched into a "rhythm chant," a page-long rendition of "My Darling Clementine." As their eyes blurred with boredom I struggled to imagine a campfire in front of me. Just as quickly as this image formed in my mind, and sixty hard-rock miners crouched to wax nostalgic for sixty lost loves, Clementine and all her troubles dissolved when I glanced back to my lesson plan.

There were several more joyful repetitions and interpretations – a page-long strategy that seemed designed to turn all the students into parrots. If I was to play the exotic pet from a foreign zoo – a strange animal that had the singular ability to read joyful English on command – then the students would be the ones who would suffer the most. An understandable goal: I wanted them to form connections with what they were repeating, so they might be able to generate sentences on their own. But they were so traumatized with indifference that they seemed close to falling asleep.

I decided to start slowly. With the help of my fellow teacher, I performed my introduction in English and then repeated it in Japanese. I am from Canada. I have a brother and a sister. They are both younger than I am. They are both taller than I am. (The class was mildly surprised by this news.) Even my dog is taller. (They perked up.) He has spots all over his body, spots on his legs and tail. Spots in his mouth. Spots under his nails.

One spotty-dog story and I reached the end of my vocabulary.

Next, I tried to wrench them from lethargy by introducing myself to one student at a time. I began with bows then gravitated to handshakes. Few of them, it appeared, had ever shaken hands with another person. They may have seen the greeting performed on television, but the idea of touching skin seemed uncomfortably intimate to them. Their hands were clammy and wet with anxiety, caked with gym sweat and lunchtime kiwi juice. And most of the students didn't realize that one has to grip and shake at the same time.

"Teacher," said one brave student, "how long to shaking?"

Two of the students grabbed for my arm, wanting to translate an honorific (deep) bow into a similarly honorific handshake. They all but shook my teeth loose with their enthusiasm. At the end of this exercise my hand felt like a sore foot: rigid and uncertain.

In Japan, both students and teachers are required to participate in one after-school sport. Filling in for a vacationing teacher, I was given kendo.

From my unschooled point of view, kendo distinguishes itself as the one sport where you wear a spaghetti strainer on your face and whack the bejesus out of your opponent with a rather long bamboo sword. The clothing consists of a black cotton skirt, a turtle-like stomach guard, and carpet-thick gloves that only marginally protect the wrists. Everything about the sport seems to honour the samurai tradition. Consequently, no head-guard improvements were ever made. The spaghetti strainer – or helmet, as it was properly called – has remained the same for the last five centuries. Nothing but a folded handkerchief separates the helmet from the skull. The sword is called a *shinai* and is made of five spliced lengths of bamboo, held together by a leather handle and a plastic hand guard – called a *tsuba*. A thin nylon line runs from pommel to point and imagines the top of sword's blade, its *kensaki*. A leather cap holds the tip of the sword, and all five splices, together.

I was to learn that spliced bamboo makes a satisfying *rhap!* when it is struck evenly, or a hollow *twang* when an edge catches a glove or an eye guard. With a perfect strike the spliced bamboo first absorbs and then recoils from the blow, so that the sword kicks back into the hands and readies itself for another attack. A scream prefaces most lunge attacks.

On my first day in the gym I watched my opponent's sword disappear behind her back. Though her feet were hidden, she bridged the distance between us quickly. I heard her leap forward with a front foot that smashed into the floor beside mine. Then, a guttural scream: "*Maaan!*" The word for *head* escaped her visor and I swung wildly to avoid a sword that cut the air and cracked the top of my helmet. Inside the helmet, I was wet with perspiration and cold fear. Matted against my hair, the handkerchief barely constrained the vibration and did little to soften the blow.

Then another scream concluded her attack, though this second voice was mine and I only recognized the word *sshiiitta!* because the spray of this exclamation caught in my helmet and dripped down the bars of my mask.

I'll be honest. From the start, my opponents were small (but mighty) children. That first day, I fought a seventh-grader named Nobuko. An hour before that auspicious battle, I'd asked her and her classmates a battery of questions (How many chairs are there in the room? What is your favourite food? How many stars are there in the sky?). They'd done so well that I decided to mix up some of the questions and see if they could improvise with each other.

One student asked, "What is your favourite star?"

I was surprised by this question and didn't expect anyone to answer – in English or in Japanese. But Nobuko responded, quite quickly, with the answer: "The sun."

When the class was over I grabbed my *Utter English* textbook and met some of these same students in the gym. I heard the muttered words, "The teacher is here."

And after that: "Teacher, how many kendo sticks are there in the room?"

When I was struck on the head by one particularly ferocious seventh-grader, she asked, "Mr. Teacher, how many stars are there in the sky?"

I recognized Nobuko's voice behind the mask's visor. A red and white handkerchief trailed behind her small head. Her bright eyes seemed to smile at me. We paired off, and listened to another instructor spout instructions from the sidelines. Nobuko seemed to sense my plight with Japanese words as much as with swords, and helped me assemble my first kendo dictionary, one movement at a time:

"*Rei*," she said, bowing once.

I bowed. "*Rei*."

"We must sit down," she said. *Chya kuza.*

I wasn't sure what to do with the sword, so I used it as a crutch to get closer to the floor. Nobuko whispered, "*Mokuso*," and closed her eyes. We sat cross-legged for an intolerably long time, and just as my legs began to lose all feeling I heard the words "*Kiri-tsu!*"

I opened my eyes and saw that most everyone was standing upright.

One action at a time, Nobuko whispered the words for everything we did. She prodded my back with the tip of her sword, whispered, "*Shi sei o tadashite*," until I straightened myself.

Sei retsu. We formed a line.

Mae e. We took a step forward.

Ato e. One step back.

And finally, *yame*. We stopped.

Over the next few days Nobuko edited my movements, fine-tuning my stance or my meditation, by giving me those small words whispered from one spaghetti strainer to another. The directions became more detailed: "Left heel, always hold up, hold out your right and left feet, point straight left foot, walk with short steps, look at your opponent's eyes, have sword without the left little finger, stand ready for me, don't walk with long strides, *right turn!*, stretch the line of your backbone, pull, *hit the head!*, hit your hips with the sword's handle, don't fall down top of sword," and so on.

We marched up and down the gym, exchanging both words and blows. During those practice hours I abandoned the idea that I was her teacher and she was my student. And while her English was improving by the yard, I seemed to measure my own success by the bruise. On a good day, I found only wrist welts. On the bad days, my ears wouldn't stop ringing until I'd driven home, sat for an hour, and sedated myself with a bowl of vanilla ice cream.

Almost immediately, Endo noticed the sword sticking out of my briefcase.

I told him it was hard to keep anything secret in a small town. He smiled.

"We are living in a fishbowl!" he said, motioning to the clouds, swinging one long arm across the line of buildings that framed our apartment complex. "And they feed us too much!"

Then he told me that an Occidental who functioned relatively well in Japan with the language, the sports, and the chopsticks, is called *nihonjin mitai*: "Japanese-looking." And the Japanese person who spent time in America, picking up foreign habits (or Levi's jeans and spoken English), is sometimes called *gaijin kusai*: "foreign-smelling." The difference between these two labels seemed more poignant when I learned that the actual meaning of *gaijin* isn't *foreigner*; the word literally means *outside person*. It seemed I was either Japanese or I was outside humanity. A more pleasant translation of this word was *gai-koku-jin*, meaning *outside-country person*, but I didn't hear this expression as often. And I was centuries from the original Japanese term for foreigners: *padres*.

Forced to choose from one of those unfortunate labels, I told Endo I preferred the Chinese equivalent. In Hong Kong, the outside world was divided into a series of colourful ghosts. The

Japanese were Yellow Ghosts, Africans were Black Ghosts and the Caucasians, I told him, were the White Ghosts. The real people – those who exist in Hong Kong – were simply People. The rest of the world was, necessarily, an apparition.

I became an outside person – an apparition made real – just a few days later. Endo relayed a message from Shacho that I was to be fingerprinted. All foreigners, he said, even Japanese-born Koreans, were required by law to report to their local city hall and register as "Aliens" within ninety days of arrival or birth.

I welcomed the diversion from lesson planning and walked to the building alone.

The Alien Registration card was laminated for its protection against the elements and was to be carried for my protection at all times. It was deep blue and white and listed my address in Japan, my sponsor, Shacho, and a requisite serial number. There was a place for my thumb print (in miniature) next to my photo. The instant I saw the card I seemed to shrink to fit its dimensions and I became that small, blue Alien in a white frame. The label was as palpable as a mouthful of sand; I could suddenly taste it everywhere.

In accordance with the official rules for Alien Registration, the alien's photograph had been taken within the last six months. The photograph also measured four centimetres by three and showed a full-frontal view of the top half of the alien's body, without a hat. I didn't have to sign the card, because my alien fingerprint was proof enough. Instead, I signed another guarantee to relinquish the card "at the point of my departure." I also promised that – in the event of my death – I would return this certificate to the mayor of my local ward or municipality within fourteen days.

I wasn't happy to get this card, but I needed to carry it when I returned to the airport to retrieve my lost baggage: one suitcase of clothes and one cardboard box of pots and pans, blankets and books. All the modern conveniences and the vanities of easy living awaited my signature and my Alien Registration card, just a day trip away – if I hurried. Endo told me that I could get there by noon if I caught a bus to the station by 6:15 a.m., jumped on the Shinkansen bullet-train to Tokyo, passed through Ueno station, and then changed trains to Narita airport. After that, he said, I would be able to return to Saitama with the other Tokyo salarymen, in time for a cup of tea before bed.

His directions were letter-perfect but it took me an extra hour to find the airport's shipping and record offices. The building was a subterranean labyrinth. With each new corridor I tried, the sound of airplane engines ripping the air became fainter and fainter, until it was completely quiet. An official silence, perhaps, in a windowless building just five floors below the passengers who came and went, travelling to places as far and exotic as Canada.

I found the complaint office (without a door) and asked for directions. From there I was sent to a mailroom with ticker-tape debris covering the floor. The temperature in these underground offices seemed to escalate; the deeper I went the hotter it became. A basement boiler heated the floors and walls. It warped the desks and made the plants flourish in exaggerated proportions.

Seeking help, I entered a room where a customs official was literally scraping the pubic hair off a photograph in an adult magazine. He looked up, adjusted his bifocals, and seemed to regard me fully.

"Lost baggage?" I asked.

"Wong womb," he said. Then he turned his attention back to the photograph. A lonely profession: running after foreign women, in censored magazines, with a big white eraser.

Next door, I entered a office where I heard a movie projector rattling from within a desk drawer, or from deep inside another, inner room. The office was empty, except for the faint sound of voices – two lovers, a man and a woman – and their chorus of bedsprings. Their voices turned ragged, breathy, then instantly conspiratorial. I'm sure I heard the word *fenestrate*, and some romantic reply, in Swedish.

In the next office I met a man in a blue-buttoned uniform. He was separating excess-baggage applications from declaration forms, in some official order. The light in his office was so dim that the papers seemed to glow in his hands. More 11"x 14" officialdom hung like curtains from the sides of desks. The edges curled into scrolls. Like sentry soldiers, two filing cabinets stood still and sweating next to the water cooler.

Most of the papers I signed were in Japanese but the last sheet was in English. The baggage official explained that this last page was an apology for my indiscretion at not declaring my unaccompanied baggage when I first arrived in Japan. Further, the paper stated that my forgetfulness was caused by my lack of understanding of Japanese law and that I would endeavour to be a law-abiding traveller from this day forward. All of this was true enough, but I phoned Endo anyway.

"They will just file the paper," he said. "Extremely usual with Japanese bureaucracy. It means nothing at all."

I could receive three, perhaps four of these warnings and still be allowed back into the country. My signature, he said, was a gesture in the name of the eternal paper chase that exists in Japan. So by mid-afternoon I was back in Tokyo, shuffling one box and one suitcase through the Ueno station, trying to find the train that would take me back to Saitama. Rush hour was upon me. And it was this day that I met the famous train-pushers and their clean, white gloves.

They are enlisted into action during heavy traffic hours, only when the herd is stalled or too polite to advance much further, at which point they soon begin to push. Caught in a funnel that squeezed toward one train, I had no choice but to move with the crowd. I actually raised my feet, covering metres before the next step, the box secure in one arm, my suitcase in the other, and I was buoyed by the people around me. I floated toward the train's open doors. Wedged in among two salarymen, an old woman with an umbrella, and twelve high-school students in matching karate uniforms, I tried not to jab anyone with my box. I lifted it toward my chest and the upward motion sent the contents of my shirt pockets fluttering. We surged toward the open door in a series of circulatory gushes and I suddenly felt my heart begin to pump with the same flush of the crowd. I looked to one side to see the old woman wearing my lost-baggage receipts in her grey hair. A penicillin-allergy alert card, an international driver's licence, a mini-edition of *The Book of*

Tea, and my Alien Registration card fell on her shoulders. But my hand was glued to the box corner a fraction too long. In another instant my cards fell from her coat and then she too was gone. The woman disappeared behind a man wearing a white hospital mask and a dark business suit. And the mask looked at me with bright, confused eyes. I was derailed by his stare until I realized that the man was wearing this mask to protect the people around him. He was sick. A cold, influenza, an allergy, something more serious – I didn't care what he had, but out of courtesy I fought my natural urge to distance myself from him.

Thankfully – at this moment – the men with white gloves gave pause. I felt the crowd's movement slow. The men with white gloves came to their moment of assessment. I couldn't remember the procedure for lost registration cards, but was sure there were rules for re-application, for more thumb prints, more apologies, a three-week application. Then there was a sudden surge, and, because I was taller than most of the people around me, I was almost decapitated by the train's low doorway. It actually occurred to me that if I died, right then, I wouldn't have time to re-apply for a new Alien Registration card in order for it to be returned to the mayor within fourteen days.

I looked back to see the commuters pressing against me and the men with white gloves fast approaching their rush-hour nirvana. A final push and I was inside with my boxes.

We were crumpled into the train, each of us assessing our individual damage and our new neighbours. Dozens of arms grasped for the train's hanging rings, then the doors began to close. Dejected, I finally put my box down on my suitcase, only to find the old woman, whom I'd seen – briefly – outside the train. She smiled and reached into her down-turned umbrella and pulled my name from the tines. She examined each card in her hand, politely, as if we were exchanging business cards or pleasantries.

Then, *sumimasen*, she said, apologizing for her supposed interruption. She offered everything to me as if I were the one doing her the favour by accepting each gift. Excuse me, she said, reading my name on the last card, my Alien Registration card, *sumimasen*.

Santa-san

June

Endo's drifting room

The ghost of Colonel Sanders

Either the woman was a fortune-teller or that day held its own inkling. I lost my identity as soon as I returned home. Endo took a certain pleasure in telling me that I was scheduled to play Santa Claus during the last two weeks of December. They needed a bandleader for all the new songs in the December module of *Utter English*.

"Besides," he said, "*Kurushimemasu* is coming."

"Christmas?" I asked.

He didn't respond, at least not in words. Instead, he gave me a tattered costume, some black leggings (which transformed my slippers into black boots) and a rib cage of jingle bells that shimmered an alarm at my slightest movement.

It couldn't be a coincidence that the Japanese verb *maruku kurushimemasu* sounds startlingly similar to "Merry Christmas," and means – roughly translated – to be roundly tortured. Endo had said as much: *Kurushimemasu* is coming, he'd said. Your misery is near.

A few days later, I grabbed my keys and jingle bells, and on my way to the car I warmed up my vocal cords for the impending *ho, ho, ho*. I drove across the Kanto plain, through bamboo groves and rice fields, wearing those red and white clothes and a long white beard, going from junior-high schools to elementary schools to preschools, playing ole Saint Nick without break. I drank through straws so I wouldn't have to drop the beard and spoil my disguise. I adjusted my pillowed belly with a gesture that was nothing short of obscene, until it finally became an appendage that I was comfortable carrying with me.

Because my students expected Santa-san to be both jolly and nimble, I learned a kind of fat man's tap-dance, or Russian folk-dance for woodcutters. Later, in the afternoon, when I grew especially tired of the extra weight hanging from my body, I resorted to an octogenarian's shuffleboard step, which employed a vague, cruise-line grace. Dragging my feet, I moonwalked between classrooms. Evenings, I hauled my stomach to private *juku* schools and my voice grew hoarse and changed into something deeper I no longer recognized. Santa's holy image gradually disappeared from my thoughts.

I knew something about fashioning Christmas before coming to Japan. Throughout the year, my father used to visit wrecking yards and broken bus shelters, collecting shards of glass. Then my mother – an artist, the tips of each finger covered with Band-Aids – would cone those shards into glass trees. She built row upon row of broken windshields, then added another layer of glue and glass, until she reached the top of a green tree with the last single shard. I marvelled that the colour was pale and clean in her hands, and that she knew the trees would gradually tinge themselves green. The colour deepened with each row she added.

Later, in the fall, when she had an assembly line of half-finished trees running through our house, she travelled from one row to another and slowly bled her way through a forest of glass cones. I admired this patient advance of Christmas.

In my family, there was only one leap toward that season: one August afternoon when Christmas exploded out of the end of my father's .22 rifle. My father was in the garage, cleaning wheat for one of my mother's craft projects. I noticed a long brown bag and asked about the gun that he hadn't used in years. Eager for a distraction, he peeled the rifle from its leather bag and forced it open. He smiled and I felt safe in that moment, though we lived miles within the city and no animals were likely to appear, at least not without turning on the television.

My mother materialized in the doorway.

"It's all right," said my father, before she could say anything. "The gun's empty."

Still, he turned the barrel to the side of the garage – toward a wall that shared the support for the hall entrance to our house. "The gun's cocked already, so stay where I can see you. I've just got to relieve the pressure."

He pointed the gun at the wall and pulled the trigger and the gun set off, as it should have. I was surprised by the blast, and by the sudden density of air that seemed to expand in my ears, as if the explosion from the gun had pushed all the walls inward. A sudden publication of air dissipated as soon as the room noticed a vacuum at the end of his gun.

Weeks later – though still in the month of August – I noticed a painting in our hallway which refused to stay level. I adjusted it twice before pulling it from the wall and examining the hook. A small hole had appeared in the back of my mother's watercolour. This hole matched yet another hole in the wall and another inside the garage. The painting itself was intact, but behind the unbroken glass, I found a bullet and the scattered remains of mat board, burst white and snowing across a summer mountain scene. The bullet, travel- and insulation-weary, had finally fallen with those white flakes and blocked a cerulean (number five) river.

In Japan, I found that the trappings of Christmas were neither patient nor sudden. The snow was simply there, from the moment I'd arrived. The freak storm had covered my path from Narita airport to Saitama, a shock of white that veiled the country one day; by the next, a cement world had emerged, reasserting its hold on the season.

Within a few days of my becoming Santa, the costume was already wrinkled and dirty. I suppose I expected some small transformation to take place – a light snowfall – each time I put the beard on, but nothing like that happened. Most days, when I looked in the mirror, I felt my cheeks blush against the whiskers. I was a bit warm but that was all.

I did notice a transformation in others.

June (short for Junichi) was a retarded boy who attended few classes beyond art, calligraphy, and table tennis. On the days when basketballs outnumbered ping-pong balls, June was allowed to drift and no one complained that he wasn't supposed to be on the basketball courts, or that he couldn't play the game so well, or that the basketballs might hurt him when he failed to catch his own rebounds. Most of his school hours were spent with the nurse or the luncheon cooks. He was a happy boy, singularly happy when gripped by one teacher, or hugged by another, and no strict rules of Japanese etiquette seemed to slow his lopsided smile.

June was waiting for me as I arrived in my black Toyota. He'd been quickly outfitted into a red track suit, a pair of black kung fu slippers and a white beard — made of cotton batting. Bandaged to the ears with hospital duct tape, his beard was delicate and full of holes. But during the first three periods of the morning, June was patched and puffed and ready to meet me outside the school kitchen at noon. The school's nurse gave him a cardboard sign that read SANTA and he fanned the word at me as I rounded the corner.

Faced with a mirror image of himself, June's smile dislodged one side of his beard, so that it hung from his left ear, and the nurse ran to repair him. She was a small, cannonball woman who was quick on her small feet, but June was intent on meeting Santa and tore from her grasp.

"Wait," she said. "Wait just a moment."

June slipped away, one side of his beard still dangling.

"*Kon-ni-chi-wa*," he said, drawing out the syllables.

"Hello there," I said. "Hello, Santa!"

June's smile brightened and his cotton beard fell to the floor beside a metal cart full of luncheon trays. When he tried to pick up the beard he actually pushed it under a bank of curry udon and no amount of digging could dislodge it.

Our meeting was brief, and surrounded by chopped kiwis, but June did not seem to mind. We shook hands and said "Ho, ho, ho," together. He understood the words "Merry Christmas" and we walked, arm in arm, down the hallway to visit the principal, who came out of his office to greet us.

In halting Japanese, June introduced us by saying, "Good afternoon, Mr. President. We are Santa Claus."

By this time the nurse had retrieved June's beard, so the principal kneeled and reached around the boy's neck and attached the cotton batting again to his ears, mouth, and chin. June froze, waiting for the principal to finish adjusting his costume. I watched them and thought that the moment was somehow perfect and intimate – and that they were both oblivious to this grand occasion before the school's photographers could arrive to commemorate something official. The moment held, then the principal stepped back and resumed his composure.

"Santas," he said, "I am honoured to meet you." He gave us two deep bows and June stumbled back, as if too proud of the honour he'd just received to speak again.

So many levels permeate Japanese meetings between superiors and subordinates that I regularly lost track of the subtleties, all the unspoken indicators that formed a social climate. Conversations, I thought, could sometimes be measured in

Fahrenheit. Each dialogue had a discernible temperature, odour, or pith, that could only be sensed from downwind. There were few direct questions and even fewer confrontations. One edged around an uncomfortable subject, using "stomach-talk" to flesh out someone's true motives and real message.

But there was something both genuine and rare in what I'd just witnessed between June and his principal. I knew the moment would not last, neither for myself nor for June, but I was happy to be there – in that school hallway – to see what was likely the first equal conversation between a principal and his slowest student. June must have somehow understood this conversation, at least vaguely, otherwise he wouldn't have been so honoured by the new-found respect he'd won.

"Good afternoon," June said again. "Good afternoon!"

In my tenure as Santa Claus, I met only five Scrooges. One student gave me the finger. Three couldn't have cared less and actually rejected my proffered candy canes. And two days before Christmas, as I stood on a street corner waiting for the light to change, a bicyclist – a pedalling grandmother – nearly ran her bicycle over my toe. She was so close to my inflated belly that my beard fluttered in her wake. As she passed she simply muttered the word *haiyiai*. She didn't glance at me. She didn't blink. Only later, within the confines of my Japanese dictionary, did I learn the meaning of what she'd said. The word *haiyiai* means "you're early."

A few thousand children may have wondered why Santa spoke broken Japanese with an English accent, but their response – on the whole – was positive. To the best of my memory, I received six punches to the groin and thirty-five pulls on my beard. Ten students said, "Hi, Shingo Balls!" Eighty-nine said that I looked like their teacher. Fourteen wondered how I had arrived in Saitama (the answer: Toyota *Tonakai* "Reindeer"). And six hundred and seventy-three said, "Santa-san! Give me presento!"

I'd gone through eight boxes of imported candy canes.

Having sung hundreds of Christmas songs in dozens of classrooms, I thought I knew something about Christmas. But I didn't realize that my students had studied the same Christmas songs each December, every year of elementary school, junior-high and high school. It was Nobuko – my small kendo opponent – who asked me about Rudolph the Red-nosed Reindeer.

She wanted to know, with grave urgency, "What were the names that all the other reindeer called Rudolph?"

"Bad names," I said.

"What bad names?"

"Nicknames," I said, unnerved by her serious face. "He had a red nose," I said. "Nobody else did. But his nose was *red*. You could see it for miles."

"Yes, yes," her friends agreed. They knew about the nose. They knew the other reindeer didn't like him. He was shunned. He was avoided. But what were the *names*?

"Rudolph," I said, "you're a jerk."

Their eyes lit up.

"Rudolph, you're nose is a lantern outside a Yakitori restaurant. Rudolph, you are Anne of *Red* Gables. You are communist. You are . . ."

They waited, thrilled with expectation.

I was searching for the worst possible thing you might say to a reindeer in Japan and June's haggard beard and smiling face came to my thoughts.

"You are *different*," I said.

Endo was something of an expert on foreigners. Though he'd never travelled outside Japan, he was in such close proximity to *gaijin* teachers, year after company year, that the other Japanese salarymen seemed to treat him as a quasi-foreigner, a *gaijin kusai*, or (at best) a bit of an oddity. He was also their intermediary, the tightrope walker who seemed to reconcile both our worlds. When one of the Japanese secretaries had a question for the foreign teachers, or some new company policy to broach, they went to Endo first. For contract discussions, Endo again. For transcribing a local restaurant menu into English, Hideo Endo.

From my own point of view, he was a strange man to watch. He seemed unconstrained by his formal, Japanese milieu. Unlike his co-workers, he'd picked up some Western gestures – shrugs, winks, high fives – and he was more expressive than most of the Japanese people I'd met. I think he enjoyed grimacing and patting himself on the back.

On Tuesday afternoons he taught a class on Western gestures and sent an entire kindergarten class into the street with the knowledge that they, too, could say "Number one" and throw up their arms exactly like a team of soccer players in Leeds. He prepared them for every Western contingency. An interesting question? "Hmmm," he said, then forty children scratched their foreheads. A bad cappuccino? "Mama mia!" they yelled, and shook their small hands at the sky. He created monsters. Revolutionaries.

He liked using Hollywood movies as a linguistic touchstone – his most important ready-reference.

"Of course I'd like to talk to you," he said. "Not!"

Wayne's World was an obvious favourite. If I closed my eyes I could almost imagine a teenager standing in front of me: a young Mr. Endo wearing a baseball cap, a Madonna concert T-shirt, and bluejeans. Eyes open, I saw a tall Japanese man with bad teeth who couldn't quite wield his huge eyelids behind those bottle-thick glasses.

When we met, at the end of a day, he was often quiet. Deep in his thoughts, he let me rattle on about my new impressions. Then he would begin to speak, winding up his English like an old Victrola, until he was laughing and talking with more expression than a schoolgirl at her first graduation dance.

"We ornamentals," he said, "are a people unto ourselves." He smiled before I had a chance to correct him and say, *We Orientals.*

"There is a Japanese proverb," he said. "*Rin chikai ume omoi no mama.* Flowers differ from one to another."

"It sounds like the French phrase, *vive la différence!*" I said.

"What does *vive* mean? Vivacious?"

"Live," I said.

"Ah," he said. "The Japanese are not so very good at living. We have talented workers, but we do not have talented livers."

He popped a shrug and wandered off to his apartment.

I remembered his proverb about the flowers and on the next evening I brought him a gift: a piece of paper that one of my students had folded into a blue tulip. He smiled when I told him that out of these six-by-six pieces of paper my students made weapons and usually armed themselves with origami throwing stars. On the good days, these Ninja weapons changed into kimono-clad figures, orchids, and cranes within colourful boxes. He told me that the students actually learned origami in elementary school.

And it was from one of these paper creatures – a crane – that Endo finally settled on a Japanese name for me. He said that without a vowel at the end of my name, I have become rather difficult to pronounce. Endo didn't differentiate a name from a person, so he simply said, "You don't roll across the tongue so very well."

Another problem: it was one day before Christmas vacation and I was still scribbling myself into the school's ledger, while the Japanese teachers used small, pinkie-sized stamps called *hanko* to ink their arrival at the start of each day. Even I was bored of this special treatment, this practice of initialing everything. My bank – actually the post office where I deposited my salary – had requested one of these stamps when I first opened an account. Compared to these ancient ink blocks, a signature seemed like a modern invention. Some were carved from wood, others from bone or jade, and each person's unique characters were registered with the government to act as their signature for a credit card or a bank cheque.

I thought that creating this new identity would be a pleasurable task, as it involved choosing the characters of my own name, and – by approximation – choosing my character. But there were horror stories, Endo said, about those foreign teachers who picked some melodic identity and suddenly found themselves saddled with a name that turned out to mean "The Round Baron" or "Little Curd" or "Wheat Head."

Images from nature are the main source for names in Japan because all Japanese surnames are derived from natural objects. Yamaguchi: Mountain's Entrance. Ogawa: Small River. Despite the modern, industrial wasteland and their blinking-neon cities, miniature forests seemed forever on their lips. So I was happy that Endo, with his knowledge of Japan and foreigners, was interested in finding something appropriate for me.

He said that we should shorten my name toward a Japanese equivalent or a couple of characters that could (in turn) stand alone, and approximate the sound of my name.

"Great," I said, eager for a new Japanese identity.

He didn't respond, at first. The pause lengthened. He took off his heavy glasses and rubbed his eyes and I noticed that the glint from the hallway's bulb had coloured his eyes blue. He returned the glasses to his face, tapped the bridge, and the frames slid back to cover a red indentation on his nose. The blue sheen was gone.

"Your name," he said, "can mean anything from *cage* to *opportunity*. Let me think about it for a while."

He walked toward his apartment. Then he waved his hand for me to follow him. At least I thought it was a wave: his hand was palm down, and he seemed to brush me toward him.

Endo's apartment was next door to mine (in fact, flat against the wall) and it was the mirror image of my own three rooms. His floor plan, the appliances, all the light switches and rooms were in the opposite places where I expected to find them. I tripped over three tennis racquets when I tried to step up onto a landing that should have been to my left, but was actually on the right.

He apologized for the mess and – by way of explanation – said that he played tennis year-round. I already knew something about his habits, just from living so close to him. He loped through his games, winning (invariably) by leaping through the air and distracting his opponent's attention. He was a bachelor, despite his forty-nine years, and his mother – who lived several blocks away – still made most of his meals for him, one week in advance. When his food supply dwindled, he ate truckloads of Instant Ramen noodles and Seven-Eleven sushi rolls. A nearby rice hut serviced his most pressing fits of hunger and the odd sweet-potato salesman helped him through those days when he couldn't dash out of the school for an afternoon snack.

When I entered the apartment I could see that he was also a man who liked to collect high-tech curios: eyeballs that rolled across the floor and never stopped staring at the ceiling, electric rugs that actually plugged into the wall and warmed his feet, neon plastic balls that could be mashed like snowballs against a window. I exchanged my shoes for a pair of guest slippers and padded past the small bedroom, toward the kitchen and his tatami-mat living room. Both of us had similar eight-mat rooms with sliding doors. A faint ink painting was etched into each screen and showed a mountain on one side and a murder of crows on the other.

The antithesis of Zen, Endo's *apaato* was chock-full of electronic knickknacks and *omiage* gifts that he had collected from years of admiring students. Two modest girlie calendars hung on one wall. Compliments of Japan Airlines, the women were pinned so that one stewardess gave him the present and the other glimpsed the next month, as if he could walk across the room and enter his future with a cup of coffee. On a shelf below December he stored Chinese trinkets, bowl caps, plastic nunchucks, a glass oil lamp, and two harvest-festival fans. A black velvet picture of Mount Fuji hung below the calendar and, below that, on the floor, sat a red Gentle Bunny waste-paper basket embossed with the words "My name is Gentle Bunny. Are you free this coming weekend? Creative gear into good space produced by Sanko."

Across the room, in January, he'd organized his pink stereo and a bookshelf, along with Italian learning cassettes, Latin dictionaries, several versions of *Pinocchio, Peter Pan,* and *The Neverending Story* beside three toothpick containers and two different pencil cases. One of the cases (a Hello Kitty variety) held pencils for his personal writing. The other case (featuring Casper the Friendly Ghost) was meant for everything else: marking student papers, writing letters, or adding the day's events to one calendar and the day's plans to the other.

Endo didn't want to be a writer, at least not in any Western sense of art or ambition. He simply believed in the habit of writing – and the profession, second – so that he might give books and fantasies to children and bring some measure of relief to the tortures of their Japanese childhood. I don't think that he wrote children stories to apologize for becoming a *juku* after-school-study teacher, but it was, rather, the only way he could fight a regimental culture from within.

From this humble undertaking, he'd begun writing stories for himself. I saw a stack of clean scribblers on the floor and another batch that was eight deep and well thumbed. I looked through one of the scribblers and saw that each page allowed a grid of pencilled notations – written in neat, but incomprehensible, kanji. Each pictograph filled one box and almost every box on the page was filled.

"They are drifting stories," he said. "Travel journals about sailors who drift back and forth across the Pacific. One day they drift to this side of the room, and the next . . ."

"Are they true stories?"

"Yes and no."

Endo had a theory that history was a frustrated bellhop who pretended that one's bags reached their proper destination.

"Of course, a bellhop can be bribed," he said. "He can be bought for a song!"

I must have smiled blankly because he read my confusion precisely. A bellhop, he explained, will close one eye while a traveller takes his suitcase and the complimentary soap. A bellhop is used to the idea that we need fragments from the real world to construct the imaginary.

"Maybe I use history," he said, "to tell stories. But sometimes, if I write well enough, perhaps I am writing the real history with these imaginary stories. Do you understand?"

I thought back to Claudio Crespi, and the butterfly that had whirled above our airplane seats: "Nothing happens in this world without a reason," he'd said. "History is a wheel! History is our front-tire rotation!" Crespi had, I thought, a kindred spirit in Mr. Endo. Here was a man who sat in one day yet expected another, more fanciful future in the next. If the future was so malleable – and just within his grasp – then why not the past as well? Endo's calendars proved that he could drift from one month to another and back again. He had taken the complimentary soap and his electronic gadgets and designed his own imaginary past, present, and future. Any one of them might have been real or unreal.

I looked around Endo's apartment for more of these fragments.

"Is Hello Kitty from the real world or the imaginary?"

"She is real," he beamed, "abso-*loot*-ally!" (Either Endo stretched the word into three gulps to add emphasis to this remark, or his mouth had trouble wrapping itself around the word.)

"Gentle Bunny?" I asked.

"Imaginary!"

I looked at a calendar. "And the woman who sits in December?"

"Ah," he said. "That depends. If she is in December then she must be real. But the next woman who waves to us from January," he paused, "she is imaginary."

I had heard Endo in the evenings, getting up from his *kotatsu* table, turning on the tap water to freshen his tea, then returning to his notebooks with a slow, inspiring shuffle. And I made sense of these sounds when I saw that his *kotatsu* had a skirt that covered the table's legs, and that an electric urn sat next to it. Fixed to the underside of this desk, an electric warmer proved the Japanese maxim, "Warm feet, cool thoughts." He lived this advice. He said he plugged in his electric carpet year-round. The heat killed the bugs in the tatami and kept his futon dry and warm. Likewise, Endo's thin frame warred against the cold. An urn of hot green tea beside him, he would free his mechanical pencil, open a notebook, and begin filling the notebook's squares with neat Japanese characters. Under the table's skirt, his legs would toast until it became too comfortable to work. Then he simply went to bed.

In the mornings I heard him wake late, hang his futon to dry, and rearrange the same desk for breakfast. If it was Friday, one calendar sent him to visit his mother. If it was Wednesday, he went to the dentist. I asked him about this habit of his – this strange penchant for seeing the dentist on such a regular basis. He insisted that the best dentists only work on one tooth at a time.

"Each week," he said, "my dentist concentrates on only one part of my mouth." He explained that his gums must also heal and that regular visits were "extremely mandatory." I imagined a theme park of bridges and braces inside his mouth, or a work-site that was curtained off, dug, drilled, and landfilled within an hour. A decade of weekly plaque shavings that could fill a wheelbarrow.

"Peanuts?" he asked.

"No, thanks."

"After next year," he promised, looking at the other calendar, "I will abso-*loot*-ally have the best mouth in Japan. Tea?"

"Sure."

This mouth, he explained, was no small dream. The Japanese have one of the softest diets in the world. Udon noodles, sushi, sashimi, even their tempura dishes are so soft that they give the teeth no challenge whatsoever. Years before Western candy made its way to Japan, the children would gnaw on chewy, sun-dried squid between meals, giving their gums the workout desperately needed to push their new teeth down, in straight paths toward proper bites.

"Now we are a country held together by dental records," he said. "Fingerprints for you, dental visits for us!"

I knew a number of adult students who seemed painfully afraid of showing their crooked teeth, their smiles, or their adult-fitted braces, so this news held a vague personal logic. Endo seemed to agree: "A Western smile can be a difficult thing. Perhaps I will teach the Western smile to my students."

"And the Japanese smile?" I asked.

"That takes a lifetime," he said. "It is a mask."

He poured the tea into two small cups and we assembled ourselves on opposite sides of the *kotatsu*. But before we could debate the inequity of cataloguing an entire country by their wisdom teeth, Endo changed the subject and asked me if I'd ever met a man named Colonel Sanders-san.

"The chicken guy?"

"Yes, that is him."

"No, I haven't," I said. "I think he's dead."

"Not!" said Endo. "You may be from America, my friend, but you do not know about the Colonel."

In fact, I had noticed that outside every Kentucky Fried Chicken restaurant in Saitama, Colonel Sanders was wearing a red and white Santa Claus suit that vaguely resembled my own. Between the Colonel and June (with his makeshift costume) I seemed to find doppelgängers everywhere I looked. If someone had turned the Colonel into yet another Santa Claus, who was I to complain?

It was Christmas Eve, and five more schools had requested Santa's presence (and presents). So I woke early that morning, took the pillow from my bed, wedged a corner of it into my boxers, and hauled my red pants over the whole bloated mess. The stuffed belly needed only a little adjusting. But the walk to the car settled my stomach into its proper proportions. In this persona, I grabbed my jingle bells and made for the parking lot. Jingled down the stairs, each step. Jingled past the wall of mailboxes and down the open-aired hallway. Jingled past a single bulb that lit the parking lot.

The morning was quiet. The grey asphalt seemed to be painted just for these tired days, with overcast skies and blurred mountains, blue in the distance. Space was at a premium, and the cars were wedged into their usual spots, backed in like tatami slippers on a rough asphalt mat. A quick getaway – the graceful exit – and I was gone, driving across the Kanto plain.

After Christmas I folded my costume, boxed it with my beard and jingle bells, then delivered it to one of the school secretaries. I knew that my students would be returning to class in one week, but during the holidays I felt strangely jobless without the Santa suit. Endo's challenge – to learn about Colonel Sanders – seemed to stick in my mind.

In a Japanese almanac I learned that Colonel Sanders came to Japan in a bid to improve domestic sales. Like most foreigners, he came here to work. In 1993 alone, Colonel Sanders grossed almost $70 million in Japan. While these details were mildly interesting, they did little more than suggest I give up teaching immediately. I mentioned the book and the statistics to Endo and – later that evening – I found a newspaper clipping in my mailbox.

The article was cut from the *Japan Times,* an English daily that was published throughout Japan. Some of my students bought the paper to practise their English, but Endo evidently studied it to learn more about foreigners. I read the headline: "Colonel, thrown in river, resumes his post in Osaka." There was a photo below. A Japanese woman, wearing a striped Tigers baseball cap, was hugging the Colonel. Both figures were smiling, but the woman had a face full of braced teeth that shimmered in the camera's lens.

Like myself, Colonel Sanders had changed occupations upon arrival. From what the article implied, the Colonel had become a baseball player . . .

On October 16, 1985, the Kansai Hanshin Tigers baseball team had won the Central League pennant for the first time in more than twenty years. Osaka went mad with celebrations. Firecrackers, singing, mob euphoria, flags, and chanting fans are the norm in Japanese baseball, but this event brought something fresh: the Tigers had soundly beaten Tokyo's Yomiuri Giants, the best team in the Japanese league. A baseball mob left the stadium and spread out across Osaka's Minami entertainment district, straddling both sides of the Dotonbori River. One by one, fans dove off a bridge into the river, each screaming the name of one of their immortal Hanshin Tigers. They called out the name of every player who'd played in that game except one: a certain Randy Bass.

Bass was from the West. Each Japanese team was allowed two foreign players, and – as the Tigers' power hitter – Randy Bass had led the team toward a miraculous victory.

After the game, there was a moment when the baseball mob looked for someone who resembled the American player, a pause that approximated a post-game rain delay. Certainly, there must have been a sense of nervous confusion, a suspension of disbelief, while they looked at each other for an authentic Bass lookalike. The mob – threatened with derailment – was quickly losing its enthusiasm for chasing its players toward enlightenment.

Quite suddenly, someone in the crowd noticed a large Caucasian man standing nearby. The man was smiling, rather confidently. He was thickset, just a little shorter than Randy Bass, but he stood – rock solid – outside a Kentucky Fried Chicken restaurant. His baseball jersey was smooth and white. He seemed to benignly watch the crowd moving toward him. Despite his white moustache, the man's smile was radiant. His cheeks bulged with possibility. And if his name was not actually Randy Bass, it did not worry the mob.

A single, amoebic thought held them together and they spread themselves toward Colonel Sanders, surrounding him, touching his head and glasses and grasping for his solid, downcast arms. At first, the Colonel did not seem willing to join them. He refused to be torn from his pedestal and seemed to lean back against the crowd's desperate plea of force. His smile thinned as his head went back, then the Colonel returned, beaming, when he was righted. He leaned forward and the crowd first pulled and pushed him toward the Dotonbori. Behind, they patted his back and his white figure seemed to bounce, jovially, through the crowd. When he reached the bridge, the Colonel moved more slowly because there were so many people who wanted to touch him, so many more people who had to lean into his narrow path, then sweep themselves out of his wake.

At the bridge's edge, the Colonel rose up above the crowd. Though his feet were unsteady on their hands, the Colonel's eyes were unwavering. The sun travelled across his goatee and furrowed his eyebrows.

The crowd cheered through this euphoric moment of baseball history. They cheered that a ragged team of outsiders had finally beaten Tokyo's Yomiuri Giants and no one heard the Colonel scream out the name "Randy Bass." To be fair, the Colonel was twisting in the air and could not properly speak a name, upside down, in that instant when a moment can sometimes hang like a tossed coin.

But he cleared the rail and the momentum of his dive sent his concrete feet over his head, tumbling, so that he appeared to dive headfirst into the river. As his head touched the water, the same momentum that propelled him over the rail pushed his heels forward. His legs splashed down together and he greeted the water with a marvellous bellyflop. No one actually saw him raise his arms, but the Colonel seemed to flail with the current as he went down into the water. His head bobbed three or four times. Smiling bravely, his head stayed above water until something unseen – something in the water's murk – pulled him down. From the bridge, the baseball crowd saw a glimmer of white, then the Colonel disappeared. No one has seen him since, in Osaka, because the Colonel was never found.

Finally, on November 12, 1992, a new statue was placed in the vacant pedestal outside the Dotonbori restaurant.

I returned the article to Endo's apartment and he nodded, slightly, and filed it in a side drawer.

"I checked the stats," I said. "Since the Colonel disappeared, the Hanshin Tigers have never come close to winning a major-league pennant."

He didn't acknowledge or contest my remark, except to say that, during the team's seven-year slump, vicious rumours spread throughout Japan. It was said that the Colonel's ghost had cursed the team and plagued it with eternal misfortune.

"So, he *is* dead," I said, hoping to incite him toward agreeing with me.

"Not!" Endo said. "*Hana de kikimasu*: you are listening with your nose. The Colonel is one of my drifting stories. He'll be back! The Colonel who washes away from Japan, riding on the Dotonbori, will win baseball games in other cities."

I smiled.

"He will return. Abso-*loot*-ally."

The summation of the tale seemed to suggest the evening's closure as well. So I thanked Endo for the tea and for sharing the article with me, then tried to extract myself from the low table. The *kotatsu*'s warmth radiated from my numb, pretzeled legs and made it easier for me to disentangle left from right. On my way through the kitchen I turned around, made a little bow (an awkward show of thanks), turned into the hallway, and opened the door to his bedroom by mistake.

I had expected to see the front door of my own carbon-copy apartment. Instead, I saw dozens of books – old books – and more loose papers, newspapers, and flutter books, completely surrounding Endo's low futon. His newspapers had overtaken the room like a dull ocean of crested paper waves. Near the centre, a solitary Hello Kitty reading lamp waved for help. His bed, a raft that safely bobbed along the surface.

I could hear Endo blush his way toward me, either to see me out or to close the door to his bedroom's chaos. And I was about to apologize but Hello Kitty caught my eye, and I saw the page she illuminated. In English, the headline read: "The prison odyssey of Ranald MacDonald."

I stared at the paper whirlpool and would not be budged.

"Another drifting story," said Endo.

He picked up the piece of paper by the lamp and showed me the article, perhaps to lure me out of the room, into the hallway. There was a black-and-white photo at the bottom of the page. In it, a dark, heavyset man stared at the camera and shrugged. Someone had drawn on the man's photo, giving his eyes a peculiar combination of grey and brown, a hazel line that circled each grey iris like a band of rust.

"They were my father's papers," he said, and the gentle tone of his voice made me look at him.

When he smiled, slightly, I knew that his father was no longer living.

"He smoked like a fish," said Endo, wistfully. "And he had a heart attack when I was still in high school."

I nodded and apologized for the intrusion.

"This way," he signalled, opening the proper door for me to leave.

I turned the corner to my apartment, on the other side of Endo's swirling "library," and said good night.

Memories of forgetfulness

Two rows of fingers

The light of the fishing torches sinks to the bottom of the waves and startles the fish; the oarsman's song on the nocturnal boat rises upward to waken the traveller from sleep.

– Noro Masashi describing Hashimoto,
a post station on the shore of Lake Hamana

Mister Endo died in 1964 after he'd strained himself lifting a box of pickled radishes. He set the box down, quickly, as if he could reverse the effects of the wrench that gripped his chest. He focused on one hand, still resting on the box. He noticed the yellow cigar stains on his fingers. Then he looked into the box and saw that the pickled radishes were clean and white. After a minute's reprieve he tried to straighten himself up, but his heart was a knot that refused to stretch. Something inside him seemed to pull and tear and shriek the instant he was almost on his feet. It wasn't his heart, he thought. It must be something else.

Hideo was sixteen, and he hadn't helped his father with the shop's opening ceremonies since he'd begun high school, almost a year before. But when he was told the news of his father's death Hideo felt a heat flash run through his body like the blue kite he remembered from his childhood. He felt his blood rush with the news. A hot wind overtook him, as if a door had just opened, and closed forever.

A few days later he watched his mother bag two packages of udon noodles, a box of green tea, a handkerchief, and a bottle of *sake*. There was also a note that she signed, in extremely formal Japanese, which read, "Thank you for attending my husband's funeral." She filled several hundred white paper bags with the same gifts and on the last twenty-five she wrote, "Thank you for attending my *father's* funeral."

Mister Endo was taken to the hospital for confirmation, then home, where he was to stay for three days. A doctor drove him home in a long black car and gave Hideo a bag of dry ice to keep him cool. Then he edged Mister Endo off the wooden gurney and arranged him on a table so that his head pointed south, for the first time in his life. While Hideo's mother dressed her husband in a long coat (with tails), and fit the rocks of dry ice along his arms and legs, Hideo watched the doctor leave. The doctor smiled at the boy. This visit was required by law, he said, a "prudent" custom from years ago, when the dead sometimes woke up, as if by mistake. He said this to Hideo with a bit of a gleam in his eye, without explaining exactly whose mistakes these were, the hospital's mistakes, his, or the body's. Hideo quickly dismissed both the consolation and the man. He was sixteen now, and he could recognize an adult's lie when he heard one.

Fifteen twenty-foot floral arrangements soon surrounded the house. They were circular arrangements, supported by three poles, and they resembled huge painter's easels. The only difference between these arrangements and the other ones that sit outside their department store, announcing a sale, were the bits of black that could be seen in the flowers and a large kanji character in the centre that read, "to bury."

At the outdoor funeral service, Hideo sat on the veranda with his mother and watched the guests file through the yard to pay their respects and wait in line. At the front of the line a bald monk conducted the ceremony. Tattoos peeked out of the sleeves of his green robe. Gongs filled the afternoon. Incense suffused the garden. Hideo was partially screened and watched the mourners mimic each other. He wondered if the next person in line distorted each successive bow. Nameless, faceless strangers pinched incense from a nearby container, touched their foreheads, then sprinkled the dust into a smouldering bowl. They brought their hands together in prayer, bowed deeply, and turned to follow the others.

He watched them sign their names in a ledger and leave an origami envelope, with a bill in the lucky denomination of three, five, or ten. The paper was folded in such a way as to hide both the money and the amount that they'd written on the corner of the envelope. Finally, they passed a reception table where they exchanged numbered tickets for the noodles, tea, and handkerchiefs. They left with these things, his mother's gifts, chatting happily about the weather and the pleasant service.

That night Hideo went with his mother to another place – a building on the edge of Kumagaya – and waited for his father to burn. It was the same feeling, he thought: waiting for his father to finish listening to someone else, waiting to be heard. He wanted to prolong the moment – quite suddenly – he wanted to wait for his father for as long as he could. But twenty minutes flew by and then they were shuffled through the crematorium, into another room that held a lacquer table and three backrests.

His father, Mister Endo, was on the table, waiting for them in a silver-blue bowl. His mother had chosen that bowl, an iridescent raku that shimmered like the side of a wet fish, and she arranged herself in one corner while Hideo faced a man who had lines drawn all over his face. The disparity between the cremator's papery face – cross-grained with wrinkles – and the bowl was shocking, because the bowl was so alive and wet with colour. Mirrored in the black table, another silver-blue bowl swam just below the surface.

The old man pulled two pairs of chopsticks from a side drawer and presented them to Hideo and his mother. She didn't wait for Hideo. She stirred the remains until she found one small bone, and then she looked at her son.

Hideo thought that he was ready for this moment: the gathering of bones. Of course he'd never practised for it. He did remember reaching for a piece of food once, and finding that another set of unmated chopsticks had already claimed the morsel. Arguments over shrimp tempura only mocked the dead, so he'd dropped the food immediately.

But he knew they should be lifting his father together, two sets of chopsticks holding a single, white fragment. He knew that the cremator was already imagining the bone, constructing its significance within his father's life. Was it a heel? Was it from the foot that carried his father to work? The patella, that floated like a rowboat upon his knee? Whatever the answer, this man was an expert at deciphering the meaning of the bones and extracting the last utterance that the dead might have to speak. And for whatever reason, Hideo did not want to listen to him.

He knew that they would be left alone for one week and that they would never see the man again. He knew that seven days later all his relatives would come to honour his father, then again forty-nine days after the funeral. On the anniversary of his father's death, Hideo would go with his mother to the gravesite and they would remember his father's words – spoken by this cremator – and together they would pray for his father's soul to come back to earth. After that, his father would visit each *obon*, on the third week of every August, for the rest of their lives.

He'd seen cabbage leaves and flowers hanging from the other gravestones. Sometimes he'd seen cans of *sake*, beer, coffee, or packages of sushi. His mother told him that whatever the dead enjoyed in life, they continue to crave in the next world. On some marble shrines he'd even noticed embossed packages of cigarettes that read, *Speak Lark!*

So while he waited for the crematory man to speak, Hideo remembered his father's cigars and his bright eyes. He thought back to that moment in the *depaato* when their eyes had met and his father had spoken to him, somehow, across a crowded store. And suddenly he wanted to be alone with his father, instead of waiting for this shrivelled old man to speak. He wanted to decipher his father for himself.

Hideo closed his eyes in the same second that he raised his chopsticks and he struck the bowl (as if by mistake) with the side of his hand. Upsetting the balance, he toppled his father – a flash of rebellion – and dashed the table with all his father's worldly memories.

Ten years later, a paragraph in a newspaper rekindled one of those memories. Within the pages of the *Daily Shimbun*, Hideo found an article that mentioned a man named Ranald MacDonald. A map marked his floating passage through the Tsugaru Straits. There was a photo of him, this unlikely sailor who might have composed Mister Endo's dictionary – MacDonald was shrugging one shoulder at the bottom of the page. He was now claimed by both Canadian and U.S. historians. During his lifetime MacDonald had watched the lines of political geography slide and blur, as if he'd gone to sleep inside British North America and woken, one February, in Oregon.

The photo was wedged between a letter to the editor and an article about the red foxes that were overtaking the streets of Hakodate.

Hideo began to search for this unlikely man named Ranald MacDonald. And he found him in the strangest places: inside a book on the Indians of Lower Columbia; on microfiche cards in a Tokyo library of prison records; and, of course, upon his father's bookshelves.

He learned that MacDonald was the second son of a princess, the daughter of the Chinook Indian chief King Com-Comly. Her name was Koale xoa, or Raven. She was named for the colour of her hair – an "Egyptian brown," said MacDonald, in a letter to a friend, as though divorcing his mother from the colour of her skin. She was the second daughter of the last Indian king of North America. And here, even in genealogy, MacDonald seemed both lucky and unlucky. He was the last royal Chinook, but not quite the last. The first American in Japan, but not quite the first. He was also Canadian, but not quite Canadian.

Near the end of June, in 1848, a sailor, named Ranald MacDonald, consigned himself to the sea and practised over-turning his boat near a small island, off the western ear of Hokkaido. His boat was seaworthy and rigged for sailing, but not so difficult to flip if he leaned into the mast and swung himself away from the boom. The foot of the boat's sail dipped into water, dragging the long spar with it, and as his world rolled into the sea, MacDonald watched his deck planks pop, slide, and float away.

The current was cold. MacDonald hung from the boom and reached out for his wooden trunk, keeping it near the vessel. When the boat and the slosh of waves and the moment itself were stable, he dragged the chest lee-side, fumbled under the knob of his bowsprit, then used one hand to feel his way down the bottom of the boat. He'd lost one paddle, but he was still pleased with himself when he found that he could lift himself partially out of the water and right the craft by dangling off the bilge keel. He bailed her with a glazed-hard felt cap, keeping his provisions close to the side. Righting the boat would be an easier job, he decided, if he had filled the chest with water, then used the extra weight to make ballast.

Unfortunately, no one saw him. Except for a few gulls and a herd of sea lions, the island was deserted. His Japanese invasion had gone unnoticed. He would have to begin again – find another place – feign a small shipwreck and pretend to walk ashore a salvaged man.

In the waves he'd lost his Hadley quadrant – a marvellous device that he'd used only once. Despite this setback, MacDonald spent the last two days of June 1848 exploring his tiny island, imagining the place that waited for him on the other side of the water. As he walked, he thumbed a rolled pipe of linen that had been torn from a ship's sail. Unscrolled, the pipe became his map where he sketched his wanderings. He'd copied Von Siebold's directives to whalers who braved the northwest passage down the edge of Yesso. Several mythical sea creatures bordered the design and hinted at the island's fantastic cosmogony. A mixture of rough Japanese and fearful Latin listed not destinations but places best to avoid: Volcano Bay, Malespini, C. Blunt, Sangar (its bay of blood), and a shoal of mid-ocean rocks that Von Siebold lists with a glass pen on sheepskin. At the far eastern edge of this country – between "Yes" and "so" – Von Siebold's hand seems to waver, as if approaching the crease in the map he must somehow ignore. And from this place, from the hollow where someone might look for the city of Yes, MacDonald could see Yankeshiri, large and snowcapped, above him. The volcano speared a thin rake of clouds.

Clock-calm, the wind was slack on this morning, so MacDonald made all the sail he could, set course for Yankeshiri, then took a mallet to his rudder. The hinge and plank would be found by a passing ship – the *Uncas* – sailing from New Bedford, some eight miles away. He decided that whatever happened to him now, he was officially "a shipwrecked sailor." Aft, the morning fog advanced and seemed to agree with his thoughts by pushing him farther away from the whaling ships, farther from the islands and everything he knew. So MacDonald spooned before the sea and used a quadrant to head north, roughly thirty-three degrees toward Russia. Thankfully, the Tsushima current swung his boat close to the Tsugaru Straits that separated Hokkaido from the larger Japan. But at the edge of Von Siebold's map, past the northern, snowcapped island of Rishiri, MacDonald finally found a place to paddle his rough craft toward land.

Inside his trunks he had stored thirty-eight books. Chock-full of learning, his boat groaned with lofty thoughts and grammar guides. MacDonald chose the books before departing America, hoping that his time in Japan could be used in some exchange of language. He was Christian, so he brought several bibles – two leather-bound, two without covers. Then he packed both Homer's *Iliad* and *Odyssey*, because they were the only two stories that can ever be written: the war and the journey.

He found no Japanese dictionary in any of the ports where they had docked, so he brought English, Portuguese, and Dutch dictionaries, grammar guides, and Church of England prayer books. He hoped that some missionaries' books may have fallen some two hundred years and four generations to the present and greased the way. Floating the Portuguese and Dutch dictionaries between the bars of his cage, he planned to use the books as buoys, meant to narrow the distance between English and Japanese. He thought a word in English could be translated into Portuguese or Dutch using books, then – once spoken, midstream – the same word could be found in Dutch–Japanese dictionaries on the other side.

Besides general history books, he brought scientific journals on the measurement of starlight, a book on longitude and the *Mundus Symbolicus* book of meanings. Looking for subjects that the known world and Japan might hold in common, he included Padua University's treatise on the circulation of blood and – within this book – sea charts that plotted warm-weather patterns for crossing the Pacific Rim. He counted on the shared trajectories of blood and wind. Months away from his first conversation he was already plotting a starting place, a skid.

And against the shogunal decree, he brought brass spoons. Not a set that resembled the Puritan spooned apostles, nor the one large soupspoon, traditionally destined for Christ, but a full set of spoons and forks and fruit knives. A walking wind chime, he heard the cutlery jangle in his bags with each step. The sand crunched under his feet and he remembered the touch of it, the way sand buckled under his arch when he was a child.

Japan had come to him the same way: during night-time storms. As a child, he had walked along the beach and found glass balls that were the size of his ten-year-old head. The balls were hollow and green and the glass was thick, but he could still look through them and see his hands on the other side. He learned that they were fishing bobbles used to buoy nets, and were dragged and left in the sea by the Japanese junks. Left to float their nets and curtain the fish below, the bobbles sometimes broke free to traverse the world. He could imagine them swirling the Pacific. He found blue sailors on the beach after every storm. Walked around their jellied bodies. A day later, the bobbles arrived, first the large then the small. Saw the tops of their heads submerged in the sand. Caught the glint of glass only from a distance, with the help of the rising sun.

If he could find employment as a teacher, he believed that his own knowledge of Chinook jargon – a trader's language – would help him in Japan. He also believed, completely without cause, that the Japanese and his mother's people shared the same blood.

When MacDonald came ashore, on the island of Rishiri, he was greeted by a half-dozen fisherman. The men tried to push him away from the beach and erase his tracks in the sand, but MacDonald faltered to one knee, fell into the surf, and left his boat to drift.

The boat was retrieved, brought ashore, and MacDonald was made to sit while one of the men ran up the beach. Within minutes, he came back with another man – the second was dressed in deep-blue robes. In Japanese, then in Portuguese, the man in blue gave MacDonald the words "Come, come."

MacDonald walked through a white town – white because his passage through the village was curtained by sheets held up by small brown hands. He walked a quarter-mile within this whiteness and never saw a face. The most he saw were wooden sandals and – above the white sheets – two rows of fingers without thumbs . . .

I didn't want to ask Endo about his father, or bother him about MacDonald, deciding to wait until the time was right, when our conversation flowed naturally toward those two subjects. But I enjoyed our evening visits and, after exactly one week of putting up with my prodding requests for a Japanese name, Endo met me one night with a story that could be called *The Crane and the Loom.*

"I think impatience is a Western custom," he said, half-serious. When I rolled my eyes he added, "But this name might actually help you. Do you remember the paper crane?"

I nodded.

"From now on, your name will use characters for *ori, hana,* or *ba,* but will suggest the words for *weave* and *wing.*"

"So what do they mean when you put them together?" I asked. "Wing-weaver?"

"I'll tell you an old story. There was a time when a young man named Yohyo . . ."

"Yo-yo!"

"Wait," he said. "Be patient."

I promised to hold my breath until the end of Endo's story.

Yohyo, he said, was working in a rice field. He was planting the shoots in straight lines of two sprigs each, making a green frill in mud that could be seen just under the water's surface. Near the end of the morning, on the side of a mudbank, he found a crane that had an arrow through its wing. When Yohyo pulled the arrow out of the bird, the moment itself seemed to brighten and the bird sat upright and looked at him. Yohyo washed the blood away from the wing and let the bird walk away through the unplanted section of his field. It was evening by the time he finished his work, and when he returned home he was so tired that he didn't see the figure standing by the door until he was right next to her.

Welcome home, said the woman.

Who are you? asked Yohyo.

I am your new wife, she said.

"This sounds rather promising," I said, letting out one breath between paragraphs.

"Not!" said Endo, smiling. "You'll have to wait. There's a little more."

The woman's name was Tsu and she said that she has come to take care of Yohyo. Sit back, she said. I have made you dinner and after you have eaten, you can sleep. Then Tsu made him promise not to disturb her while she worked in another room.

As he fell asleep Yohyo heard the sound of a loom chafing through the night. By morning, she had returned from the room and had a gift of cloth in her arms. Tsu was visibly tired, but she walked toward Yohyo and placed a batch of purple silk at his feet.

The next night was the same, and the same after that. A gift of dinner, sleep. and a morning batch of silk. Tsu grew tired with each new day, but Yohyo asked her to make more cloth. He didn't like planting rice and he wanted to sell the cloth in the city. He asked his wife to make more cloth each night, and each morning she appeared with a new bolt of silk.

"This is the origin of silk in Japan," said Endo, "from the crane . . ."

"Please hurry up," I said. "He has to break his promise, look into her room, find out that she is the crane and then she flies off, right?"

Endo smiled. "That may be so. He is as impatient as you! This is a good name for you, I think. The story fits."

Weaver. (Or was it Wing-weaver?) I liked the name well enough, but I didn't subscribe to this idea that my Western impatience was part of my "essential character." It sounded like a trap (even a prison) in the guise of a beautiful label.

"Not!" he said. Endo explained that a name is a kind of vehicle – a boat, perhaps – that could carry me along. I could get out at any time.

The story wasn't really a cautionary tale, then, but a gentle suggestion to listen more and ask less. "You can learn many things in one year," he said, "if you have patience to discover them."

I took his suggestion and started formal Japanese lessons the next week. Endo arranged everything. He said he would help me with conversational Japanese, while another teacher – a family friend – taught me grammar and calligraphy.

Her name was Etsuko Kobashi. She was sixty-seven years old. Her hair was cut sharp at her shoulders and she wore a tailored business suit that looked purple in one light, green in another. She spoke no English, but when addressing foreigners she seemed to enunciate so clearly that the tone and force of her words carried a certain translatable impact. When I first met her I believed that her lessons were confrontations, designed to incite or coerce me into following her. She marched through the Japanese vocabulary with regimental fervour, building an army out of the Hiragana sound syllabary, five steps at a time:

Ka, Ki, Ku, Ke ... *Koh!*
Sa, Si, Su, Se ... *Soh!*
Ma, Mi, Mu, Me ... *Moh!*
Pa, Pi, Pu, Pe ... *Poh!*

Once I learned the Hiragana alphabet – for writing home-grown Japanese words – we pressed on toward Katakana, spelling words borrowed from other languages, words like *beddo* (bed), *apaato* (apartment) and *canzone* (Italian song). Foreign street signs and mysterious advertisements gradually became intelligible. Then, once I had read and understood those signs a second and a third time, they ultimately disappeared to their rightful place within the mundane.

Endo's conversational lessons reinforced these signs until, at five months, I was suddenly having trouble with Japanese. The words seemed bent on confusing me, or they bent themselves for that purpose. I called a ceiling a genius (*tenjo* vs. *tensai*), a child a fruit (*kodomo* vs. *kudamono*), an orange some free time (*mikan* vs. *jikan*), and cute became afraid (*kawaii* vs. *kowai*). All this led to exponentially more interesting conversations: "I was just going to buy some free time when I saw your beautiful fruit. How old is she? She looks like a ceiling. Very afraid."

Endo didn't help. He deliberately used a wrong word, steering me toward some conversational disaster, for as long as he could hold a straight face. He didn't seem "Japanese enough" to keep his emotions masked for very long. Or perhaps I was just beginning to understand his facial giveaways, hints, and expressions.

"Be careful," he said, smiling. "*Kuso* can mean fantasy, but *kuso* is also the word for insubstantial, and *kuso!*, with exclamation, is shit!"

At eight months the whole planet changed. A framework swung into existence as if I could suddenly piece the language together. Whole paragraphs sprung up, fully formed with oranges, ceilings, whole shopping centres, parking lots, and people. Kobashi-san gave me more words, alphabets in the form of pictographs. She brought concrete blocks of nouns, then verbs that I placed at the end of each sentence like hinges that suddenly swung my thoughts into action. Roughly eight months into my studies, an architecture of language suddenly appeared around me. And through these new signs, sounds, menus, and cities, I began to learn kanji. With the more difficult pictographs, Kobashi-san spoke her drawings into sight by explaining the meaning behind each that I encountered.

"A ghost," she said, threading her brush through the pictograph of three mountaintops, "winds its way through the mountains because it is alone. This is the kanji for *dark, obscure*, and *lonely*. The words for *mystery* and *netherworld* come from the same place."

After that kanji lesson, Kobashi-san made calls to three local schools in Saitama. She spoke softly to the principals and the next day I was put to work labelling one hundred and fifty soccer balls, at each school, with the words *flower* (part of the town's name), *middle, high*, and *school*.

"You needed a project," she said, by way of explanation. "This will keep you focused on the brushstrokes, not the ghosts inside words."

But she wasn't solely a kanji teacher. Kobashi-san was also a Shinto priest, someone who blessed buildings, promised good marriages and good deaths.

After one lesson, I watched Endo walk Kobashi-san to her car. Suddenly it must have occurred to her to give him a bottle of wine that she'd left in the car's front seat. Endo accepted the gift graciously and bowed, while she said something in Japanese. Then she noticed that I was nearby. She reached into her shopping bag and gave me an orange. I said thanks and she went back to Endo, placed two ripe peaches in his hand and went back to the car to collect some chestnuts. By the time she'd gone through most of her bag she remembered Shacho (unseen, somewhere in the school) and gave Endo an apple for him. The secretaries were forwarded oranges. And the new teacher (who was scheduled to arrive that afternoon) was given an fistful of tiny eggplants and a plastic, watery pouch of vegetable roots that resembled a bag of black guppies. Kobashi-san looked back at me, hoping to even the gifts somehow, and suddenly remembered a bottle of rice wine in her trunk.

The varied sizes of these vegetables created a problem for her. She paused, judging the size of a twisted sweet potato next to a bag of pearl rice. She'd begun a roller-coaster of vegetable altruism and seemed bent on continuing until she had virtually nothing left in her car, trunk, purse, or hands. After she'd presented the last, bright persimmon to Endo her arms were empty, except for a package of fish. She was unsure of the smell that came from the bag, so she kept this questionable item for herself.

In her clear, ironclad Japanese she explained to me that she often received food and much of it goes bad, so please take it.

After that day, Kobashi-san continued to give us bags of vegetables. These were the religious offerings that were given to her after she appeased the gods and fulfilled her religious duties for all the buildings she had blessed. Each Saturday we ate with the gods, eating what they couldn't finish.

I was looking forward to meeting the other teacher when she arrived. Her name turned out to be Charlotte. She was from Chicago and possessed a self-assurance that surprised me, at first, until I recognized that this was her protective instinct kicking in. She had thin blonde hair and a sharp nose that seemed to give her face the visual equivalent of an exclamation mark. She spoke quickly – all her thoughts a menu to choose from – and it was such an added surprise to hear full-blown English that I had trouble keeping up with her rapid-fire conversation. My own words came slower and slower. I tried to focus on her questions, her travel, her plans, until our "discussion" resembled a car, running over a startled deer in slow motion.

She noticed my blank stare and, finally, she asked, "So, where ya from?"

"Canada," I said.

"How do you spell that?"

"What?"

"Canada. How do you spell that?"

"The usual way," I hedged.

"C–eh?–N–eh?–D–eh?"

"Yup," I said. "As in Yup–eh?" I hoped to make her laugh at my only successful response, but she turned the joke completely around.

"You mean *yuppie*. So what's there to do here?"

Good question, I thought. A good question that hadn't even occurred to me.

Because news from the West was a premium, Charlotte and I began to trade books and magazines. Within a week we walked around quoting the same archaic references from *Mirabella* and *Rolling Stone*. To buy a new English magazine in Tokyo, the trip entailed the sacrifice of one day, railing our way back and forth, and roughly twenty dollars American to buy each magazine. As a rule, imported books were three times the cover price, so Charlotte usually just made the day trip into Tokyo and read all of the magazines on the shelves. Glowing with fresh memories from *People* magazine, she would return to Saitama with all the latest statistics for Hollywood marriages, divorces, and scandals (which usually involved five women wearing the same style of dress).

Occasionally, she'd call me over to watch Japanese commercials.

"Get this!" she screamed. "Sylvester Stallone is doing a commercial for Honey Hams!" Or, "Charlie Sheen is here for Modello Shoes!"

Charlie, alone in a phone booth, whispered the words: "Lost . . . in your eyes." Finally, at the end of the commercial, the camera travelled from his face to the shoes and we heard a quick battery of Japanese. Charlotte positively chortled, thrilled with the idea that an English phrase – some nonsensical declaration – could be used so freely.

"It doesn't matter *what* you say here," she said. "They just want to hear something English!"

Another time, Charlotte cancelled her Yomiuri newspaper delivery and took a mid-week trip to Tokyo. When she returned, the newspaper refused to start her subscription up. They insisted that Charlotte had cancelled her newspaper delivery *forever* on Tuesdays and Wednesdays.

Undeterred by her communication troubles, she made plans to visit someone in Kumagaya for a late dinner, the same day. By eight o'clock the buses had stopped running and her only salvation was a taxi company that might, or might not, come to pick her up. The more she argued with the person on the other end of the telephone the more adamant she was to handle this situation by herself and get to Kumagaya for dinner. Her plan to escape the town became the Foreigner's Quest, a preoccupation that suddenly justified her existence and – she said – summed up what's really wrong with Japan.

"What's that?" I asked.

"This flagrant discrimination," she said in English, without covering the phone with her hand. She turned to me while someone on the other end of the phone talked into her ear. "I may be new here," she said, "but I know how to handle this sort of thing. Watch and learn.

"Listen to me," she said in Japanese, "I want to go to Kumagaya. I am in *the sticks*! I want to go to Kumagaya *now*." Her accent was strong. Like a train that hurried toward the inevitable, all her syllables were in place and – for the moment – I was quite impressed by her linguistic prowess, the sheer force of her conviction. She pummelled her words with a certainty I'd heard in her voice only once before . . .

The very week she arrived, Charlotte had tried to define and translate every Japanese sign and symbol she saw. She actually memorized the kanji for *Enter Here* and another phrase that she'd found on a bus window. To my amazement, she could remember these characters the next evening, and she drew them neatly on a restaurant napkin for Endo to translate. This involved a complicated set of slashes, boxes, and scribbled flourishes that Endo could not quite recognize. Only by squinting his eyes, then by turning the napkin around to read it from the back, held up against the light, did some genuine meaning filter through.

"What does it mean?" she asked.

"You found these on a bus," he said.

"Yes," she said. "How did you know?"

"You read these from inside the bus and you were sitting near the back of the bus, next to the door, with the ticker-tape machine rattling behind you."

"Yes!" she said.

"There was only one driver and you entered the bus from the back, instead of the front. Then you found a place, next to the window."

"How can you possibly know all this?"

Endo didn't want to tell her that the characters were written exactly backwards, and that she'd memorized the mirror image of the phrase *One Man Bus*. Her backwards, mirror image might have read *Bus One Man*, or, more appropriately, *Bus One Dyslexic Man*. But he didn't want to curb her interest by telling her the truth. Rather, he usually preferred to delve into the history of a word before giving up its modern meaning.

Bus, he explained, or as the Japanese say, *basu*, was taken from English and used so widely that almost no one knew that the old Japanese term for bus was *oogata noriai jidoushya*. The kanji translates into *big, get in/mix*, and *car*. Just as *taxi* wasn't really *takushi*, but *nigata noriai jidoushya*. *Small, get in/mix*, and *car*.

Charlotte, like many others he'd bored with such etymology, wasn't interested in this history. Her impatience gave him a kind of licence, I thought, to tell her anything she might have wanted to hear.

"Well, you've drawn these characters very well," he admitted. "Once you learn to read them, you can place the writer within a kind of frame, as I did. The script – not the words – will define this frame, as if you could read exactly how the writer recorded some moment, on a bus, where she was sitting, the hunch of her shoulders –" Charlotte straightened her back at this news – "as if you could sit right next to the writer, nudge her a little to abandon the armrest, and inhabit the very moment of her description . . ."

"Christ," she said. "Just tell me what the words fucking mean and skip this *ornamental* bullshit. You can *inhabit the moment* some other time."

"All right," he said. Then he told Charlotte the truth. Despite what she asked for, she didn't seem happy about her talent for reproducing backwards, inside-out kanji. Later, she blamed us both for prolonging this simple deception over the "ridiculous difference" between mixing people in cars and buses. This moment seemed to colour her Japan. Rather, it changed her perception from colour to black and white, and strengthened her resolve to define (and cheapen) Japan's mysticism wherever she found it.

Personally, I preferred a little mysticism to clean derivations. A backwards story always seemed more interesting than the inevitable Moral. So that day, I left Charlotte with her cold vivisection of the world.

After fifteen minutes of bantering for a taxi to Kumagaya, Charlotte gave the man her address, hung up the phone, and I said nothing when she smiled at her sudden success. She disappeared into the bathroom. Some five minutes later I heard the nasal tap of a horn outside our building.

I looked out the window to see a two-ton moving truck backing up to Charlotte's door. Three small men in matching blue jumpsuits dropped out of the truck's cab.

"Your ride's here," I said.

"It's about time," she said, without looking through the window. "Tell him to wait, I'll just grab my purse."

The three blue men walked to the back of their truck and began untying the hoist. An electric ladder unfolded, then began a slow descent. When the doors opened I could just glimpse a couple of dollies and a rack of green blankets inside the truck's cavern.

"Have you got enough money?" I asked.

"Yeah, everything's peachy," she said. "Chalk one up for the good guys."

"Hear, hear!" I said. "One for the good guys."

"Well, I'm off!" she said, emerging from the bathroom. "How do I look?"

"Just fine," I said. "Enjoy your evening."

The sky was clear. The blue mountains of Chichibu were moving from purple to black, merging into the night's sky. And that evening Charlotte walked out to a new appreciation of Japan. The next day, in the even light of global understanding, there were elaborate apologies and papers to sign. Our Shacho was scheduled to make an apologetic visit to the other Shacho for the moving-truck business. And when the mayor got involved, briefly, on the subject of foreigners in Japan, our school was commissioned a new project: a manual for future foreigners in Saitama, complete with bus routes, taxi numbers, and local club activities. Charlotte volunteered for the activity section, and let Endo and me fill in the rest.

"Hey," she said, "I got my ride to Kumagaya, didn't I?"

Most sunny weekends, I sat on the school sidewalk and read the sports page in the *Japan Times*. If it was Saturday I could usually hear Kobashi-san inside, teaching her weekly lesson to Charlotte. I wasn't just trying to pick up everything I heard in Japan; I'd actually grown fond of hearing the sound of Kobashi's marching voice, whether or not I was taking one of her classes.

And one day, after she had finished her lesson, Kobashi-san appeared above my sumo page and invited me for a walk. She told me that those who cannot afford a horse (and pay for its upkeep) must walk to the temples and present a tablet with a painted horse.

"We shall think about horses," said Kobashi-san, "and go on foot."

We walked toward her favourite temple in Saitama and passed a noodle hut, a bakery that refuses to sell anything sweet, and the only Seven-Eleven in town. There were sheets drying above Seven-Eleven. A band of slick-haired youths stood in the parking lot outside. The road ended beside a men's hair salon and at that point we turned south, walking farther along this road – the "Main Street" of Kounan-machi. On one side of the road, a patch of bamboo gave way to a tangle of thorny plants that scraped our legs as we walked. Beer cans, speared on bamboo sticks, marked the borders of each farmer's land. As usual, the cars were driving on the left-hand side of the road – almost all of them were white today – and we stood to the side to give them room on the narrow artery. Instead of waving to us, most of these drivers bowed their heads down to their steering wheels to thank us for making way.

As we walked beside the moving cars on one side, the marsh on the other, Kobashi-san told me a story. The Kappa, she said, lives in the mud and marsh, moving about in the night. He is a greedy ghost, a river boy who sniffs death and feeds on cows, children, and unwitting travellers. Sometimes, he resembles a boy between thirteen and fifteen years old; other times he is an upright turtle, with claws, shell, and beak. His skin is invariably green. And almost everyone says that he had a wide, stupid grin and that his eyes look up, from time to time, as if to check his eyebrows. His hair is bobbed, with a bald spot on top, in the style of monks who call this fashion O-Kappa, "Honourable Kappa."

Actually, said Kobashi-san, the Kappa holds a bowl of water on his concave head. The water is probably from the marsh, but wherever it is from, the fluid gives him strength. This water, she said, is the reason that we honour the Kappa with a bow. When the Kappa returns this bow the water on his head spills and his power disappears. He must run away in search of more water and this is our only chance for escape.

A poet and essayist named So Sakon wrote a group of poems dedicated to this monster. The Kappa, he said, feeds on his victims by reaching up into their intestines and "regaling" on their livers.

"Can you imagine," asked Kobashi, "a liver that hangs like an arbour of grapes? Can you see the sun that glows through those grapes at the end of a day?"

"I've seen that," I said. "Yes."

"That is the light that a Kappa sees when he looks at a liver," she said. "He runs his fingers across those glowing bulbs. He's intoxicated by the warmth and the trick of inner light."

In payment for this feast, the Kappa leaves behind a lantern that slowly burns itself out. When the victim dies, this lantern becomes a Kappa tomb that the creature revisits at will.

"Why does the victim die?" I asked.

"From lack of light," said Kobashi-san, touching her side, as if this translucent light was within her.

It struck me that this creature might be well suited for entry into Grimms' fairy tales. A bow that diminished a monster's power? Red Riding Hood protected herself with a similar decorum of flattery: "What big *teeth* you have, Grandmother!" But the fear of something black rotting *inside* a person seemed more insidious than a wolf in grandmother's clothing. The Japanese version also borrowed something from the Kappa's surroundings. Water, mud, and graveyards were no place for a wolf who hides in a white-cotton nightie. In this wet place it made sense that the Kappa lived beside the cockroach. A cockroach that left her eggs on dead insects, so that the larvae would have something to eat, for breakfast, when they woke.

But this is only a background for the Kappa, said Kobashi-san. There is more. The Kappa is a river-dweller and every town in Japan blames him for its drownings. He is said to be fond of cucumbers, so mothers customarily throw a slice into a river at the beginning of each swimming season. And each village in Japan has a different tale about this creature.

In Idzumo a Kappa was caught and begged for its life, promising never to drown another child. He was released and the promise was kept. In Kumamoto, a samurai jumped into a river, seeking revenge for the child that he'd lost to the water's current. After an afternoon of search and a night of battle, the samurai managed to cut off one of the creature's arms. A similar promise was secured from the Kappa and the samurai gave back the arm.

In Saitama, where Kobashi-san had lived her entire life, a Kappa once came out of the river and visited a woman. Her name was Sachiko and she had become, only recently, a widow. Her hair was cut short; the locks filled a small box within her husband's coffin. In keeping with tradition, she had shaved her eyebrows to prove that she had truly renounced the world. She gave up the day as well, sleeping through the afternoons with a fierce, solitary enjoyment. When the evenings were too long for sleep, Sachiko had the habit of sitting by a window to let the night's breeze cool her skin.

One night she felt a hand – a hairy hand – touch her own and she jumped away from the open window. The next day she told no one about the hand that had visited her. In fact, by the next evening, Sachiko had convinced herself that a hand could not possibly have reached in to touch her. She must have been dreaming. She'd fallen asleep, she decided, and her arm had fallen from the sill.

The next night – one more time – Sachiko sat by the open window and let the breeze run its course. She wasn't dreaming when, an hour or two later, she felt the same hairy hand reach for her wrist. This time she pulled herself back from the sill and, with a widow's clarity, made plans to fend for herself the next evening. Sachiko bought a knife, a blade so long that it should properly be called a sword. With a little practice she found that she could wield the blade with one hand.

The next evening, when her suitor came to call, Sachiko was ready. The knife was high in her other hand. She felt the breeze, then the unmistakable touch of someone's hand. Finally she brought the knife down, stabbed into the hand's warmth. The hairy hand broke off with the blade's touch and changed into a branch with five green twigs. In the even light of the next day, Sachiko found a trail of water that led from her window to the river, so she kept the strange branch and waited until evening for her visitor to show himself. She had an idea about the hand, and – if it proved true – she wanted to make an exchange.

The man who came to see her that evening was missing his right arm. He was curious, he said, about the rumour that he'd heard in the village, a story about a widow who had protected herself against a tree.

"Was it true?" he asked.

She said nothing, preferring to let him speak.

Next, he wanted to see the hairy hand and the twig that she'd found.

"Kappa," she said, "is that what you really want?"

He bristled. "I want what is mine returned."

"So do I," said the woman. "My husband is dead. And not even you can bring him back."

Now the Kappa was quiet, enjoying the possibility that his silence offered her.

"What will you do with this twig?" she asked him.

"I have some medicine," he said, "that can mend the past with the present. If you give the arm back to me I will show you how to make the medicine."

Sachiko agreed. She gave him the twig and watched it transform into an arm the second he slipped the branch into the cuff of his *happi*-coat. A Kappa always honours his debts, she said. Show me the medicine that can mend the past with the present.

The Kappa reached toward the woman and turned her around. His hands, suddenly translucent, scrawled down her back, then reached through her skin to touch her liver. This organ, he said, is amphibious. It grows and changes when the heart cannot.

Sachiko felt his fingers, tickling the details of her liver.

In death, a liver is divine. Death, he knew, hardens a liver until it becomes a right-angled, triangular prism, showing five smooth surfaces. (It was at this moment, holding his next thought in his hollow head, that the Kappa almost forgot his promise.) But in life, he said, a liver is fluid. A liver moulds itself to neighbouring organs, spreading to cover the diaphragm on one side, filling even hollow viscera with what can only be described as a greedy sense of delight to explore the world.

The Kappa found her liver – the traveller's organ – exactly where he expected it: slightly to the right side of her body, in the upper part of her abdominal cavity. To the left a shallow groove stretched like a river toward her aorta. Further still, a gall bladder, shaped like a ripe pear, and to the left of this sat the stomach, and finally the Kappa returned – full circle – to the left lobe of her liver. With his hands stretched across her stomach, he found an empty bridge that could be called the umbilical vein of a fetus, if she'd had one.

He held one hand across her abdomen and with the other hand he softened that place with some liquid, moulding her liver into the shape of a bowl. He wanted it to stretch like a trough toward the springs in her body that already existed. With a thumb he smoothed her liver toward that heady, liquid seat of emotion that she called her past.

Sachiko felt a cool sensation that began to burn like nostalgia gone sour, and when she woke up she found no sign of the Kappa.

In the weeks that followed she imagined the place in her stomach – the largest organ in her body – where hope was already collecting. She touched her stomach and remembered her husband's hands, pulling her toward him, his nocturnal need for reassurance. She knew that the Kappa had kept his promise.

More memories will come, she thought.

After her story, Kobashi-san walked lightly along the side of the road.

"You can still buy this medicine," she said, "in a few drug-stores in Kumagaya. It is called Kappa no Myoyaku, 'Kappa's mysterious medicine.'"

"What's it for?"

"The memory," she said. Then, "Memories are all we have."

The drivers continued to bow as we edged toward the curbless brush. And I imagined what we must have looked like: two roadside travellers who seemed to wait for the cars to pass. The light of the day and the glint of their windshields coloured us green. I remembered my mother – suddenly – and her broken windshields that forested hundreds of Christmas decorations.

It took us half an hour to reach the temple. The building was hidden by sad, overhanging trees. A long path met the road so suddenly that the steps leading from the temple seemed too surprised to continue. So we bent our bodies around the branches and I looked back at the road to see that pavement began, rudely, just past the veil of shadow. I could no longer hear the white cars that whizzed past, and we seemed to have entered a place that was apart from the real.

Kobashi's temple was small – with room for only one god on any one day – and completely surrounded by conifers. A news board, with a miniature roof, was pegged to the right side of the entrance. But instead of notices and meeting times, the board framed a dozen-odd children's bibs. Some of the bibs were old, stained with bad weather. Others were as white as business cards. Letters, folded into origami ribbons, hung from most of them. "Offerings," said Kobashi-san, "for those lost babies who do not complete the journey of birth."

Abortion, she said, was legal in Japan. I already knew this from reading comic books to improve my Japanese. Even the most generic comic *manga* had references and ghostly allusions to the aborted fetus that haunted a woman's future. The *hentai* (adult) *manga* presented a version of this abortion ghost that was nothing short of apocalyptic. A distorted baby – left in a garbage and crippled with neglect – usually grew into a monster that eventually killed its parents.

We moved closer to the temple and a nearby cast-iron cauldron. Kobashi-san reached into her purse and pulled two incense sticks from a paper wad. She put the incense into the cauldron, then lit a match that had materialized from nowhere. She waited for the smoke to waft toward her, then she helped it along with her open hands – splashing the white smoke across her face – until she was entirely immersed in its whiteness, washing herself in an imaginary sink of fumes.

Golfing with the Yakuza

The riddle of the sea

Marlboro girls in Electric Town

In Saitama, most winter mornings were so foggy that the cranes were trapped inside pillows of silence. They woke late, between eight and nine, and I could hear them – slow and lethargic as bleating sheep – outside the school's second-floor window as soon as the fog lifted from the trees.

Like the cranes, my high-school students preferred to sleep through this weather and through all their early-morning routines.

The older boys arrived at school, changed into plastic slippers, and then disappeared into a bathroom to repair their pompadours. The girls let down their uniform skirts that they had raised for the walk to school. And after an interval of gossip and chatter, they settled into their desks and usually fell asleep for the entire first period.

One morning in February I tried to shake my class out of this first-period fog by announcing a class composition. One by one, the students were supposed to come to the blackboard and write a single sentence.

"We will write a group short story," I said.

No one stirred. "Together," I added.

I found ten reluctant volunteers (nine girls and one boy) in a classroom of forty-five. Nobuko, Akemi, Kumiko, Makiyo, Ayako, Yukiko, Asako, Rie, Setsuko, and Yoshimi, one writer at a time, they dragged themselves toward the blackboard. In a matter of seconds, without any planning or discussion, they composed the following story: *A strange thing happened to me. Yesterday I woke up but I didn't hear anything. I became like Helen Keller. I became famous. I got a lot of money. I built a big house. However, I was only dreaming. So I went to school. Every day is the same. One day I even dreamed the same thing.*

I came to understand this fog and experienced it myself – first-hand – one day when Endo knocked at my door at six in the morning.

"Fresh morning" he said. "Do you want to go golfing at this moment?"

"No," I said.

"I have an employee-request form. We can take the day and go golfing with a very important student. You would like to meet him."

"Please," I begged him. "I'm so tired."

Before I could close the door, Endo jammed the piece of paper between the door and the lock. I opened the door wide, letting more of the morning inside, and looked at the page.

"Just sign the date for February fifteenth," he said, even though it was already the nineteenth. "It doesn't matter, you know." Endo's personal *hanko* stamp was already at the bottom of the page giving our day off executive approval several days in advance of our request.

"Ah," he stopped himself, "better write February fourteenth on it – I wasn't here on the fifteenth. This employee-request form cannot be valid if I'm not here. It must be sitting on my desk for several days."

I didn't argue with his logic. I signed the form and left to get dressed for a day of golf.

I once saw a film documentary that skirted the origins of golf in Japan. Just before the Second World War, Will Rogers arrived in Tokyo and was met at the airport by dozens of Japanese reporters who were anxious about his travel plans. Vacillating between national pride and a desperate need for approval, the reporters crowded around Rogers seconds after his arrival and asked him these three questions:

Press: Mr. Rogers, you must like Japan very much?
Rogers: Yes, I do. You might remember the last time I come over here – you were at war. I'm glad to come over here in peace 'n' everything. Mr. Roosevelt told me: "Now, Will, don't you go over there and jump on Japan; you just keep them from jumping on us."
Press: Then you're on a goodwill tour?
Rogers: I ain't on any goodwill tour – see, that's what's a matter with our country, sending so many people around with goodwill. I bring no goodwill at all – none at all. I'm not here for that.

Press: Mr. Rogers, Mr. Rogers! Have you heard? Japan has adopted your favourite pastime. Can you guess? It is golf.

Rogers: Now that's the beginning of the end. Now you've gone in for golf, it won't be long till you are right where we are – in the business of supremacy of the world.

Endo's student was definitely in the business of supremacy of the world. He was also a well-known and well-respected Japanese mafia man.

"A Y-guy," said Endo, preferring not to use the word *Yakuza.* "Mr. Sato-san has only these fingers." He lifted his hand and showed me his index fingers and thumbs.

"If you make mistakes in the Yakuza, or if you change from one family to another, you must give up one finger. They usually begin with the pinkie and alternate hands until the knife has travelled all the way toward the thumb."

"A travelling knife?"

"When you finally give up this," said Endo, waving his index finger at me, "you abso-*loot*-ally learn respect. What good is a hand that has only a thumb?"

Endo went on to explain that Mr. Sato was fond of instilling lessons of respect in his underlings – especially while he played golf. The game demanded a certain focus and utter patience, ideals he wished to instil in his subordinates. Only one disappointment had blemished an otherwise perfect record of mafioso respect.

Two years ago, Mr. Sato had examined the tee on the last hole, squatted to measure the ball's flight toward the green, and used one hand to pinch a sprig of grass between his thumb and his one remaining finger.

Regardless of the other players who waited for him to move from the last tee, Mr. Sato tested the wind at leisure. Of course, no one disturbed his concentration. The underling, who held Mr. Sato's bag, solemnly waited for him to decide which club to use and nodded, imperceptibly, when Mr. Sato asked for a four iron. Mr. Sato's opponent looked away, back over the course they had walked, as if to regard the slow progress they had made as they whittled a passage through a wooden afternoon.

When Mr. Sato had finally chosen the ball's flight path he sidled up to his tee. He focused his thoughts completely through his opening shot. He practised twice, then let his swing carry itself down his arms, past his two remaining fingers, through the ball, up and out. His club moved through the ball, picking up some grass, as he'd planned; the club swung right past his mental trajectory toward that small white flag in the distance. The ball arced dangerously close to the tree line, then changed its course and veered south, bobbing its way down the fairway. A half-second later Mr. Sato's four-iron slipped through his fingers and followed the ball. His club seemed to transform – mid-flight – into a tomahawk.

The underling laughed – just once. And later that day he lost his first finger.

"Whatever you do today," said Endo, "you must not laugh."

I'd seen a few Yakuza near our school. None of them, to my knowledge, ever took classes within the building. So I was surprised by Endo's story. Most of the Y-guys I came across were probably Sato's "underlings," men who drove "Benz" cars and stood (briefly) outside the local Seven-Eleven eating junk-food rice-rolls and octopus-on-a-stick. They were well-dressed, wore dark suits one day, light purple suits the next; underneath their jackets they wore T-shirts. Their hair was almost always short and "punch-permed," gelled to shimmer in the sun, sometimes coloured with a tinge of burnt orange.

Once, from behind a bowl of shark-rice soup, I did see one – an underling – at Denny's Restaurant. He wore a black leather jacket, a monk's collarless shirt, and a young woman – which is to say that she seemed to accessorize his life, like a necklace. She sat close, wearing dozens of rings and a white fur coat. On the table they had six huge bottles of beer and a single ashtray that was heaped to overflowing. I bent to tie my shoe and saw what looked like a game of patty cake played out under their table, though she seemed too reserved for the spirit of this game. She liked the attention, though; that was clear. Her hair was sculptured black. Her lips were off-red, I thought, perhaps maroon. They were so sharply defined that she could not risk eating food. So she guarded her mouth – and the colour maroon – while the rest of her face was a mask of white.

I nudged Endo away from his chicken strips and he nodded glumly.

"Yes," he said. "Y-guy."

"He's so young!"

"Shhh," he said. "They will hear you."

"So?"

"So he can be more trouble to us if he is young," he whispered.

"How?" I asked.

Endo tried to cut the subject off with a series of quick statements. "He is unpredictable. He is wild. He is John Wayne and Mickey Rourke rolled into one!"

I laughed out loud and the whole restaurant seemed to teeter in our direction.

Endo quickly fumbled for the plastic dessert menu and I feigned complete interest in a picture of a lemon meringue pie.

With one eye, I watched a waiter approach and change their ashtray, but he did not speak to them, even to take their order. He seemed to know that he'd be tipped better if he left them alone. So the boy looked out the window as he gave them a new ashtray and retreated back to the kitchen. The two sat and smiled at the other patrons, their backs to the window, as if they had figured out something important and amusing about the rest of us. And we – individually – stole glances at them. All of us, living the high life at Denny's.

If Endo was nervous about playing golf with Mr. Sato, he didn't show it. He smoked a cigarette as we walked toward a small lake, which, depending on the season, could also be a large pond or a bed of white rocks. I could see seven abandoned pedal boats on the other side of the water. Endo said that too many boaters drifted toward Mr. Sato's property to glimpse his pet tiger. Deciding he did not want to become a tourist attraction, Mr. Sato bought all the pedal boats, the business, and all of the land on one side of the water.

Just beside the lake and a rash of bamboo trees, a clean Mercedes-Benz waited for us under a *tori* gate. The engine was running.

Endo dropped his cigarette on the ground and pretended to stamp it out, all while the butt safely burned next to his other foot.

"Please do not laugh," he said, as we approached the car.

A door opened and a man with black curly hair emerged.

"*Hajimi mashite,*" said the man, bowing slightly. We didn't shake hands but Endo made deferential introductions with deep bows. I returned the greeting. With a slight flourish of one quick hand, Mr. Sato pointed us into the car's leather world. I was surprised that Mr. Sato was driving us himself, unchauffeured, and that it is just the three of us careening toward a day of golf.

The morning traffic was thick, a steady line of cars seemed to block our way, but the Benz veered around these cars with the grace of a figure skater at a buffet table. A comfortable smile on his face, Mr. Sato drove with the window open beside him. His right hand rested on the door until he needed it to signal a lane change, and for this he simply put his arm outside and showed them his one pointer finger. The other drivers moved out of our way – avoiding the finger's unspoken power – and shifted to other lanes. Several cars turned off the road as if an ambulance had crossed their paths.

"*This,*" said Mr. Sato, "is a fire car." Meaning one of two things: the Benz was a fire engine (authorized to pass other vehicles), or (more likely) the Benz was a chariot used to transport sinners to hell. This latter Buddhist translation meant that his car was suffering the flames of hell before it actually reached its destination. The Western translation of this translation meant that Mr. Sato was tired of spending money on a gas-guzzler.

He shrugged away our appreciation of the Benz with this self-deprecating phrase, then suggested, in Japanese, that the Yakuza had a bad reputation in the West. He looked in the rear-view mirror to read my reaction, then reminded us that he was a businessman. A new law, he said, was passed last year in Tokyo's Supreme Court and made it impossible for the Yakuza to act as bodyguards. I'd heard something about this law and remembered that most of the organized leaders – the Yakuza unions – had flown to Tokyo to protest this unfair treatment. The national news covered their plight by filming the union leaders who picketed on the streets outside the courts. But the newspapers skirted the real story by framing it in a summary of Tokyo traffic jams. The Yakuza eventually faded from the day's news back into the shadows.

"These days," said Mr. Sato, "the world is economics. Big business." He and some business partners owned pachinko palaces, game rooms, the Pleasantland-Open-24-Hours-Hotsprings, and the only indoor ski hills in the prefecture.

"Do you know how much artificial snow costs?" he asked.

"No," I said, "I don't."

"You'd be surprised," he said.

Mr. Sato swung his finger, then the car, away from this sensitive subject and we turned off the thoroughfare toward a batting range. I saw a what looked like a hundred-foot net, and a bunker complex on the edge of a hill. Fifteen to twenty men were swinging at machines, popping baseballs deep into the centre of the net.

Beyond this diamond I saw another five-storey building that faced a park. In all respects the building looked like a rather short office tower, except that it had no outer walls. Crossbeams and columns supported it, and I could see a man (sometimes two) on every floor and in each of the building's compartments.

Outside, the lawn was littered with golf balls. I thought that this was the equivalent of an executive's wet dream: each man stood at the edge of his office, swinging a golf club through an imaginary wall.

Mr. Sato parked the Benz by backing it into a space beside the clubhouse. He announced our arrival with a diminutive nod, and pointed us toward a small hut, which was shaped like a golf ball.

He paid for all of our admissions by reaching into his pocket and putting his *hanko* stamp on the counter. The hand disappeared by his side and a young cashier accepted his offering with both hands. She bowed and stamped the ledger for him. Having lost so many fingers, he appeared reluctant to bare his hands in moments that did not require his forefinger's authority.

"Do you want to warm up?" asked Endo. "We can begin at the range."

"That is a good idea," said Mr. Sato. "An Olympic idea. It will give me time to practise my English."

So, I thought, the real lesson had begun.

Three swings and Mr. Sato asked, "What is the difference between scandal and tragedy?" Then, without an answer in hand, "What is the difference between a man who kills himself and a man who is murdered? Why is only one scandal?"

These questions had even Endo curious because, for the Japanese, everything is scandal.

"It is an interesting problem," I began, walking toward the edge of our room. "If I fall off the driving range this morning it will be a tragedy for my family, a great loss for my boss, Shacho, and a scandal for the golf club. If, on the other hand, your golfing is so superior to mine that I kill myself, *seppuku*-style, on the ninth hole, then it will be a tragedy for my family, a great loss for my boss, Shacho, and an embarrassment for the Canadian government. Now, look at the examples: if he kills himself, if he is pushed, if he survives . . ." and so on.

Endo smiled, weakly. Mr. Sato was listening, intently, but a change in clubs gave me an excuse to stop this insane lesson and actually think about what I was saying. Mr. Sato approached the edge of the office and sliced a ball into the horizon.

Endo pulled me aside and asked, quietly, "Are you crazy at this moment?"

"What's he going to do?" I whispered. "Fit me for a wooden kimono?"

He looked doubtful.

"Don't worry," I said. "Foreigners can ask insane questions."

Endo nodded, a bit too quickly.

Mr. Sato returned.

"Before we begin," he said, "I must ask, do you know Amari?"

"No," I said.

"Amari, Amari, you must know Amari. You are Canadian," he said, suddenly doubtful of my origins. "You must know Amari. She is very famous."

He frowned – an easy gesture for this man, I thought, because he immediately found what he wanted: my complete attention. My mind reeled back to Canada. I was about to admit that I have been away from Canada for half a year, when Mr. Sato gave me one more clue.

"She is a singer," he said, which brought the words *Anne Murray Anne Murray yes of course Anne Murray* out of my vocal cords and a quick smile to his face.

The rest of the day's golfing went very well. Endo bent a pink aluminum putter when he leaned on it just a moment too long. Mr. Sato seemed genuinely pleased with his game and his English prowess. And – like most days – I survived the day without laughing.

Teaching English in a small town often gave me several versions of the same story, from different students. And no more than two weeks after my "golfing lesson" I met a man who gave me another side to the Yakuza's story. Mr. Tanaka owned a small stationery store in Kounan. His wife was the town potter. Over a long table, completely hidden by glazed teapots, he told me about his greatest passion.

"I am a hunter," he said.

He wanted to meet me because he'd learned that I was Canadian and he wanted to share some big-game stories. He was a small man who held a heavy English dictionary in his hand the whole evening we spoke. Instead of drinking tea out of his wife's pottery, we drank out of gold *sake* cups. They were decorated with official seals from the police department and commemorated the day that Mr. Tanaka tracked and shot a missing tiger on the streets of Kounan.

The tiger had escaped from Mr. Sato's mansion on the other side of "pedal-boat lake." The police, without any experience in tracking and killing wildlife, looked through their records and found Mr. Tanaka. He was one of only a hundred Japanese hunters who had passed a dozen character tests and was allowed to own a gun. Over the years, he had killed mostly partridges, small birds and – by mistake – a few Hokkaido foxes. He usually found them hiding in quiet places: near rice fields, roadside thickets, or in the rocky reservoirs where Japanese rivers used to flow.

After a sweaty hour, exploring the pedal-boat garage, Mr. Tanaka found the cat's footprint near a local power plant.

"These power plants," he explained, "are very strange. The river is dry, but smoke keeps coming out of them. I don't know what they make there, but probably it is chemical."

I knew the place because a supermarket had just been built down the road, and I'd seen the plant's concrete chimney from the parking lot. A fenced area and a *senshin biyoin*, a mental hospital, stood between this market and an exclamation of bamboo that rose sharply, into smoke. Some nights, strange hoots and cries could be heard from this place – from the woods, the hospital, or from the smoke itself.

The police were anxious to capture the tiger before school began the next day. One saleswoman was chased through an apartment driveway but she managed to outrun the cat on her moped, losing only her batter's helmet, three flats of yoghurt, and one white saddlebag. And a sweet-potato salesman suffered minor burns by hiding inside his metal cart for a half-hour.

"*Yakimo! Ishi yakimo!*" said Mr. Tanaka, imitating the salesman's trademark cry, "Sweet potatoes! Stone-baked sweet potatoes!"

He might have become a stone-baked sweet potato himself, but he was rescued by some teenagers who opened the cart's hatch looking for food.

The cat was also hungry, and angry. Mr. Tanaka said that the police ordered him to kill it. There was no time to find tranquillizers or construct cages. The Yakuza would have to do without one pet. And so, on the gravel tributary of an abandoned river, he shot his first tiger. It was, he said, an indescribable feeling.

"I will not forget it, but I do not want to relive that moment." He thumbed through his dictionary. "It was," he said, "a hollow day."

At the end of his story, Mr. Tanaka gave me one of his gold *sake* cups. And then he offered to walk me back through the streets of Kounan – it was a nice evening, he said, and he could use the walk. He disappeared from the pottery room and, seconds later, reappeared with a jacket and a flashlight.

"Maybe the tigers are out," he said, kindly. "I can't tell you that story and ask you to walk home by yourself."

The air was crisp and clean. A cool February night. Tanaka-san's small feet seemed very light on the pavement. He'd swapped his indoor slippers for a pair of black karate slippers. And as we walked, I listened to his gait – a *clack-clack-clack* that seemed to bounce off the storefronts and echo across the nearby windows.

He said it wasn't the first time his family had something to do with the Yakuza. Having spent a life selling imported American trucks, his uncle became a rich man and (consequently) well-known to the local Yakuza. At that time, a woman ran the Yakuza in Saitama prefecture. The family's trade in organized crime was handed down, from father to son, from war to war, until they had run out of sons and wars, and a woman was finally selected to carry the Yakuza honour.

"She was very clever," he said, "to control all those men."

Tanaka's uncle refused to pay the mafia their business premium, so the Yakuza sent him an invitation to meet them by the river. He told no one. He left the house with a contraband samurai sword hidden in his overcoat, and that morning he walked into the trees alone.

At this point, I wasn't too surprised by Tanaka's story. Most of my students had a sword tale with which to regale "the foreign teacher." Even a fellow teacher, named Mr. Ueno, kept one, despite the laws against housing long, sharpened blades. He'd said that one night he met a prowler with it and almost hacked him toward enlightenment. The burglar escaped out the front door and, eight years later, Mr. Ueno had still not repaired the blade's gash in the side of his doorframe. A badge of honour, perhaps.

I had asked to see Ueno's sword but he said only that "it would be difficult." I let the matter drop. But the next day he came to my desk with an open shaft of severed bamboo and fifteen different photos of himself cutting his bushes. He gave me a tube of bamboo as proof.

"With one stroke," he'd said. "Very clean."

I didn't interrupt Tanaka's story, or ask to see *his* sword, because (deep down) I thought that he might actually have it with him.

"The Yakuza met him by the river with knives," said Tanaka, with a faint smile.

Next to a stretch of Japanese cedars, Tanaka's uncle pulled the sword from its sheath and said, "Now, I will kill you."

The Yakuza took one look at the sword and escaped into the woods, never to bother him again.

"What about the woman," I asked. "Was she there?"

"No, she was not. She was very smart, I think, not to be there."

We turned the corner to my street and passed Endo's favourite rice hut. A metal scroll covered the gap above the counter. When I looked up at my apartment complex I noticed that Endo was still awake; his reading light glowed through his bedroom window and an outside curtain of clean laundry. Charlotte's light was on too, but I knew better – she was likely visiting "friends" in the city.

"Don't wait up," she'd said, on her way to the bus stop.

I looked back to Mr. Tanaka and was surprised to see him about ten feet away, heading toward the patch of unschooled weeds on the other side of the street. I'd grown accustomed to hearing his footfalls, but without nearby windows perhaps he was in his element: camouflaged in the depth of open air.

"Good night," he said. "Please visit me again."

Then he slipped into the weeds and was gone.

I knew only one person who could tell me something more about the Yakuza. A policeman in my Kumagaya adult school had come up to me at the end of one class and corrected my only reference to the Yakuza – some joke about my severe practice of correcting their papers.

"Mistakes," he said, "cost a finger or 500,000 yen, not 50,000."

Anxious to learn more, I made plans to meet the policeman at a nearby seafood restaurant. A huge crab hung from the outside of the building. The restaurant's entrance, just below a pair of robotic claws, opened up to a small lobby and a wooden wall of lockers to shelve our shoes. While we changed into slippers, a woman in a green kimono spoke to herself, softly, a black headphone device barely visible against her perfect net of hair. She motioned us toward her by bowing twice and we walked past her into a tatami-floor elevator. Another hostess greeted us as the elevator doors opened and, without asking, led us immediately to a table set for two.

Over dinner, the policeman told me that the Japanese police force is scattered into prefectures. Usually, an officer will live in one prefecture, then do a tour of surveillance and undercover work in another.

"What sort of surveillance?" I asked.

"This is a good question," he said, "because generally these are mixed problems. The police have many sections: drugs, traffic patrol, politics, murder, looking for missing people, and also Yakuza. Some crimes are violent, some are heinous, some are only moral offences. Each officer has a black belt in at least one martial art. But there are many families to watch: the T——,

Y——, W——, I——, and the S——. These groups are in Saitama, Kansai, Kobe, all over the Kanto area. Since our – how do you say *mumei?*"

"Anonymity."

"Anonymity is crucial. The police became great students of dialect and provincial nuance. But these particular days, the Yakuza are in the towel-rental business: *oshibori.*"

The policeman pointed to a small plastic roll on the table, then picked it up and examined the bag. When he tore it open he unravelled a wet cotton napkin, and I could see steam rising from his hands.

"There can't be much money in cotton hand towels," I said.

"There is large profit," he said, as he fluffed the hot towel on his palms like wet pizza dough. When the towel was cool enough, he polished his fingernails, then put the towel on his face and leaned back. I expected to see his face emerge refreshed, but he seemed to wince when he returned to the conversation. Then he exchanged the wince for a smile. An appetizer arrived and he offered me a small, dried fish.

"The Yakuza," he said, "charge restaurants for clean, rolled napkins. This is the Japanese tradition: we freshen our hands before eating. Do you imagine how many restaurants, festivals, and food huts in Japan rent these towels for their customers?"

"No."

"There are over five hundred thousand restaurants in Japan and the same number of bathhouses and laundries. The pachinko parlours number only fifteen thousand. The Yakuza know that there is more money in renting expensive napkins than in providing bodyguards. Besides, these two things mean the same to a business owner. One law calls this protection, another calls it a wet towel. *Oshibori*."

"Do the restaurants pay the Yakuza the same number of yen for each service?"

"This," he said, "is a difficult problem."

A "difficult problem" usually signals the end of a Japanese conversation. The policeman – he should have no name – dropped the subject by picking up the remains of a small fish he had just finished eating. The head, ribs, and spine dangled from the tail he held between his fingers. He smiled, as if to say, This doesn't really matter, does it?

"Ah," he said kindly, "this is my destiny."

I smiled and he changed the subject to ghosts. Some two weeks later, I found my notes from that macabre conversation. When I finally made sense of the policeman's odd phrases and my haphazard scribbles, I suddenly realized how dark the restaurant must have become . . . our sunset inside a crab! On the page, our conversation looked gloomy and difficult to read. He'd spoken about his job – which is to say that he'd spoken *around* his job, giving me clues to the nature of finding clues. It was like using a metaphor to describe a metaphor.

Small birds, he said, are sometimes trampled into the pavement like broken umbrellas.

I imagined the policeman's birds, flat as shoe leather and pressed into the ground. I saw the people, the crowds who marched over them, oblivious to their singularity. Then I remembered what he'd said about the life that still pulsed inside them. A clue, he said, did not come from watching maggots and worms, but from imagining flight. A trajectory. Even the dead tells stories, he said. And you don't know if a death is the beginning of the story, the middle, or the end.

Obviously, he had a fascination with death. I read the words: *Chichibu, Ongaku temple, a ghost appeared. Then gossip. We kept going to the temple to investigate during the summer. We saw nothing. But gossip. Gossip kept growing like a shadow. Summer came and we found a girl's body. Two weeks later we caught her killer – the boyfriend.*

His favourite story, no less cryptic, became the following riddle.

Too many boatmen bring the boat up the mountain.

— Japanese proverb

Between the seventh and eighth stations, two thousand metres up the bushy steep of Mount Fuji, two hikers pushed through a tangle of persimmon trees and found a body completely clothed in scuba gear. The diver was wearing his oxygen tank, flippers, and a mask. The hikers could smell the scent of tea on their hands when they covered their mouths and quickly pushed their way back through the trees. Then they retraced their steps down the mountain.

The trees on that side were spread out like the sea – a *jukai* sea that curled above five mirrored lakes and the bottom of Fuji. Hikers routinely lost their way near the volcano because a natural magnet formation surrounded Mount Fuji and pointed each hiker's compass toward a different city. Each compass seemed to say, *Yes*, you are walking in the correct direction.

The diver's name was Shiguro Maruyama, and his family had reported him missing the previous summer, on August 6,

1965. At the time of his disappearance, NHK news presumed that the young man had run into trouble somewhere in the Pacific, and that he had drifted into the shipping lines en route to Yokohama Harbour. The evening report closed the story with a warning to the diving community about the dangers of swimming alone.

Eight months later, when Maruyama was found mid-stroke on a mountainside, the second round of media inquiry gave him more serious consideration. An autopsy listed that he didn't drown – there was no water in his lungs – and the actual cause of his death was, in fact, severe hemorrhaging. Somehow he'd broken his left femur, both tibias, one side of ribs, and fractured his skull. The police had no idea how he'd made his way out of the sea, how he'd skirted two fishing villages without being seen, or how he'd climbed a hillside and come to rest on the edge of Fuji-san.

Faced with so many unanswered questions, a third inquiry was ordered by the Minister of Shizuoka prefecture and a second autopsy found that Shiguro Maruyama had also broken his pointer finger and, furthermore, there was no way of knowing if he'd drowned, since the water in his lungs might have evaporated between the months of September, October, and November. The body was then moved to Tokyo and a third, lengthy round of tests began, to see if the Shizuoka officials had missed anything more that the Yokohama investigators had failed to notice.

Slighted, and tired of waiting for yet another round of tests, the anatomist in Yokohama wrote back, "If the Tokyo police want to know if the boy drowned, they should wait another year to see if salt crystals materialize inside his lungs."

The police returned to the crime scene and combed through the grass looking for footprints, Yakuza calling cards, or some sign to help them solve Shiguro's murder. Had the finger been completely removed, it might have pointed the investigation toward the Japanese mafia. If the ground nearby had been softer, it might have held a footprint for several months. Perhaps Shiguro wanted to slide down Fuji. Perhaps he wore the scuba gear to protect himself from the mountain's cold.

"In August?" cried the investigators, who were losing patience fighting suppositions that became more and more implausible.

The first lead in solving the mystery came when one especially young police officer happened to find several small bones fifteen feet from the place where the hikers had discovered Shiguro's body. The bones turned out to be cartilaginous.

"Dogfish," said the officer. "My wife made me the same dish for *asagohan* this morning with *natto*. The beans were fermented without remorse. I will never forget it."

Dozens more dogfish, eels, bony fish no one recognized, as well as two octopus beaks and a single starfish were later found on the grassy hillside. Most of this cache was suspected to have fallen from the boy's side pouch. But when the investigation spread into the bushes, the police discovered the charred remains of one small chestnut tree. The nuts were still warm with the day's heat, easy to crack, and (the officer reported) delicious to eat.

He picked at the shell and looked up at the crater's edge. The sun, retreating from the horizon, cast the outline of Mount Fuji on the clouds to the west. He'd heard about this phenomenon. He knew that it was called spectre of the Brocken. So the young policeman watched Fuji clothe those western clouds and mountains and from this vantage point, between the seventh and eighth stations, he looked up to see a hiker who stood on the lip of the crater. When the policeman looked back at the mountains, he saw the hiker's magnified shadow above the crater's outline, a figure that was briefly transformed into an enormous god. The sunset's prismatic colours framed his head with concentric rings, like a halo.

Standing below the remains of this chestnut tree, peeling the shells of those burnt chestnuts as though they were boiled eggs, the young officer solved the case of Japan's lost scuba diver. And because the solution was his, the honour fell to him to call a press conference.

"The poor boy was picked up by a fire plane," he said, "when the aircraft dipped into the sea to fill its reservoirs. Trapped inside the plane's tanks, the boy had no way of knowing he was being flown over Mount Fuji to extinguish a fire."

Allowing himself one foreign reference to corrupt his official police report, the young officer added: "He was our Icarus. Shiguro Maruyama came back to Japan having touched every element known to man – water, air, fire and earth. Ultimately, this was his undoing."

I scribbled all this down because I thought Endo would like the policeman's tale. I thought it subscribed to his own idea that travel journals mix variable ingredients of history and fiction. If all travellers re-invent the places they visit, then Shiguro Maruyama's is the sort of fantastic arrival that makes travel writing a singular concoction. He becomes the unnamed traveller who (secretly) wishes for some accidental quest to find him – the traveller who is transformed the moment he boards a plane and cartwheels through the clouds. A drifting storyteller, he grasps for hope, as would any flying scuba diver over myth-inspired seas.

The policeman didn't tell me the name of the young Japanese officer or even the names of the hikers. These were details that he left out – I suspect – for a reason. A few unanswered questions encouraged his fiction a little, toward the realm of the possible.

And yet, what could be more plausible than an "accidental quest"? A boy stumbles over a bean, an old book, or, if he's a little older, a beautiful woman, an airplane, or a ship. It is the moment where most stories begin. History, I thought, is made from such accidents.

Endo thanked me for the policeman's story. I could see that he liked it, by the way he discreetly filed it in one of his crowded drawers, on the imaginary side of his room, just below the calendar that read the next month, March.

"I haven't been to the sea," he said, "in a long time."

I was surprised by the sadness in his eyes (magnified in his bottle-thick glasses) and by his voice, thick with nostalgia. I honestly didn't expect such a show of emotion from a Japanese man. He squinted his eyes. His pock-marked cheeks turned red. It was as if all his regrets couldn't quite fit under his mask of self-control. Endo, of all people, pining for his own country when it was (so obviously) all around him. The idea seemed – there was no other word for it – foreign.

While Charlotte had kept herself busy – travelling, here and there, every weekend – I was busy denying my own version of homesickness. I had written a few letters home, but I'd spent most of my time exploring my nearby surroundings, trying to save money and learn Japanese.

But perhaps it was the same with Endo, for different reasons. He may have been stuck inside his calendars. Regulated by one month and held prisoner in another, he seemed in dire need of a spontaneous vacation.

The Marlboro girls in Akihabara don't come out until just before noon. Endo and I saw them on our day trip to Tokyo because we arrived early in the morning, in time for a hot bowl of curry udon. Fat buckwheat noodles, shredded beef, and a bowl of soup large enough to bob for apples. After this breakfast, the hour was near and "Electric Town" spread out across our vision like a modern Dodge City at high noon.

False-front advertisements for Sony, Panasonic, and Toshiba loomed above the buildings. Feverish neon sputtered and sweat on the corners of most shop signs. And as we walked through this electric place, silver objects glinted in the sun like the closing of so many windows. There was something mildly depressing about the whole milieu. The side streets were dark and littered with wall-to-wall repair shops; make one wrong turn and enter the backside of a radio. But Endo – wide-eyed and one pace ahead – seemed to be in his absolute glory. So we continued past the Nintendo game floors that blinked, shot, and gasped like automated barroom brawls.

At each corner he stopped and described our travels, or he talked about his father's *depaato*. Much had changed. Now, Akihabara was the centre of modern Tokyo. Akihabara was the testing ground for all of the electronic goods that came out of Japan. The technological advances that flew through the Asian marketplace, through copycat warehouses in Hong Kong, Taiwan, and Seoul, actually began here. Endo said that it took roughly three years for most of these aeronautical watches and electric toilet seats to make their way out of Akihabara's showrooms to Western shores. In a country with no central heating, it made sense for toilet seats to warm to body temperature as soon as the lid was raised. In a polite society, musical accompaniment should always mask the timbres of a toilet's embarrassing flush. Modern science must keep up with society's quest for civilized life.

Such luxuries would probably never reach America. But what of the cargo of Panasonic coffee tables, chocolate squeezepacks, robotic vacuum cleaners, tricoloured Apple laptops, and all of those individual, identity-driven Walkman stereos?

"These are wonders," Endo said, "that are already on ships sailing to America."

At the subway stop for Akihabara, an outdoor sign read, THIS WAY TO ELECTRIC TOWN. The sign was easy to miss because it hung behind a pillar on only one side of the tracks, as if Electric Town *should* only be accessible from one side at a time (i.e., the wrong side). Under this sign, we followed the stairs down into a narrow tunnel that swung left, then right, past three concrete planters and three revolving laptops. We went past several telephone-service advertisements and two rows of green telephones. We dodged one low-flying dolly – stacked high with television boxes – and then light finally hit my face. The day was near.

And outside the station, if noon has indeed passed, the Marlboro girls meet all the commuters who venture into Electric Town. They wear matching red cowboy boots, white hats, white vests, and silver spandex. They give away sample packages of moist towelettes, candy, and cigarettes under billboard-sized televisions. Their costumes promise the West, sex, and an open-range golf course for each and every man.

Tokyo is full of such Western apparitions. On weekends James Dean lookalikes can be found in Harajuku, combing their hair or dancing to rockabilly that jumps out of fridge-sized stereos. Young Natalie Woods wear sweater-sets and white bobby socks. Traffic along one stretch of road is abandoned to shoppers, tourists, and the Western icons who form small groups in the middle of the road. The "Natalies" sit on leather jackets while the "Deans" squat in perfect circles – hard to tell if they are watching behind their black sunglasses. A single dancer – at centre-lane – twirls his leg, taps one blue suede shoe, and gyrates his hips.

But Electric Town was our pilgrimage. Endo wanted more electronic gadgets for his collection and the Marlboro girls were more elegant gatekeepers than any nostalgic, big-eyed, brooding characters from the past. Instead, the Marlboro girls welcomed the future.

I thought Endo chose Akihabara because he was in love with the modern technology. Blinking lights and tiny instruction manuals mesmerized him. So we had made our trip to Tokyo to pay our respects to curry udon and the future. But when I saw the Marlboro girls I realized that there was another reason he'd chosen this place: he was looking for another of his floating stories. The Great Floating West, in all its grandeur.

Electric Town necessitates a sideshow commercialism of biblical proportions, a welcome-come-all-ye-who-believe-the-future-is-here mentality. Not *the end is near!* but *the future is here!* Endo's Marlboro girls wave hello to this future. They cross the street and, in their wake, the Marlboro girls drag pocket-radio vendors, vegetable dicers, icers, and splicers. Tomatoes turn into roses. Watches become television remotes. Chairs turn into vibrating stereos with hidden, surround-sound, assault-type headphones.

Out of refrigerator parts and old Walkman sound-boards, electronic birds hatch from their *tamagochi* eggs and live or die in the palm of a consumer's hand. Only Electric Town can imagine a creature that mimics mortality: a toy that is programmed to die if neglected. Electronic fate is uncertain here. Push a button to feed the birds grains of rice or cookie crumbs and they may outlive their owners. Though which comes first – the product or the consumer – is impossible to know.

So electronic fish dodge electronic lures inside video fishing holes. *Printo-club* photo machines personalize postage stamps.

Bouquets of flowers drop like potato chips from vending machines. And the Marlboro girls watch all these marvels arrive by truck and leave by hand.

Soon, another stagecoach will come to Akihabara full of new supplies and another train-full of people will take the wrong exit into Electric Town. They will walk down this "Main Street" and reach for a joystick. One stranger at a time will test Nintendo, pit one electronic life against another. And the Marlboro girls will reach into their white holsters and congratulate the winner with a cigarette or a moist towelette.

We fought our way out of this labyrinth. We tunnelled up the stairs to catch the Circle Line back to Ueno. By the time we boarded our Shinkansen, Endo announced that he wanted us to take another trip. Hopefully, during the summer vacation.

"There is another place I know," he said, "that is even better than Akihabara."

The thought left me cold.

He leaned toward me, and in the reflection of his thick eyeglasses I watched myself grow large and misshapen.

"Rita Hayworth," he whispered, "is also in Japan."

I admitted that I wasn't interested in finding the West in Japan. I hadn't come to find Rita Hayworth, the Marlboro girls, Colonel Sanders, or even Santa Claus. I still clung to the idea that I would be able to discover for myself the real Japan.

Endo dismissed my preoccupation with "discovery" as the most common obsession he had observed in a long line of English teachers. Each of us wanted to claim Japan, he said, as if a whole country, in all its depth and complexity, was either a prize to win or a riddle to solve. We aspired to be conquering heroes or, failing that, we could always be "Taipan-Sams."

"I call it Asian Discovery Sickness," he said. "Harmless, but abso-*loot*-ally contagious."

As we railed home to Saitama, and as the cities scrolled past our window, the day gently faded into night. Almost everyone on the train immediately fell asleep. But with each brief stop, a few salarymen woke up and shuffled out, until we were the last two people on the train. Endo spoke again of MacDonald, someone who, long long ago, was searching for his own mystical Japan. I could almost see MacDonald's rough-hewn features, his deep-set eyes, and the weathered map that he carried.

And in the darkened train that shot through the night, somewhere between Urawa and Kumagaya, Endo described the Japanese ideal of the traveller who aims to repeat the journey of those who have gone before him. A journey to Mito, he said, could recall the poem that once described that city's plum blossoms. It would not matter if the trip was made in winter, if the trees were bare, or if the city had changed beyond recognition. In Edo-Japan, the traveller bends the months and years backward, until one journey finally glimpses another.

MacDonald revisited

Toole

The Captain's story

The bread's ear

When we returned, we settled into Endo's tatami room and surrounded ourselves with newspaper clippings. His smart-machine tea urn quietly boiled between us. Self-regulated to hold water at the brink of ninety-five degrees Celsius, the machine percolated a soft, contented burble, like pigeons on a window ledge.

Endo continued to describe MacDonald's life, as he understood it. I looked at the newspaper clippings and the broken dictionary on the table and began to assemble the story of this man, named Ranald MacDonald.

You must understand, Endo said, that Japan has always been found by castaways and *hyōryūmin* – drifters. He told me that rumours of Japan first spread among sailors who travelled to China. In the thirteenth century, Marco Polo heard the story, and happened to mention that there might be something more to be found in the sea, just beyond China's grasp. Later, in 1542, a lost

Portuguese crew finally drifted out of the regular trade winds and stumbled – as if on a shoelace – on the unexplored latitude of thirty degrees north.

I learned that Japan lies completely above this thread, twenty degrees beyond the most reliable sailing course. Historically, the Portuguese were more comfortable following the trade winds, along latitudes that traversed the Sandwich Islands, the Sandrones, and Singapore, en route to the western coast of the two Americas. The trip was called "the lady's run" outside of hurricane season and meant sailing from Portugal to the West Indies, "south till the butter melts, then due west."

By 1611 red-seal permission to trade with Macao was given. A black ship from Macao brought silver and great cargos of raw and woven Chinese silk to Nagasaki. Then Hasegawa Fujihiro, Minister of Ships, begged the elders of Macao to send the Black Ship each summer, for the sake of friendship and profitable trade to both countries.

He liked to close his letters with the words *Please do not hesitate. Bowing twice.*

The friendship with Macao was short-lived. On the last day of August 1639, Japan announced its departure from the world.

"You must know," said Endo, "that even a country can drift!"

I tried to nod sagely – imagining the tectonics of an island in motion. Then he refilled my cup and pushed the table's skirt from his legs.

He went into the kitchen to prepare some small dishes of salted peanuts, fermented beans, and rice snaps, and I flipped through his books and clippings.

In almost every account, Portuguese missionaries were said to be troublemakers – they had a habit of distracting the Japanese away from their "bounden duties." When the Dutch were caught celebrating their trade monopoly at a thanksgiving service, they too were banished from Japan. The shogun ordered the Hollanders to tear down all their buildings which bore the date of the Christian calendar above their doors. He also banished their Ten Commandments, the breaking of bread, spoons, the crucifix, holy water, the Bible, the Lord's Prayer, the Creed, Moses, Mary, Maria, Sunday, baptism, foreign burials, God, the Prophets, the Portuguese Christ, the Dutch Christ, Christopher Columbus, the Whole Race of the Portuguese with their mothers, nurses, and whatever belongs to them, the king of Spain, and all of the apostles.

It was true, the Dutch Christ was named *Christus* and the Portuguese was *Cristo* or *O Nosso Senhor*, but the similarity in name seemed only trickery, designed to fool the shogun. Despite his head-smacking fit of recognition, the shogun concealed all his anger with a thin, bitter smile.

I read his words to Endo: "We have known long since that you were Christians but we thought that yours was another Christ." Then the shogun allowed himself the luxury of turning his face away from his listeners. They could barely hear his last words on the subject: "But you Hollanders are all Christians like the Portuguese."

An envoy from Macao was dispatched to Nagasaki in 1640, carrying no cargo but presents of gold, silver, and four of their most respected citizens. They brought a petition declaring that no missionaries had ever been sent to Japan from their harbour.

And when they arrived at Nagasaki on July 1, their ship's rudder, sails, guns, and ammunition were immediately confiscated. Seventy members of the ship's crew and the four envoys waited one month to hear the result of their petition.

On August 2, 1640, they were summoned to the governor's hall and given the chance to renounce their faith and live. Each one rejected the offer, so fifty-seven sailors and the four aged ambassadors from Macao were led out to a hill and decapitated. The day was hot and especially muggy, because two of their galleons were being burnt in the nearby harbour. Thirteen men were spared to bear witness.

"That is an unlucky number, isn't it?"

I nodded.

Then they were returned to the governor and given a message:

Do not fail to inform the inhabitants of Macao that the Japanese wish to receive from them neither gold nor silver, nor any kind of presents or merchandise; in a word, absolutely nothing which comes from them. You are witnesses that I have caused even the clothes of those who were executed yesterday to be burned. Let them do the same with respect to us if they find occasion to do so; we consent to it without difficulty. Let them think no more of us, just as if we were no longer in the world.

MacDonald must have known this edict, known he would be imprisoned, or worse. By the time he fell into the sea, as if by mistake, Japan had been off-limits to foreigners, upon penalty of death. Endo had read a partial transcription of the imperial decree in MacDonald's ledger, but he found the rest, "too blasphemous for expression," in a Tokyo library:

So long as the sun warms the earth, let no Christian be so bold as to come to Japan, and let all know that if King Philip himself, or even the very God of the Christians, or the great Shaka violate this command, he shall pay for it with his head.

Since then, even Japanese sailors were left alone. If they drifted away, during storms, many of them were afraid to return to Japan. There were a few daring Portuguese traders and scores of American whalers who had come within sight of the Japanese junks. But they met only briefly, when they shared the same current in the Sea of Japan, or hauled the same wind.

Endo pulled a photocopy of an article from one of his drawers. He gave it to me with both hands, and I accepted it quickly. It was from a Honolulu paper, *The Seaman's Friend*, and was dated December 1, 1848. The words were thick with over-exposure, or the page had been copied many times.

As the reading world is not likely, for some time to come, to be favored with an account of the conquest or opening of Japan by the naval forces of England, France or the United States, our readers on ship and shore may not be uninterested in the following facts and documents relating to the adventure of a sailor belonging to the American whale-ship "Plymouth" of Sag Harbor, Captain Edwards. If his plans were not upon so gigantic a scale as those which might emanate from a board of admiralty or a naval bureau, yet to answer his purpose they certainly indicate some head-work. It appears that a man named Ranald MacDonald shipped on board the "Plymouth" when she sailed from the United States. After remaining in the vessel two years, while in Lahaina in the fall of 1847 he requested his discharge, unless Captain Edwards would consent to leave him the next season somewhere upon the coast of Japan. Young MacDonald is a son of Archibald MacDonald, Esq., formerly in the employ of the Hudson's Bay Company, Fort Colville, Columbia. On application to the agent of the company in Honolulu we learned that this young man received a good education, but instead of pursuing a mercantile life on shore, betook himself to the sea. Soon after the "Plymouth" left Lahaina, he began to make arrangements for penetrating the hermetically sealed empire of Japan. Captain Edwards allowed him to make choice of the best boat belonging to the ship. The carpenter partially decked her over. Having gathered his all together, he embarked upon his perilous and adventurous enterprise.

I tried to imagine MacDonald in his Japanese prison. His room, so much darker than the open sea he'd just left.

Endo reached for his mug and seemed to burn his lips on the hot tea. He put the mug down a bit too quickly. When he removed his glasses, I saw a dark ridge across his nose and one under each eye where the frames had pressed into his skin.

He told me that MacDonald had orchestrated his own shipwreck, that he'd practised overturning his boat, that he'd washed up in Hokkaido, as if by accident. A "light traveller," MacDonald had arrived with little more than an old map, a compass, and a handful of books.

And while he spoke, Endo pushed the odd book across the table, prodding the facts, the genealogies, and the history just a little, as if to give all of these dry statistics some bit of life. He gave me a reproduction of MacDonald's map and said that it marked his landing spot, off Yankeshiri. Another book gave me his mother's birthdate. In yet another I found a drawing –

MacDonald's? – that approximated the Japanese pictograph for silence.

At some point in the evening, I began to pay more attention to these pages than to Endo's voice. He did not seem threatened by losing my attention. Instead, he pushed himself away from the *kotatsu*, lit a cigarette, and let me rifle through his library. He blew the smoke away – toward the kitchen – and I wandered through his papers and newspaper clippings alone.

His parents' wedding was a splendid feast, by all Hudson's Bay accounts and by those of the traders who were stationed there, on the Pacific slope of North America. MacDonald had heard the stories and relished their details: on both sides of the river there were cakes and ale and potlatch gifts. Furs stretched across the ground, from table to shore.

There was no priest, which bothered MacDonald, slightly. The marriage was royal, he said, trying to let the matter drop. If pushed to explain a Christian absence, he would answer that no Christian, no missionary, no Roman Catholic or Protestant had ever passed through Astoria before his birth. They were not known to be good with an axe, he said. The country was too wild for God's messengers. Pushed further, MacDonald would add that all of the Indians in North America – and the Japanese, too – were essentially monotheists, that they believed in the God, or the Great Spirit, and that his mother's marriage was sacred, a law unto itself.

Raven died during salmon-running time, in June 1824, immediately after MacDonald's birth at the mouth of the

Columbia River, Fort George. His father moved to Norway house.

With two young sons to care for, Archibald was a suddenly an extremely busy Hudson's Bay clerk. The abridged minutes from the Hudson's Bay council meeting, one year later, recall that Archibald MacDonald sat for hours while one hundred and forty-seven resolves were passed for another term of three years from the expiration of his contract, at terms affixed, viz. $100. His new duties: Resolve #108: Indians: Industry encouraged, vice repressed, and morality inculcated. Spirituous liquors gradually discontinued. Ammunition supplied even to those not possessed of means. Resolve #127: Plot inventory tariff for country produce, viz. bark birch, barley (rough, bush, hulled), canoes, corn, fat, flour, geese (fresh and salt), meat (pounded, dried or piece, fresh, salt, buff'o, salt deer, and oiled), sturgeon, pemmican, rice, buffalo robes, salt, shakanapie, snowshoes, skins dressed (buff'o, red deer, reindeer, and moose), sugar maple, tongues, wheat, dogs, sleds, horses. Resolve #138: Religious improvement. Divine service to be read Sundays. Resolve #139: Religious books to be furnished. Resolve #140: Immoral habits checked – opposites encouraged. Resolve #142: Women and children to be always addressed in English or French. Resolve #143: Parents to instruct their children in ABC.

Archibald was lost in these commandments. They swallowed his life. So, on September 1, 1825, with a measure of relief, he walked into a church in Red River and married a woman named Jane Klyne. Reverend M. Cochrane, wearing a black shirt and a new pair of boots, directed the ceremony. The priest's name was listed in the MacDonald family Bible, though no mention of Princess Raven or the king was ever penned above Ranald's name. He was – as always – an early adventurer who slipped into the genealogical listings of "Births, Deaths, and Marriages." *Ranald – 3 Feb'y '24.*

Archibald and Jane soon began having children of their own. More names appeared on the page: *Angus, Archy, Alexander, Allan, Mary Ann, John, Donald and James (twins), Samuel, Joseph, Benjamin.* At the age of six, young Ranald was sent away to live in a private school with several other Hudson's Bay children. Winters, Archibald corresponded with his son and with the schools that were charged with his care. His letters were affectionate and seemed to poke at Ranald's ribs.

"How fares my little Chinook?" he asked. Or, "How is Toole?" as he was sometimes called. *Toole* was the Chinook word for *bird.*

Through no fault of his own, MacDonald eased away from his Native heritage. He had moved away from the Columbia and had relocated so many times that there seemed to be something natural about this loss, as if memories should truly be vague and uncertain things. He could remember furs, a few warm faces, but none of the people were recognizable. Even his grandfather's grave was empty, proving their Chinook memorials were similarly uninhabited.

Years later, he'd found his grandfather in Dunn's *History of the Oregon Territory:*

His head is now in the possession of some eminent physician in Edinburgh and, strange to say, although he had been buried about five years, his skin was quite dry and not decayed. It required a very sharp knife to penetrate the skin and his hair was still on his head.

Another account blamed Dr. Meredith Gairdner of the Hudson's Bay Company, who "removed" the skull six years after the king's death, and sent it to a museum in Portsmouth, England, in 1838. *The skull lost only its lower jawbone during a bombing of the museum in World War II, and it was returned to Oregon in 1953. After a short trip to the Smithsonian Institution for study, the skull was returned to the Chinook Nation.*

His first drink in prison came as a gift. A man in blue robes brought MacDonald a pottery urn and settled it on the floor of his black room.

"Grog-yes?" asked the man.

MacDonald shook his head, too surprised by an English phrase to distil its meaning. Finally, he answered, "Grog-yes."

The man in blue poured some liquid from the urn into two porcelain cups – paper-thin – and made motions to drink from one. MacDonald took the other cup of grog-yes, sipped once, then braced himself for the assault of alcohol that jumped up from his lungs to his nose to his thoughts as though running up a flight of stairs.

"*Sake*," said the man, finally giving him the Japanese word.

This was, MacDonald learned, a popular word on the islands of Japan. The villagers in Hokkaido had assumed that the English translation for *sake* was *grog-yes*, because every sailor who had tried the rice wine had said, "Grog – yes, bring it on!"

After another drink, bowls appeared. Some were filled with rice, others had pickles and small bits of fish that MacDonald's jailers laid out on the floor, as if for an honoured guest. The portions were not so large for him to believe he was being fattened for some impending feast, but this thought was alive in his mind. Even his guards seemed to be waiting for someone to appear and decide MacDonald's fate. So here he waited with his jailers, for some word from a man called "the Captain."

"Who was he?" I asked.

Endo's research proved this man could not have been Gorogoro Imai, the captain who brought MacDonald by palanquin from Matsumae to the Eramachi. Nor could he be Captain Katoda Araida, who greeted MacDonald in Matsumae, nor Captain Tan-emon Ujiye, who later transported him to Nagasaki. The unnamed Captain is lost between the Japanese records and MacDonald's diaries because he was not a captain of a ship, but (most likely) the captain of the guards.

"It doesn't matter," said Endo, relinquishing this detail to obscurity. He threw up his hands to emphasize his defeat, but the gesture didn't seem to fit.

He seemed a little irritated by my question, but I wasn't just nitpicking over trivia. I had already learned that, in modern Japan, a name becomes a man and vice versa. The mere presentation of a name began with intimate gestures of immense significance. A man's business card was offered with both hands, palms opened slightly. The business card, his *meishi*, was meant to be read immediately, so script itself was presented to the receiver. After a polite pause, perhaps some small remark about the logo or the card's design, the meeting resumed.

I knew that a man's name and (by approximation) his business card was not unceremoniously stuffed inside a back pocket. To say the word *meishi* was to say these words literally in medieval Chinese: *name slice*. The card was a thin slice of the man. Even in MacDonald's time, to give a name must have meant to truly offer something.

Despite this lack of name (or cards), the unnamed Captain – the man whom MacDonald befriended during his prison odyssey – would become MacDonald's self-confessed "close friend." MacDonald will record the Captain as "kind-hearted," a man with "a marked intelligence and sympathy."

But their first meeting began somewhat differently. Several months after arriving on Yankeshiri, MacDonald was summoned to visit this Captain. He was taken from his small hut at night, and marched – within sheets of darkness – toward a place that MacDonald would come to know as intimately as his own cell.

The Captain did not lean toward MacDonald when they spoke. Nothing in his manner was so direct as to confront him with a question about his motives for coming to Japan. The Captain had heard that MacDonald had left his ship after some disagreement with his commander. And while he didn't believe the shipwrecked story, he decided to let this problem sit for a time. His interrogation, instead, seemed to walk around MacDonald and reach MacDonald's ears from one side or the other. MacDonald felt no immediate reason to lift his guard, until that time when he was back in his cell, re-imagining his conversation with the Captain, and flipping through their discussion as if through a series of daguerreotypes. The words were black and white within his mind, more clear in the darkness of his cell than in the confused light of the Captain's room. Their shared words came and went, circled and slipped away to a place MacDonald could not – at first – see.

"Time is an enemy," began the Captain. "Let me tell you about time, because it is the reason you are not allowed in Japan."

MacDonald walked toward the man, but stopped in the middle of the room when he noticed the ink drawing on the floor. To cross the narrow room he would have to walk across the body of a bearded man stretched out on a crucifix. The drawing cut the room into four sections and the Captain stood to greet MacDonald, as if to balance on the top of the crucifix.

MacDonald paused. Then he looked up at the Captain and held his eyes as he walked right across body of Christ. It seemed like a bridge instead of blasphemy, but he knew that walking across the figure was actually a test.

"Do you know the name Hideyoshi?" the Captain asked.

"No," said MacDonald.

"Do you know his edict to punish foreigners in Japan?"

The Captain explained that Hideyoshi was favourable to Christians. He'd accepted the Jesuits in 1587. He'd accepted the calendar of worship, the months of July and August, and he'd accepted the day of Sunday, the moment of prayer, and he'd even allowed Christians to hang their clocks from their walls. He'd let them string these clocks through their jacket buttons and hide them in pockets.

Hideyoshi was a tolerant man until 1597, when he was close to death and suddenly realized his mistake. The Franciscans were fighting with the Jesuits, arguing over the property of the soul, when the noise of this argument woke his suspicions. Even to his failing ears, an organized Christian treason sounded both near and conceivable. If the soul is conquered, he reasoned, the heart would follow.

Quite suddenly, Hideyoshi realized that a heavenly afterlife was not a promise but an actual threat to his immortality. His name, he believed, could live only if remembered. And Western Time, he decided, was already overtaking the names of Japanese rulers. The names of Japanese years were never relegated to numbers – those were base instruments used to catalogue property and tax.

The Captain counted out the words for "one, two, three, four ...," spelling out the kanji with his fingers to show his dismissal of mathematics.

In this moment of awakening, Hideyoshi abolished this instrument of mortality and banned Western Time from our names. He left numbers for taxes and standardized Japan's property, measuring the world into lengths of tatami mats. He excluded the foreign devils from Japan and killed time only months before it found him.

"Without calendars," asked MacDonald, "how do you plot the years?"

The Captain did not understand the word *plot*, but guessed that MacDonald meant to seed the years with memories. From the Jesuits he knew that the Greek notion of time looked backward, watching the world retreat, growing smaller and smaller.

Time was a wind where scraps of the present continually blew past the ears, through the hair. Time retreated from the eyes while the mind tried to grasp a moment's significance with open eyes and outstretching fingers. Time escapes them.

"For you," said the Captain, "time began when your ancestors looked at the universe as a pin-scarred blanket. Through many deaths, these stars were handed down to you. You may own them, these illusory blankets, but they are only property. Your possessions become antiques; they are your tether, the only kite-string for memory.

"For us," said the Captain, who had begun to lean toward MacDonald, "to say a man's name is to bring him close – close enough to see with the eyes or with the mind. He is always within reach of the blade."

MacDonald held his place, on the floor above Christ, and looked up at the Captain. The two men settled into the pause that followed, as if sinking into warm water. Finally, the words MacDonald expected to hear: "Why did you leave your ship?"

"My captain," said MacDonald, "let me go."

They were silent as they approached the sea. If anything betrayed this silence, it was the sound of their bamboo brushes rattling deep inside their *yatate* pipes and the black ink at the base of those pipes that gently sloshed with each footstep.

But here, the Captain interrupted his story. He wanted to tell MacDonald something that seemed important to this strange tale:

They called themselves the Heike, but they were also known as the Taira clan. Blindly, they believed that no one could recognize the sound of words from an inkpot. What is unwritten, they said, did not yet exist. The ink was not distilled from crows, but from black cormorant feathers and brought all the way from Fukushima because the birds in that prefecture were rumoured to be mute. The cormorants, they believed, had bartered with the sheep and traded their voices for a streak of white upon their breasts. A trade they regretted their whole lives.

But pen and ink released them; they could speak again. With the help of a coarse brush, a cormorant could turn into an insolent, chatty crow or (under a finer hand) a cormorant could regain its voice, finally, and speak of flight.

Their words were often composed by painting two character pictographs, side by side. This collective image was an ideograph, a pictorial metaphor that hinted at abstraction. To the Western imagination, a metaphor was a twin-pointed ladder pushing through an apple tree. Two images began in the real world and let the reader climb toward the imaginary. But for the Heike a metaphor was not a climb. It was descent. To say the word *metaphor* was to say *hidden under* in Japanese, as if all our ladders led to the underworld, as if the fantastic was always at our feet. The Milky Way, *amanogawa*, was always "Heaven's River."

These words came to Japan from another river: the Yellow River region of China. About three thousand different characters have been found in this river, most of them inscribed on bones and tortoiseshells. Some of these characters were said to be carved in stone by the sheer force of a master's brush. Yet another story tells of a fourth-century calligrapher named Wang Xizhi, who practised writing the dot stoke each day on his belly, and this is the reason we now have belly buttons. He was said to have discovered the brushstroke of his name in the backward curve of a goose's neck. And on the third of March, 353 AD, after an afternoon of drinking wine and composing poetry, Wang Xizhi wrote the *Orchid Pavilion Preface*, three hundred and twenty-four characters that were immediately recognized as the most inspiring example of handwriting in history. Wang was not the first, you see. These bone-carved pictographs were mashed, painted, drawn, and carved to create meaning, to divine the future and the past, since 2000 BC.

Now, said the Captain, we can come back to the story. The Heike approached the sea in silence. But in the ideograph for the word *silence*, the Heike tribe of Japan saw a dancer, and – next to her – a needle with a box that resembles an open mouth. The dual painting of this word required nineteen strokes of a brush. The needle may have represented the dancer's teeth. The mouth may have been the hole for the thread. Or the box could have been simply a box, "japanned" with black enamel, lacquered with the benefit of a single crow-feather brush. This much was clear: the woman had tattered sleeves and as she swung across a paper room, without spoken words, a story was woven from her dance. With the right set of ears even silence could be heard and understood.

So it was fitting that a bird's open mouth – an unwritten word – should burble in an inkpot and betray the Heike's efforts for a silent death. We heard them on their way to the sea, as if the cormorants were speaking. The Heike did not wear armour that night, but silk robes and gypsy-moth kimonos. And when they jumped to their deaths, the ink from their brushes mixed slowly with the cold water. The cormorants began to sing and dance and speak of lost battles.

Roughly translated, this was the first story that a man named "Ranarudo Makudonaruto" heard in his Japanese prison near the end of the Tokugawa period, in June 1848.

This is how MacDonald composed his Japanese dictionary: he traded the language, word by word, story after story.

His cell was clean, or nearly so. The floor was hard and black, made of planks that MacDonald could only guess were once wood. The walls, too, were black, windowless, and soot-damaged from an open hearth that let MacDonald view the moon and the stars. The roof itself was thatched with grass and thin rods of bamboo, woven into a pattern that absorbed his attention for however long he set his eyes upon it.

He was given a soft mattress to be rolled across the floor and a pillow that was not unlike a sack of corn flour. These small comforts were offered with a hushed word that sounded like an apology to MacDonald's ears: *sumimasen.* A useful phrase this, because it covered both interruptions and excuses, salutations and apologies, gratitude and remorse. Excuse us, they seemed to say, for bothering you. Excuse this small offering, this room, this bed, this tea. The accepted response was the same phrase: Excuse me for the effort you made to make me this tea, this mattress. This jail. *Sumimasen.* One word and already his dictionary was full.

In spirit these men seemed absurdly gentle jailers. Their calculated politeness was disarming. Backing out of his cell, they bowed twice. Having no word of thanks to proffer, MacDonald learned that even his guards did not know this expression. Instead, they seemed to grasp something from his Portuguese dictionary, by smudging the word *obrigato* into *arigato. Obliged.*

How right, he decided, for a country to *borrow* a phrase to express gratitude. More sophisticated graces followed and MacDonald whetted layers of politeness from their language until there was nothing left. The words *tsumara nai mono desuk-eredo, dozo* offered a gift and translated directly into the phrase *not good thing though please.*

He was given a rude spoon, a cup, and three bowls. After a lengthy exchange of hand signals, he was made to know that the bowls should be covered whenever he finished eating. The cockroaches were relentless. They were the same destructive, foraging animals that he remembered from whaling ships, but their variety surprised him. By his third month in this cell he would know thirty-one separate kinds by sight, and know – by increasing his vocabulary from *thank you* to *cockroach* – that there were sixty-eight separate species in Japan. He would learn the words for *egg, larva, pupa,* and *imago,* as if he were mapping his own life's span.

Larvae, he said, "Immature insects, wingless. A feeding stage. From the Latin for *ghost, a mask."*

The cockroaches bit and chewed everything from the grains of sugar and rice between his floorboards to the salt on the inner lining of his slippers. They thrived at night. They sipped milk, nibbled dried and fresh blood. For dessert they gorged themselves on his precious bookbindings. They ate dead insects, their own dead and crippled kin, and – most repellent swab! – their own castoff skin. He would learn to find sleep quickly in those first few months. He practised sleep, falling into dreams, as he had once practised overturning his boat in the Sea of Japan. He hoped to find those dreams before he felt the tickle of an insect moving across his face, in search of a drink from his eyes.

He seemed to dream more in Japan than he did in America. He didn't know where he was in Japan, so an onslaught of image and fear assaulted his thoughts each night.

Dreams, he thought, were the day's tangents. They began in the familiar and quickly strayed toward metaphor, reaching for ideas that the day's logic could not fathom. He didn't understand the words, much less the bizarre images which shocked him numb upon waking.

The straw mat under his body nudged him awake and each day began the same way. Bamboo and paper barred the view to the one room, but light from the hearth stretched high on his southwest wall. He watched the progress of that beam and followed the day as it began an early descent, and he watched it move across the floor and disappear by mid-afternoon.

The room remained bright enough to read in, and for this he asked a guard for each of his possessions. They arrived, one at a time. He was not encouraged to keep his books and photographs in his cell. The Captain had decided that too many foreign objects would distract his men from their actual duties. So MacDonald described a book, each cover, the size and weight of a dictionary, then another, and he began teaching his guards how to read.

"The Bible," he said to the man named Shibayama. "Please bring me the small Bible with the blue trim."

The samurai, the foot-samurai, the superintendent of the foot-samurai, and the physician all reported on MacDonald's questions and they soon learned the words *King James Edition* as quickly as they recognized MacDonald's other common phrases: *Good morning. Who is it? Water. Good. What is this?*

On his trips to visit the Captain, MacDonald asked questions. He asked one question of each man he met and pieced together the Captain's house and language, one room at a time.

The building was three storeys and MacDonald and his foot-soldiers passed through the Main House, through the arched bridge corridor, then up into the Northern Annex, where he found a room with blank walls, called the Room of Purity. The other resting rooms had drawings: the Room of Plums, the Room of Bamboo, and the Room of Maple. MacDonald glimpsed another room with latticed windows on his way into the building and the next week he learned that it opened to the Room of Cherries. The following visit he learned that only commoners over ninety years of age were allowed to visit this room; retainers must be at least eighty. The room's chief use was for the composition of verse, and none of his guards had travelled through it.

But the Captain usually waited for MacDonald in an annex sitting room – the Room of Bush Clover. MacDonald examined this room with each visit, memorizing the dimensions, the leaves upon the wall, the blue veins across the door panels, and finally the false ceiling that seemed to be made of wickered cedar.

"Cryptomeria bark," said the Captain, noticing MacDonald's upward glance. "This tree is part fish. Scales hide even the seeds. Let us begin."

And then, the Captain began his second story.

In the first years of the Tokugawa period, Emiko Murakami gave birth to a son with clouds in his eyes. She named him Hoichi because she believed the character *Ho* would protect her child, and *Ichi* simply because he was the first one she had wrapped in blankets.

She didn't know that the boy was blind and that he could see only clouds.

His father was a potter who worked in the back entrance of his small house. He spun a potter's wheel using one callused foot and wedged himself (for support) into the corner of a tatami shoe closet with the other. It was a runner's art; one foot ran a clay mile every hour. The other foot propped him up, strained against the small closet, and his thigh bulged against the wall's weight as if he needed the whole building's force to construct a single teacup. His dexterity with his one potter's foot was so great that he seemed shamefully inept – almost awkward – when forced to walk to the market on both feet.

Hoichi was seven when his father began a new series of pots that he said were meant to hold not rice, but meaning. On the surface of each clay pot his father inscribed a word in kanji. It took sixty pots to bring the boy up to the first grade. One of the first words he learned was *day*, which was interchangeable with the word for *sun*, and the pictograph grew out of the design of a real day's sun – a single dot in the middle of an oval groove. He told Hoichi that this was the history of the sun. Over centuries the word had evolved from that one sunspot, until the sun was divided and spread out across an oval sky. His father's finger stretched the spot lengthwise until it became a line that separated the sun into two distinct boxes.

When his father smashed this pot against the floor, he wiped the universe clean and threw a modern day's version of the sun: four clean imperial strokes across clay which became two square boxes, one on top of the other. He used paper mitts to bring the pot out of the kiln and he sanded the bottom of the bowl while the clay was still hot. Later, when he placed this present in his son's outstretched hands, Hoichi ran his fingers over the surface of the sun and felt its dull, solid heat.

One hundred and seventy-four pots later, the boy would find this same character – *sun* – between two gates, and recognize that the light was pressing through the doors to form the word for *a space in between*. Hoichi had never seen the light, of course, but inside this new character his fingers felt the heat from his first day's sun, pressing through the two simple gates.

And from this second, shattered lesson he learned that the writing of kanji begins inside a pictograph. As the potter leaves, he works his way out – finishing his last stroke, the final hinge on the right-hand side of a door – and he sweeps his brush out and away, closing the gate behind him. There is no return. Once the kanji is written, the moment in time cannot be corrected. It shows poor judgement and indescribable presumption to return to a word, reach into the page and adjust the sun's angle.

By his tenth year, Hoichi found music to replace his sightless world. He soon played the biwa like the masseur who hears a man's regrets between vertebrae. And it was this ability that gave him some measure of fame and, later, a small sense of embarrassed pride.

His pride did not last so very long. Hoichi was seventeen when his mother and father died and after that day he went to live with the priests in the blue mountains of Chichibu. He could not see the short forest of mushroom logs that surrounded his temple. Hoichi stayed inside and thumbed his way through dark stanzas and dark rooms. He never found the temple's forgetfulness.

But one day – in the middle of a song – he *did* find a knock on the door and a stranger's voice through the wood. The voice commanded him to follow and Hoichi soon found a path that took him elsewhere. The path was impossibly long and Hoichi began to smell salt in the air. Never having visited the edge of Japan, he didn't know the taste of the sea on his lips. He only knew the songs of the Heike – their songs of lost battles – without ever hearing the sound of someone actually slipping into water. He also knew the song of the rising river that geishas sing when they raise their kimonos. He knew all the songs of water, but never dreamed its smell until that night.

It may well have been a dream. Hoichi played three nights for the stranger's voice that commanded him to follow this path and play the songs of lost battles. Hoichi thumbed through graveyard symphonies without knowing that he was playing for Heike ghosts, who lived, briefly, in his song. The ghosts were foot-soldiers who commanded him to play these songs and Hoichi – anxious for sea – gave them everything. He kept their secret and told no one.

Weeks later, at the monks' temple, a different Hoichi appeared before a general assembly. This Hoichi was ragged with dreams, thin in spirit. Despite the delay of their meeting, the monks could not help staring at him. His eyes were clouds – as usual – but dark lines had suffused the boy's brow. His eyelids were thick and trimmed with red veins. He thanked the monks for their concern, but offered no explanation for his appearance. They thought that he had the look of someone who had truly seen the world: an old man who had readied a shrug, a smile, for the passage of time. This was remarkable, said one monk, for a blind boy who had never left the building. Walking dreams, said another. And Hoichi smiled to avoid this attention, the questions, as if to suggest that there was nothing more to say.

The monks were suspicious of Hoichi's sleeplessness and walking dreams. They could recognize the telltale languor of a boy who was haunted by dreams and secrets. But they had no idea that Hoichi's dreams were actual ghosts and that the boy was playing songs for dead spirits; neither did Hoichi. It was only later, the next evening, that two monks quietly followed him and watched the boy make his way toward a graveyard, alone. Blind, Hoichi effortlessly navigated the night then played his biwa to an empty stage of headstones, flowers, cabbage leaves, and burnt offerings.

The next day Hoichi was surprised with what the monks told him. At first, he didn't believe that he had actually played for spirits. Hoichi could remember the smell of the sea, the wind, even the bitter taste of salt on his lips. The monks said that they were too far from the water and salt for these things to be true and real. The wind was real, they said. The water was real. And so was the salt from your eyes, but not the sea. So the monks painted Hoichi, covered his body with Shinto prayers, Zen inklings across fingers, eyelids, foreskin, and the words made him as invisible as thought. The prayers, said the monks, would hide him from haunted travels.

That night, when ancient foot-soldiers came to knock they could not see Hoichi hiding behind words and prayers. Hoichi was silent. The Heike saw only a six-mat room, an imperfect teacup (made perfect by its slight imperfection), and scrolls of seasonal poetry, words meant for one god or another. But hidden in the folds of this poetry, the ghosts found one set of ears that (they knew) belonged to Hoichi. This was the only imperfection they found in all these words and scrolls of papered prayers. A set of ears that sat like a wrinkle on the page.

So the dream soldiers took these ears as proof of Hoichi's loss, his disappearance, his demise. And Hoichi, silent as cabbage, stayed hidden in his prayers while his ears were quickly torn from his skull.

In Japanese, a crust of bread – *pan no mimi* – is called *the bread's ear*. Any baker in Japan can tell you this story. Then he will carefully wrap up your selection, write the price on the outside of the package, and send you on your travels.

I watched Endo pull a box of baked buns from his kitchen cabinet. The package was clean and seemed new, but the absence of an expiry date had me worried. He opened the box and I saw that each bun was individually wrapped and vacuum-sealed to last a century. On the outside of each package, the words, written in Japlish: "Leaf Palette – Soft and light leaf pie baked thoroughly as if time piles up."

He opened one package, bit into the crustless bun, and I watched black bean sauce leak out of the corner of his smiling face.

There is rice

Hiroko

Dreams, geisha, & insects

Fly kites

For all her artistic accomplishments, it is her skill in conversation that Japanese men claim to appreciate the most. She has become fluent in the news of the day, the gossip of the theater or sumo world, the naughty jokes making the rounds, and flattery both refined and outrageous. She has studied the male ego and tends it like a garden. She knows a man's moods and his seasons. She fusses, and he blooms.

– Jodi Cobb, *Geisha*

One morning, I arrived at school and each of the junior-high teachers had something new to say to me – in English. This was unusual because, for the last six months, most of them had said no more than "Good morning" before switching to fully feathered Japanese.

"Herro," said the math teacher. "There is soup today. There is milk. There are oranges. There is cucumber. There is rice!"

"Thank you," I said. "That sounds very good."

The physics teacher was hiding behind a hospital mask in the opposite corner of the staff room. When I met him at the tea urn, he greeted me with a roster of English questions: "How old are you, how tall are you, how many sisters do you have, how many brothers do you have?"

I could see the edges of his mask strain with the force of his smile.

Before I could answer, the music teacher arrived, leaned against a filing cabinet, and asked, "What's new?"

When my own students translated this question, I would get the usual literal repetitions, "What is *new* kana?" then a series of worthy attempts. "A new coat? A new pencil? I have nothing new. Do I need something new?"

Usually I faced utter student meltdown.

But with this new onslaught of English, I could feel my own meltdown approaching, and the music teacher didn't wait for my response. He left for his tambourine room and I was left to wonder what else the teachers had been hiding from me for the last half-year. They could all speak English? But what a conspiracy!

By lunchtime, over a tray of soup, milk, oranges, cucumbers, and rice, I learned the truth. Mrs. Tani, an English teacher, had been in the hospital for the past week with a back injury. While she recuperated, each of the other teachers had taught her class one crucial lesson from her textbooks. Suddenly, the math, music, and science teachers – in fact, every teacher in the school – could speak one line of English. If I put her co-workers up against a wall I could have had a single conversation from one end of the room to the other.

That day, before I left for home, I passed by the math teacher's classroom. He was still there, marking tests, but he looked up from a thicket of papers and seemed ready to attempt some new English phrase. By this time I knew that the words for *see you tomorrow* were from some other teacher's lesson, but the math teacher waved a tired arm from across the room.

I waved back. He seemed to know that our English conversation was at a standstill, but he smiled anyway. Then he said, "There is soup today. There is milk. There are oranges. There is cucumber. There is rice!"

With Mrs. Tani's absence, my public-school workload suddenly doubled until I had almost no time to prepare my lessons. I cut back on kendo, but my increased teaching commitments and my Japanese studies left my head all the more bruised by the end of each day. My classes dragged toward completion. Each one might begin with the clock's minute hand falling toward 30, but it seemed to take more effort to push the same hand up, toward the top of each hour.

My adult evening classes also changed dramatically with the addition of a new student, Miss Hiroko Kawato. She was a bright-eyed young woman who instantly made me forget my horrendous teaching responsibilities. When I asked her to introduce herself to the class she said that she had started a law degree – which she'd recently abandoned – and now worked, instead, as a radio DJ. She wanted to leave radio and take up painting, but at present she said she was "between jobs and hobbies."

"That is the phrase, isn't it?"

I nodded dumbly.

She admitted that most Japanese thought she was very strange not to stick with one interest. Voracious to learn as much she could, she'd also tried piano and now English. She seemed to swallow her hobbies whole. The other students seemed jealous and awestruck by this freedom. She was twenty-two years old. She was also quite beautiful. And, of course, the men started dressing better. They were now punctual and attended every lesson. Conversely, the other women in the class seemed to grow quiet.

For several weeks I tried to cajole the others into speaking English. But I was secretly thrilled that Miss Kawato was challenging some of the students to speak, asking questions and completing all her homework – not just the homework for each lesson but all the homework from the beginning of the year. She caught up on some thirty lessons (which we'd been doing for six months) in the span of a few weeks. Her notebooks were littered with Japanese definitions, scrawled reminders, and synonyms for words she didn't understand and had to look up. There were extra pages stapled in her workbook for those passages which required essays and longer answers. I glanced at her exercise book and saw that she'd already pencilled in her answers for next week's lesson. The lesson was titled "Polite Responses."

Statement: My dog bites everyone who visits my house.

Her retort: *He must be a good guard dog.*

Statement: My uncle is in prison.

Her retort: *He must be innocent.*

Fortunately for me, all the men in this class were married. As soon as I emerged from my classroom, Endo questioned me about this point at great length.

Then, looking at me carefully, he finally said the words I'd been waiting for: "She is, how do you say, a babe?"

"Her teeth are a little crooked," I said.

"Are you crazy at this moment? She is beautiful. Shawing."

"Sha-wing?"

"Sha-wing," he said. "Don't you know this word? It means a great state of perpendicular excitement from a male speaker in particular."

I nodded.

"It is," he said, "gender specific."

"Uh-huh. I was just wondering where you'd heard this expression."

"Don't make fun. *Sha-wing* is a common expression in American films. You are trying to change the subject, but you must tell me if you like Miss Hiroko Kawato immediately."

"That would be confidential information," I said, "between a teacher and a student."

"I am a teacher," he said. "And I am also your teacher," reminding me that I had a class later that day and a conversational test the next week. "Maybe I can help you with her tutorial work," he said, grinning his perfect set of teeth.

There were more bribes, begging, suggestions of professional impropriety, and promises extracted. I admitted that I was interested in her. Finally, I told Endo about the exercise book and her polite responses, then – anxious for more clues about her character – he opened my briefcase and fumbled through the class assignments to find her bona fide answers to my questions. The lesson was "memory" conjugations.

I remember making a big mistake on the stage.

I remember painting on my friend's face for fun while she was sleeping.

I remember being moved by a composition which one of my friends wrote about me.

I remember spending every summer vacation in Kamakura.
"What do you think it means?" I asked.
"Wait," he said, frowning slightly, "there's more."
He stopped at the florists to buy some pink roses.
She stopped eating in expensive restaurants eight years ago.
She stopped going out with wild men eight years ago.
"Well?" I said.

"This is going to be difficult," he said. "We have a lot of research to do." For the next few weeks Endo became my confidant. I avoided Charlotte's invitations to dinner or "to come over and watch commercials" and fed Endo details about Hiroko's homework and her imagined past. He told me what he thought her answers meant about "her general character" and (specifically) about "her romantic life."

When she wrote the words, *He is drunk on his piano playing,* Endo decided that she absolutely had a boyfriend.

"How can you be sure?" I said.

He didn't answer, but kept rifling through her homework. He seemed fascinated that she had contributed the words *Neptune* and *catastrophic,* culling her new vocabulary from the stars, while the other students had written answers involving generic *animals, gardens,* and earthbound *flowers.*

"She's very smart," he said. "Neptune could mean trouble though."

"What do you mean?"

"She is not – how can I say this? – a traditional woman."

"You can tell that from the word *Neptune?*"

"Of course," he said. "How many people do you know can talk about Neptune over breakfast?" He pointed at the page.

"Instead of flowers she wants a planet! Show her a puppy and she says *catastrophic*! The words are absolutely specific."

Endo put the notebook back in my hands.

"And remember, my friend," he said, "Neptune is very difficult to reach."

At the end of one week's lesson I invited Endo out with my adult students to the Rail Club. This bar was a reconditioned antique train that sat below the Kumagaya Bridge and the railroad tracks. The two trains, welded together in the shape of an L, rattled pleasantly when the Shinkansen railed past and shook all of the whisky lockers as if looking for a key. Client name cards hung like pendants from each bottle and swayed in unison with the bullet-train's passage.

Hiroko was already there when we arrived. Between one whisky cabinet and Hiroko's boyfriend, Endo and I spent four torturous hours looking into her eyes. A happy, gorgeous girl, dressed all in black. She had the most expressive face that I'd ever seen in Japan. A way of crumpling her chin when she laughed. She didn't play to anyone in particular – not even to her boyfriend. She simply animated any thought that was put in front of her, following the conversation wherever it happened to drift. Her face: a pool of self-confidence.

Every Wednesday I watched her come to class – late, usually – and I looked forward to her apologetic smile. It was the same one she flashed when she left early, running out to some new mission, project, or hobby that awaited her. She seemed singularly grounded in youth and wonder.

After five Coronas in the antique train, I simply wanted to steal her away. I wanted to put the car on rails, let the other passengers off, one by one, and wake up in another prefecture.

Instead, I insulted her boyfriend. It was a small attack, inconspicuous within the crowd of untranslatable ideas and gestures that swirled around us. But I actually relied on a language barrier to blur my intent. I asked him if his white shirt was actually underwear, and while our stationary train seemed to slow within that tangled pause, Endo told him that whatever it was the shirt looked great.

Hiroko slapped the boy until he thanked Endo for the compliment. Our train seemed to move again, as the conversation followed its own itinerary. I wanted to jump on, somehow, and join the group. And a question about the weather – the recent spring showers, a downpour that we had all shared – seemed like a good place to begin.

Endo described the cherry blossoms that had almost completed blooming in Hokkaido. The blossoms were a wind, he said, a pink front that began to blow from the warmer, southernmost prefectures and gradually pushed north. Racing up Japan, a wave of flowers had bloomed, peaked, and fallen.

Canada's winter – a popular subject of horror in Japan – was quickly broached. I told them about the time zones in Canada, how I'd traversed an hour on Sunshine Mountain by skiing from Mountain Standard Time to Pacific. Three o'clock, four o'clock, three o'clock, four o'clock, back and forth, my two skis straddling the border between Alberta and British Columbia. I'd travelled within this netherworld of time, a boot in each province, three-thirty in the afternoon, on a typical day in Canada.

Hiroko smiled. Her chin danced for my benefit, so I went on with this monologue, beyond the size of my country to chronicle the frozen deaths that occur – quite a usual problem, I said – as Canadians go about their business, skiing from one province to another. An hour can pass over you like a white sheet and you can be frozen in your dreams. She smiled again. You can, I said, tuck yourself inside an hour.

But suddenly I became aware of my own voice, talking, talking, onward ho, and all the others politely listening. I'd almost forgotten Endo's advice to listen more and insert less. I looked at him, apologetically, hoping that he might come to my rescue and actually say something.

St. Francis Xavier, he said, landed in Kagoshima with his Jesuit mission in 1549. Against all warnings, the priest took a walk in the woods during a sun-shower and witnessed the marriage of two foxes. I smiled at this quiet tale – the idea that someone could only find the magical under a blanket of weather. It seemed so different from the ubiquitous frozen-Canadian-death story I was about to describe. Finally, the conversation veered away from my end of the table. And I sat back to listen to the passing trains and the sound of frightened bottles.

Hiroko spoke too. She described a childhood picnic that she'd taken, with her family, to a place called Monkey Mountain. They had spent a perfect afternoon, playing games and eating rice-balled *onigidi*, and on the walk down they were attacked by a brazen group of monkeys. Apparently, the monkeys could smell the rice that she had dropped inadvertently on her skirt.

As Hiroko talked, a waiter arrived at her side and she had the presence of mind to help him pass four small bowls of nachos down the line to each of us. Chopsticks soon followed; each wooden set she carefully placed by our right hands. We started to eat and she described the crazed monkeys, who were agitated by the smell and taste of short-grain rice. She examined her skirt and brushed the imaginary grains from the fabric, as if (at that very moment) the monkeys were running up, under our table, to attack her legs. I didn't realize it, at the time, but I had stopped chewing, as if I was consciously trying not to interrupt her story. Hiroko described the wild anxiety in her father's face. She said his eyes looked more feral than protective. She described the basket that he swung at the animals. Then she described the monkeys' small black hands, pulling at her skirt, in a series of quick, clawed grabs. And then, just as her father was about to swat one of the monkeys away, I felt something coarse scratch my leg and I positively jumped. It was Hiroko, a natural storyteller, with a hairbrush and the oldest campfire trick in the book.

The story – true or not – had a relaxing effect on me and on the three others. Perhaps I'd had enough beer for one night and felt a comfortable numbness in that warm moment. But her story also seemed to end the evening on a happy note, so we left the bar together and quickly parted ways.

As Endo and I drove home, I told myself that I would relax into the country's own rhythms. I even convinced myself that there was nothing wrong with being attracted to one of my own students – a student who was also eight and a half years younger than I.

But that night I slept fitfully, dreaming of monkeys that clawed at my arms and legs. And somewhere, within those drunken visions, while my air conditioner kicked on then off, I glimpsed MacDonald. I saw him fumble through his own dreams, and I saw his hand that tried to swat at the mosquito netting above his bed. His gossamer curtain strained with each tug. Outside, the wind began to blow, pushing itself into his room, and a southwest monsoon finally billowed his walls.

After that night at the Rail Club I didn't see Hiroko for a week or so, maybe more. When she came back to class she had gifts for everyone. She handed me a set of leather drink coasters that read *Mystic Kyoto*. I noticed that some of the others received key chains or blank cards (for them to send on to someone else). All of her gifts were inexpensive souvenirs, but throughout the lesson I caught myself trying to map the significance of the one present she gave me.

Mystic Kyoto, I pondered. Were these coasters meant to remind me of the Rail Club? Even vaguely? Was Mystic Kyoto remotely close to Romantic Kyoto? I could almost hear Endo, in the background, screaming the word, "*Not!*"

When Hiroko gave us her small gifts, we spoke about them in class. I learned that the word for such souvenirs – given to every co-worker and friend you have – is *omiage*. It is a sort of traveller's gift. You buy it for someone who may have noticed your absence.

Of course, I *had* noticed Hiroko's absence, but I didn't tell her that I'd also visited Kyoto. That would have seemed like too much of a coincidence. Instead, I let the class speak about other travels, other souvenirs, and other customs. I didn't tell them that, in Verona, I once watched tourists line up below Juliet's balcony and pose for photographs next to a brass statue. Juliet's left arm was slightly outstretched and her hand was open so that her fingers seemed to shoo the tourists toward one side of her green figure. Over several decades, the statue had become smaller and smaller, rubbed thin by the multitude of hands that groped her waist and by the arms that hung about her neck.

Juliet's collarbone and part of her brass dress wore out in 1967. By 1975 her left breast glimmered slightly when the sun, the moon, or the flash of a camera entered the courtyard. Each year peeled an onion-skin of brass from her chest, diminishing her so completely that her left side became concave by 1990.

When I saw her in 1991, I noticed she had been given an implant. I caught sight of her between the giggling tourists who took turns hugging her and I saw that a blowtorch had travelled a rude path across her chest. Even a new swathe of metal was eroding under the touch of so many foreign palms. Her left breast was already clean and shiny. Certainly, the scars would fade with time. Pollution's shawl and her outstretched arm will keep her right side veiled and unexplored. Unknowingly, the people who left Verona took away microscopic vestiges of Juliet – souvenirs that they gave to friends and co-workers as soon as they touched hands.

In Rome, Saint Peter feels the same wear of tourism on his disappearing marble toe. Pisa's leaning tower has marble stairs that resemble a series of empty bowls, piled high.

After seven months in Japan, I noticed that the wear of tourism was more difficult to see because most historical sites are kept beyond arm's length. It is a country of partitions, a place where a tourist can take away only photographs. But Japan seems to anticipate her march of visitors, the school tours, and the memento-hungry Japanese who keep tourism alive. Mystic Kyoto coasters, cards, and Hiroshima knick-knacks help Japanese tourists souvenir their travels.

Like everyone else, I suppose I'd travelled to Kyoto in search of beauty and memento. I'd also hoped to see another Juliet – the geisha. Most of them disappeared after the Second World War, though not strictly from the touch of men's hands. In a mad panic to embrace Hollywood and McDonald's *Bigga Maku*, Japan has almost rubbed the geisha out of existence.

She is so well hidden from tourism that she can only be seen, in outline, from outside an exclusive restaurant's windows. To shuffle in and out of the restaurant she lifts her kimono, flashes a steel-blue undergarment in her departure, then she disappears into the streets like a Venetian boatman stepping into a gondola.

I may have caught a glimpse of her before she vanished down a side street, but that was all. A small creek ran through Kyoto's Gion district, and though the water was little more than a wide trough, I'd found a small pathway that bordered only one side of the water. On the other side, where the restaurant district backed, lived the other world where the geisha and their apprentices moved about and where they could be properly imagined.

I couldn't afford these restaurants, but I did find myself listening for the sound of a geisha's wooden clogs, *pocketa, pocketa,* on the pavement. I may have watched for the odd taxi that slowed to a stop near the entrance to a restaurant or a fancy building. In lieu of meeting a geisha, I could only imagine her distant figure and her intimate gestures.

So I thanked Hiroko for the leather coasters. I knew that her gift was not charged with meaning, and that it was just the sort of *omiage* souvenir she had intended it to be. And I believed – fervently – in the idea that I did not want to touch her, or brush against her, or take some part of her home with me.

The next morning I woke up to find two grey praying mantises stuck to the window screen outside my tatami room. I shooed them toward a large glass with a bootleg copy of *Lolita*. Then I brought them inside and dropped them into a clear Tupperware canister. I wasn't sure if they were male or female (or one of each!), but the larger one was hardly moving, preferring to wait, surveying the new surroundings without actually expending any effort to walk around. She must have been female; she acted far more secure than the darker, more paranoid mantis who kept glancing over his shoulder.

But they had necks. This was my most startling discovery. Like miniature dinosaurs, they actually turned their heads to look at one another, or at me, watching them from the other side of their Tupperware hotel.

According to my kanji dictionary, the praying mantis is called *kamakiri* in Japanese, or *sickle-cutter*, and now that I had seen one with my own eyes, I rather thought the Japanese name suits them best. They didn't pray (unlike the Buddhist fly, who clasps his hands together and saves his life from the fly swatter), they preyed. Hanging upside down from the top of the lid, the female drew her sickles slightly back, then briefly slingshot herself toward a moth, grabbing it around both wings as if to demonstrate a wrestler's full nelson. Silver moth dust shimmered down the sides of the Tupperware while the mantis calmly turned the moth upside down and – in one gloriously fluid movement – plunged her head right into the moth's fat underbelly, between its open wings. The moth's wings were pinned, but against that pressure one wing seemed to stutter, evenly, like a clock with broken second hand. The mantis head – hard and triangular – stabbed into the moth, then pulled the cotton insides out as if deflowering an antique pillow. She had two larger jaws on the sides of her mouth which pulled the food inside. Smaller teeth encircled her mouth, acting as fingers or stabilizers that gripped her prey and seemed to shred whatever they touched.

I wish I could say that nothing but the moth's wings remained, but this is not true. Lolita (as I began calling the female mantis) left a mess. Yellow moth stuffing, as dry as pollen, fell from the top of the cage, heaping in piles below her. The head and one large chunk of abdomen were entirely forgotten when she broke off a wing and returned to eating the muscles that drove the moth's flight. A moth leg actually hung from her claws until she brushed it away, slowly, methodically, during the clean-up afterward. She positively licked her scissors clean. And it suddenly occurred to me that I'd never seen a carnivorous insect up close.

Before watching this feeding spectacle, I was completely charmed by her careful, refined grace. Her practised movements. She made me think that I'd discovered a miniature stork or opened a desk drawer to find an impromptu pencil ballerina.

My extra classes and new hobby kept me occupied, and stopped me from dwelling on Hiroko. But it wasn't long before Endo caught me hunting for insects in the school parking lot. One night, around midnight, he leaned out of his apartment window. He pulled back inside to retrieve his glasses, and a few seconds later he stepped out on the landing. His robe hung down to his bare kneecaps. He squinted, obviously curious about what I was doing beside a lamppost, leaping for moths with a muffin pan.

There wasn't anything that could be kept private in such a small town – he'd said as much – so I didn't try too hard to keep my sickle-cutters a secret from him. If I was living my own sort of Tupperware existence, my "life in a fishbowl," then a collection of insects was the least of my worries. The more laughable scuttlebutt was a rumour being circulated that I was romantically interested in Charlotte. Many of our elementary-school students had assumed that we were, at the very least, "an item."

Apparently, they'd seen me waiting outside her classroom, while I listened to Kobashi's lessons. It took only one day for several students to crowd around me.

The bravest asked, "Is Charlotte your lover?"

"No," I said. "And the question is not polite."

They usually left giggling.

For a time, Charlotte had called our apartment complex "Caucasian Corner." These days she said it was "The Bug House." Whatever the change, she left me alone – sensing, perhaps, that my attention had shifted elsewhere.

The bug collection gave me an excuse, I thought, to harbour a semi-private interest. It was also a passion, or mania perhaps, that distracted everyone (including myself) from my romantic imaginings.

As for Endo, I thought that he had seen enough *gaijin* teachers over the years to dull his fascination for Occidental oddities, so I didn't hide anything from him. Not Hiroko, not the mantis farm, not my new interest in collecting bugs at midnight. I simply waved hello to him.

He squinted at the muffin pan in my hand. He looked at his watch. Then he shook his head, sadly, and went back into his apartment.

The next day, in Kounan's only Log Cabin restaurant, he pushed his hand between two Kirin beer bottles and gave me a list that his father had passed down to him. The list, he said, was a samurai's rules of conduct:

A man has to be man.

A man must not show his emotions in public.

A man must be kind to others.

A man must not bully the weaker.

A man must be polite to others.
A man must not tell a lie.
A man must have his own dream.

I never learned why he gave me something so personal. Either he considered me an ally or I'd broken one of his seven rules. Of course, I was thinking about Hiroko and felt unaccountably guilty most of the time, so both scenarios seemed likely. I chose not to ask about it.

A week later, I let the smaller of my two mantises go and found another one, just as small, but a little darker and more robust than his predecessor. The large mantis was, indeed, female. I learned this through acquiring a book with insect illustrations from our school library.

For hours I watched my beauties hanging from the top of a new terrarium I bought in Tokyo. They walked over miniature logs, through a pebbled landscape, to climb the glass walls and poke their talons through the plastic roof grating of their strange surroundings. I was hardly self-conscious about my new-found occupation (or, perhaps, preoccupation). Across Japan, during warm summer evenings, children routinely collected rhinoceros beetles in wicker baskets. Fishermen once manufactured their lines out of moth cocoons. Cultural history was suddenly working for me. So, *genjiki-mushi, Caligula japonica*, the most common moth in Japan, I collected with rod and pillowcase.

A few of my students actually encouraged my hobby by collecting new specimens. I found one mantis in my desk and two were given to me by elementary students in school stairwells. My collaborators multiplied. A school principal had delivered my most recent mantis. His student had insisted that he buckle up the mantis in the front seat of his Jaguar.

"I have brought this bug from a student *in the city*," he said, shaking his head. "Do you know how many of these bugs I can find in that bush over there?" he asked.

"Dozens?" I said, hopefully.

He smiled and put the container in my hands.

Discharged from his paper cup, the new mantis spent comparatively little time looking around my terrarium. He flew at Lolita and straddled her wings. She didn't move. He descended a few steps, turned, and wrapped both sickles around her waist. They were both hanging upside down, but his hind legs held on to her wings, hugging her body like a frog attached to a stone, his body curved in an S so that his abdomen would wind under her wings to meet her body near the topside of her valvules. Still, she moved very little. Whenever she adjusted a foot or turned her head to look around, he rasped her with a sickle, quickly, four to seven times on her left side until she stopped moving. Conversely, her sickles were immobile, unused. Neither of them moved. It was hard to tell if he was just hanging on to avoid her arms or if they were really mating.

Then, after fifteen minutes, they started to swing. The female had her sickles up and ready. She was the one swinging. The male was just hanging on for the ride. She wiped her eyes, moving back and forth. The male rasped her, but she kept swinging, wiping, and cleaning her hands and face.

A half-hour later they stopped moving altogether. The male was noticeably thinner than before. His body was thin and flexible. He pushed off her slowly, unwinding his body while still hanging on to her wings. For thirty seconds he hung on as if preparing himself for something. Then he did the most extraordinary backflip, landing squarely with all four feet on a tiny log below. She didn't even see him. He looked back at her – tipped his hat, perhaps – and then simply walked away. She stayed exactly in the same spot. Her posterior throbbed slightly, pushing out a little ball of whiteness that grew to the size of a pearl. It looked sticky, malleable, and she seemed to squeeze it out, positioning it within the two spiked ends of her posterior. Three times, she tried and failed to free the white ball with her long rear legs. The fourth time she was successful. She reached back and caught the pearl with one foot, bringing it up to her mouth with both sickles. Then she ate it.

The male nibbled on his scissors, washing his hands and face. Then he began making his way from the log to the window. He didn't seem to be in a great hurry to leave. Without a moment's thought, he scaled the wall and walked around Lolita. Hunched over, she turned her neck and flashed him her full face, looking at him so directly her eyes and face seemed to grow. He froze. One foot at a time, he backed away the entire length of the cage. He just backed up. Lolita ignored him for five minutes before making her move. She seemed to be throwing out jabs as she walked, but she was actually cleaning her hands as she went.

He struggled more and more to find a way out. For ten minutes they did little more than circle one another. She lunged at him occasionally, toying with his fate, and each time he would run and freeze, run and freeze, trying to blend in with the meagre landscape I'd given them.

I felt sorry for him – sorry that I hadn't left him more places to hide – but I couldn't tear my eyes away. I wanted to see how it all ended.

He crouched next to a log and feigned sleep. She walked by, turned, doubled back, and when she pulled herself on top of the log she seemed to loom above him, like a dangerous mobile above a crib. Either indifferent or in denial, he turned his head and looked away. She took him then, whirling her sickles against his in a flurry of moss, leaves, sand, and gossamer. I almost lost sight of them in the struggle, but their storm was brief and they seemed to hold each other at the end of it.

I watched her break his knee-joint in two, and eat part of his left front leg. She severed another leg, using one sickle, then reached higher and squeezed his torso, so that it bulged with the pressure of her grip. She looked suddenly comfortable, as if she had decided to sit down to dinner while he slept in her arms.

She moved her head close to his – their eyes met – and then she bit into his throat. It took an hour for her to chew from his thorax down to his chest. Then she worked her way back up to his head and decapitated him. In her arms, his body could not move, except for the lowest part of his abdomen – his sex – which seemed to push its way toward her, in a vain attempt to get closer. She allowed this. She lifted her wings and let him in and they mated again, as he gradually disappeared from her cage.

In lieu of a bug funeral I chose the pub. There were a couple of pool halls near Kumagaya, but their tables had so many rips and tears that the game had more in common with pinball than billiards. However transient, a Western fix is sometimes mandatory.

I knew one bar in Tokyo that guaranteed the West with every imitation Corona and chopsticked nacho. It was called Books & Bait and it sat in Ogikubo, an artsy section of the city, just down the street from the Royal Host Coffee House. Frequented mainly by foreigners, English teachers, and ex-pats, the walls boasted an American flag, a hockey stick, and five antique fishing rods. By the window, a sombrero and a fake samurai sword. A bamboo screen ran next to the bar. A Macintosh computer sat by the Scotch bottles. And wall-to-wall paperbacks were shelved on two-by-four bookshelves everywhere else.

Three wooden picnic tables took up most of the space in the room. The clock face above the bar was perpetually set to midnight. A photograph of a woman, whose breasts were barely constrained by a white bra, dangled from a large nail in the wall. Another woman, a well-known comedian dressed in a black tuxedo, laughed into the camera lens, and, beside her, a handwritten message read, "To Bob. Thanks for the orgasm, it was the best." These photos seemed to contradict the sign on the door that read: RESPECT THE WOMEN IN THIS BAR OR GO TO ROPPONGI. Apparently, everyone in the bar took this advice literally, because the pub was empty.

The owner, Bob, was an ex-military man who had left the U.S. after serving an uninspiring tour of duty in Vietnam. He came to Tokyo, married a "national," and opened up his own pub above a Japanese magazine shop. At Books & Bait, his first idea had been to sell books and American sushi (what he termed "fishing supplies"), but beer drinkers had quickly outnumbered fishermen.

Bob's T-shirt was always stretched to accommodate his girth, but this never worried him. He routinely pulled his hair out in clumps, looked at it for a moment, then said, "Shit," and dropped the fuzzy brown tangle on the floor behind the bar. As an escape route from the modern, cemented world, Books & Bait was as good as any – that is, if you could tolerate Bob's convictions on the meaning of life.

"Overfill a girl's glass so the beer runs over the edge a bit," he'd say. "You can always tell she's going to be a good date if she rushes to save the head. If she licks the glass, you're in business." This, a bartender's shot-glass epiphany.

That night, as Bob poured, I consciously let the foam run down the side of my glass. The words across my Suntory beer mug read,

A glassful of drops.
Each drop is tomorrow.
Sip your dreams by drops.

Just about everything starts to look like a Zen koan for enlightenment when you drink local beer in foreign countries. Japanese Twinkie ads flirt with Einstein's theory of relativity. Pencil-case slogans lead to *gaijin* nirvana. And Bach's Toccata and Fugue in D Minor is reduced to a television jingle: *Ti da riiii, hana kara giu nyu!* Roughly translated: "Milk comes out of my nose when I laugh."

Each day, I saw Creap coffee whitener, Pocari Sweat bottles, Peek-A-Boo dessert bars, Well Come auto dealerships, and Lusty Baby clothes. They were just some of the words that had bombarded my English sensibilities since I'd arrived in Japan.

I was stewing over my beer, mulling this ever-present Japlish phenomenon, and hoping to somehow get away from it all, when I noticed the television at the far end of the bar. On the screen, a woman in a kimono was trying to catch a fly with her automatic vacuum cleaner. She swung the nozzle around her living room as if she were a samurai clearing out the village invaders.

"*Hai! Hai! Hai!*" she said. "Take that."

End of fly. And end of commercial.

Bob was rinsing out a soapy glass in the sink, watching the television with one haggard eye.

There was a heaviness hanging above the bar. I thought it was the heat and Bob's oppressive curtains, hanging to blot out the sun. They hung so low that they collected in great pools around the windowsill.

In an effort to keep himself cool, he'd left his bar fridge open and all at once an idea seemed to shiver through his ragged head. He turned to me.

"Have you ever flied a kite indoors? Ever seen a fly kite?"

I didn't bother to respond. Since acquiring my collection, I seemed to find insects everywhere I went.

"No, really," he said. "Have you even seen one?"

"No," I said, "I don't believe I have."

"Today's your lucky day. Get me a fly."

Bob left, disappearing into the bathroom, while I sat at the bar, waiting for further instruction.

"A fly," he said. "Get me a fucking fly."

"What kind of fly?"

"A fly, a fucking fly. How many flies are there? Just go find me a fucking fly. Not dead, though. I can't show you the kite trick unless you get me a live one."

This project was no easy thing. In the end, the bar curtains actually helped me trap a fly for Bob's bizarre experiment. His fly kite turned out to be a simple procedure, involving one fly, a glass, the refrigerator, and approximately two feet of dental floss. Trapped inside the bar fridge, the fly was quickly drugged into submission, and Bob, seizing this moment, spent an absurd number of minutes tying dental floss around the fly's tiny legs. When the cold wore off, the fly – on waking up in a strange, cool glass – climbed out with heroic effort and tried to balance itself on the rim of his glass. The dental floss didn't bother him. Flight seemed imminent.

Ten minutes later, Bob had eight flies tethered to the bar, spinning circles round Sapporo glasses, a private circus for every empty stool. For a while, I watched the glasses. From one side of the glass the reflections bent reality so that a fly moved one way and its image went the other.

"Nature," said Bob, "is a beautiful thing."

I went to the bathroom. It looked unsafe to attempt any bodily activity, because the walls were pock-ridden with cigarette scars and pen holes. Graffiti covered every surface, even the toilet seat. And there were three packages of toilet paper in the sink. Bob's habitual scam was collecting free tissues from the various advertisers on the street. He bragged that he'd never passed one without taking a package or two that listed HAPPY RESTAURANT on one side and an English school on the other.

"After fourteen years in Tokyo, I don't ever need to buy toilet paper again."

I moved the paper and washed my hands with a drizzle of cold water. (The soap looked toxic green.)

A few people had entered the bar by the time I returned to Bob's flies.

"This," said Bob, "is the key: always act as if she is the mother and you are the child." Another pearl out of the mouth of a nosy bartender in Japan.

Bob brushed his crag of hair, then smiled. "Just a theory."

Ten minutes later, when I decided to leave the bar, I heard Bob helping someone order a pizza.

"Tell them you want it for Ogikubo. *Oh-gi-ku-bo*. Ogikubo. Give me the fucking phone, for Christ's sake, I'll tell 'em myself."

I finished the last of my beer and decided to go home to Lolita. I walked out into the warm air and caught the last train home.

With one less mantis, my apartment seemed suddenly quiet, as if to accent my lacklustre life. Even the crickets – too far from my bedroom window – were silent.

In my dreams, I drive my car down the wrong way on one-way streets.

An old white-haired man pulls onto the street from the proper direction and stops beside my car. He asks: Am I going the right way? I say *yes*, and a moment later the white-haired man is walking toward my car. He asks if he can just talk to me for a second, it won't take long, please, and he slips into my car, into the back seat, without anybody pulling the seats forward to give him adequate room. But he is inside suddenly, and pulling something from his pocket. I say no, suddenly aware that something bad, something terrible is about to happen. He says, Don't worry, I just want to help you. I know where you are going tonight and I have something for you. And all of a sudden I realize that I am going to meet the devil tonight and this wiry-haired man knows everything. Every one of my thoughts.

There is a long, fearful moment when he takes a pin, a single pin, from his pocket. He says, Don't worry. This will protect you. I can cut a small triangle behind your ear, just a scratch, and when the devil comes to take your soul it will stop him, like a crucifix that bars the minions of his night. I say, Okay, thank you, when suddenly my car antenna goes up and down as if by an act of God. It startles both of us, and as I look away from it to calm the old man – saying that the antenna goes up whenever it wants, it sometimes sticks you see, nothing to worry about – I see that the old man has changed. He is now a huge hairy beast with sharp teeth and his hands are coming around my throat and I wake up with a yelp.

Other nights I dream about teeth (a sign of an approaching death, I'm told). I crack my teeth opening a bottle or I actually get my teeth stuck on the cap while trying to avoid snapping my one false tooth. Or my molars crack at the back of my mouth. One entire dream involves sorting the pieces of my teeth, bit by bit. Gluing them together with Liquid Paper. Days later, I cannot recall if this actually happened to me.

I'm not sure if Endo's regular trips to the dentist are somehow affecting my own sleep, or if I'm watching too many bugs die during the day, but my broken teeth figure nightly in my dreams. Most nights they just fall off and I swallow them whole.

In my favourite dreams I meet a woman with long, blue hair. We make love while this colour moves like a shadow across her face.

One night the woman backs up against me in the small bed – apparently we do this to keep warm. After an hour my side hurts – the weight of my lungs seems too heavy – so I turn around and spread out, until her ass swallows my knee and I have to move again to keep cool.

The wall heater blows air down to the bed and grants me a headache when I wake. The heat has filled my head with heavy thoughts and I wake twice as lethargic as the time I left the world. My brain wobbles to a standstill and I leave my dreams, reluctantly.

When I wake, I immediately look for her – this woman with blue-black hair. She's so fresh in my mind that I can almost imagine that she exists. The light is dim but discernible. It's almost morning. Lighter still, and I realize that I am alone.

I touched Hiroko's hand – briefly – on a pedestrian bridge.

It was our "chance encounter." I had manufactured some

question to keep her after class, and when we were alone in the room I invited her for a coffee. I was surprised how quickly she accepted the offer. Outside, she led me through the streets, one step ahead. I finally caught up to her, and walked *with* her, as we climbed one side of an overpass. A rail hid our hands for the length of the bridge. None of the drivers witnessed our acrobatic display of emotion.

At the top of the stairs I touched her hand, and felt several small scars that criss-crossed her knuckles. I asked her what had happened, and she said, "Cold, very cold, the cold killed it." Frostbite, I asked, *in June*? She shook the hand away, without responding. We walked a little farther along the overpass. Near the middle of the bridge, an arc above droning cars, I touched her shoulder, and she turned to face me. I held her face, briefly. Finally, I kissed the side of her narrow mouth and when she broke free I let her go as if she had escaped me.

By the time we'd reached the other side of the bridge, I was already wondering what had happened between us. I asked Hiroko if she thought that we both lived, inherently, in a world of aliens. Against my better judgement, I went further: Was a date with a *gaijin* such an alien occurrence? A danger? A risk? Is that why she'd pulled away?

She seemed to understand risk. But the word *alien* troubled her. She frowned, briefly, though if this happened I could not properly describe her face. A screen or mask had somehow materialized, and her eyes were without expression. Hiroko turned away, and I saw her hair gleam sharp and silver in the top of a truck's headlights. Below us, the truck passed and her hair quickly returned to black.

———

"You don't have one of those cards," I said, "a foreigner's Alien Registration card."

We'd spoken about these cards in class, several times, so she already knew my thoughts. During one particular lesson we'd covered the words for *quarantine, difference,* and *discrimination.* Another student, named Mr. Misawa, had read *Crime and Punishment* in his youth and he admitted to demonstrating against Americans after the Korean war. Most of us were surprised by that confession, by the fact that he was, of course, sitting with us and learning English. But Misawa said that he'd learned a lot by the experience.

Actions, he said, can shape a conscience.

On the bridge, some of those loaded words – *difference* and *alien* – were still buzzing about my head, but I seemed to forget Misawa's good conscience. I wanted to get at our difference, somehow, and knock it down. Then I wanted to offer Hiroko some fact that might underline how similar we really were.

"Don't you know what I'm talking about?" My question was rhetorical, but so was her response.

"Yes," she said, "I do not."

And when we descended, she ran ahead of me, breaking that moment, those contradictions, running past the rest of our conversation so that I could only look at her thin figure skipping down the stairs. *Tap tap tap,* she reached the sidewalk, turned, then smiled brightly to dispel whatever differences between us I might have touched upon. I remember that I felt relieved (for some reason) that she had not answered me.

She stood on the sidewalk, waiting for me to catch up to her, waiting to begin a different conversation. Both our masks were renewed.

The telephone rang early the next morning.

The whispered voice was frantic: "No sex Hiroko, no sex Hiroko, no."

The speaker hung up quickly. Hiroko's mother, perhaps a grandmother, had obviously heard about our walk across the bridge and the cup of tea in the Royal Host Coffee House.

I was elated by the mysterious phone call. I knew she'd told someone about me – her own confidante – and this seemed less a warning than a prediction of what was soon to follow.

Safe inside the confines of my good mood, nothing could derail me, not even my most boisterous elementary student, a certain Kazunori Hirasawa.

That afternoon, Kazunori came late, slammed the door, and entered the class with a belt tied around his forehead. While the other students fought to ignore him, he tiptoed through the room and, with one overhand swing, he smashed a bloated book bag onto his desk.

I smiled.

"I am sorry I am late!" he said. "*I am sorry I am late!*"

I asked him to sit down, before he repeated the phrase again. And during the class he hummed, kneeled on his desk, and knocked his eraser to the floor only so that he would have to run after it.

That day I let him get away with everything because he was, like me, so completely out of the ordinary. While Hiroko's image swirled about my thoughts, Kazunori answered everyone's question twice, correctly, and proclaimed his homework *dekimashita!* (finished) well before the rest of the class.

As Kazunori called out the time in ten-minute intervals, I imagined the clock's hand beginning to spin faster than normal, edging us all toward recess. We sang songs, and Kazunori insisted that "She'll Be Coming Round the Mountain" was a Chinese song, since the woman was eating chicken *dumplings* when she comes. And through all of these absurdities, I managed to hold on to the thought that something good might have happened, between Hiroko and me, on our bridge.

"How are you?" I asked.

"I am *super!*" Kazunori said, mirroring my own thoughts. He raised his arms to flex his small muscles. The other students stared at him, surprised by this colourful change from Japanese composure to pink English-garish. Obviously, he was one of Endo's students, having taken the class on Western gestures.

I should have restrained him, but that day I let him run the class.

At the end he offered me a gift, which looked like a metallic potato-chip bag. Inside, I found the latest advance in Japanese technology: each candy was individually wrapped in its own mini-bag. Curry Snake flavour pictured a grandmotherly figure who was knocked off her feet by the force of the flames coming out of her mouth. The Sour Death Ball variety (which was dipped in alum dust) showed the same woman, but this time her lips were pursed. She had large, melted eyes that were four times the size of her spectacles.

Next to her, a cat – who looked suspiciously similar to Hello Kitty – was also melting in the background.

Somehow, I missed all of these warnings. Kazunori held out his hand, gave me a Sour Death Ball, and the alum imploded my mouth so severely that I couldn't help but spit it right across the classroom.

And I still went home smiling.

That night I went to Endo's apartment and ate the last reserves of his mother's ginger chicken and rice. During our meal he played Whitney Houston on his metallic pink stereo and then he brought out one of his more recent acquisitions: an oval projector that shot a beam of light toward the ceiling. On top of the projector was a blue dish the size of a magnifying glass, which Endo filled with tap water. Then he dimmed the lights and plugged in the projector. The dish began to rotate, jiggling the water inside and shooting the semblance of a pool's blue reflection across the ceiling of his apartment.

"Welcome," he said, "to Aqua Fantasy!"

That night, gazing upwards, we drank plum wine and ate chocolate ice cream out of Dixie cups by his new pool.

I was enjoying his company, but I decided to check in on my apartment around nine. There were three terrariums, containing two praying mantises, eight crickets, three rhinoceros beetles, and a large yellow spider who seemed to demand regular attention. My fridge was full of eggplant and cucumber to feed the crickets, and I enjoyed listening to them sing, so they were never in danger of being moved from their safe terrarium to another, more volatile place. I usually kept the praying mantises away from the other "in-house" bugs, but the spider was becoming lethargic of late, and on this particular evening I was sure that a praying mantis could outlive a spider.

I opened the spider's terrarium and tipped her into another world containing two praying mantises. She scuttled toward them and then seemed to rest, or dig herself into the sand, like a soldier preparing for battle.

By the time I looked in on them they seemed wholly content with their lot, the mantises taking a few threatening swipes at the spider, just for show. The spider, large and yellow, with black flecks on her fur, merely scrawled at the glass, begging me to let her out. I didn't realize that she was, in fact, going around the cage in circles. She couldn't climb the glass because her black talons were long and difficult to wield. They seemed suctionless. But I began to notice that bits of dirt and pebbles were moving about the cage, as if tied to some transparent puppet string.

She was spinning!

When I left the room at ten p.m., she'd made about seven turns around the log and spun seven invisible circles. When I woke up to the sound of the wind at three a.m. the spider was hanging from the top of the cage and three-quarters of my beautiful cage was webbed. Incredibly, the mantises were now rooted to the ground, and I noticed that one was missing an antenna. The spider had only five legs, so I went back to bed. The odds looked rather good.

By eight a.m. the scenario was much the same, except the brown mantis was doubled over, visibly tired and probably dying. Strands of spider webs were gumming his leg joints.

Enough, I thought.

I felt more affinity for the mantis and I still wanted him to win (at least vicariously) so I fished out the spider with a mug and tried vainly to flush her down the toilet. Even after I added a wad of toilet paper, she just kept coming back, using her (seemingly) ineffective legs and an invisible safety thread. After one more try I finally gave up and let her outside, shooing her down the hallway with a cardboard notepad, until she found her freedom. She'd earned it.

I put the terrarium on the kitchen table and cleaned the webs out of the cage with chopsticks. Then I separated the mantises and actually hand-fed the sick one. To coax him to eat I had to slice the belly of a grasshopper with a pair of scissors. But water seemed to be what he was craving. I filled a bottle cap and watched him submerge his head in the water for what seemed like a long time. I cut up some cucumber and left him to rest.

When I came back, several hours later, I was amazed to see that the grasshopper and the mantis were both still alive. The mantis was hovering over the bottle cap of water as if it was about to be sick. I touched his back to test his strength and he made a feeble attempt to strike me.

Oh, but then he started to die. I was sure of it. Even his intestines started emptying, more and more, draining out black scum that coiled out and became longer than his body. The line kept growing and twisting as it left the mantis and suddenly I realized that it was some kind of parasite: a worm that finally escaped my shrunken mantis and left him for dead. The worm was shiny black and impossibly round. It curled and writhed all about the cage, overturning the bottle cap, pushing the pebbles and the miniature logs back and forth.

Stunned, I watched the mantis begin moving. Having rid the parasite from his body, he looked thin but wholly alive. Eyeless, the worm seemed to explore the cage with both ends of its body, wrapping itself around whatever it brushed, while the mantis struggled weakly to stay clear. Repulsed, I was about to toss them all outside when Endo came in and saw what was happening in my kitchen.

"Let's burn it," he said, to my sudden relief.

Outside, I folded a piece of newspaper into the shape of a hat. Using two nearby sticks, I transferred the parasite from the terrarium to the classifieds and then I began lighting corners. I could hear something sizzle and pop as it burned.

Watching the smoke rise above the parking lot, Endo stood on one side, while I stood on the other. Both of us were still in our indoor slippers, watching for any new transmogrification that might creep or fly out of the burning newspapers. We were, I suppose, just two more people in Japan burning our morning garbage. But there was something determined and twisted in both our faces. Something in our eyes jarred with the clear fall afternoon.

When the fire was nothing more than black ripples shrinking into carbonized paper, I looked up at Endo. He smiled and shook his head.

"You can call me Enzo," he said.

"Enzo?"

"I like that name quite a bit."

I nodded, as if I understood what he was talking about. He wanted a Western pseudonym, I suppose – something Mediterranean – as much as I wanted a fresh start.

Minutes later I let go of all my bugs, everything: Lolita, the crickets, the beetles, the cucumber rations, the leaves, the tiny logs, everything. Gathering up the remnants of her cage, I noticed the top of one of the terrariums where Lolita had spent most of her time. Wedged into a corner, just hidden under the lid's grating, I found a shiny grey wad, about the size of a discarded piece of Juicy Fruit.

I left the wad on the lid and stored the whole terrarium outside my balcony. I knew that I'd be leaving in the fall, so I wouldn't be in Japan to see the birth of any more sickle-cutters (even if I wanted them). Inside my apartment, I cleaned up the kitchen, concentrating on the area where the bugs had lived, then I decided to go next door.

Enzo was inside, and he had already switched on Aqua Fantasy by the time I entered his apartment, without knocking. He handed me a beer as I passed his kitchen and, even though it was still late morning, I took the drink without a second thought.

He closed the curtains, then joined me next to "the pool." He fumbled with the buttons – searching for some new setting – and when I looked up, I saw a ceiling of stars.

Moving bundles of loose clothing

A pork moon

Hiroko's beginning-of-the-end

Six months across the page of his prison term, MacDonald had not yet seen a woman. His diary notes that his unnamed Captain once asked him permission to bring his wife, his daughter, and three other women to visit him.

In the weeks that followed this visit MacDonald noticed the man's sudden absence from the day's schedule of guards.

The Captain, he was told, had his head chopped off – which was how they expressed it – for breaking the law. About this crime, written in a brief entry in MacDonald's dictionary, only a description of the women remains. The Captain, it would seem, paid for this entry with his life:

Their dress, especially the headgear, was strange to me. After they left me, I made an attempt to sketch it but found I was not artist enough. Let me attempt a description: They were dressed alike, or nearly so. Wore a gown similar to that of the men, but longer, of cotton, striped with wide sleeves, wider than those of men; dress bound round the waist, loosely, by a very broad belt, of stuff like raw coarse silk. As to their under and foot dressing I cannot say. They shuffled in and out, and squatted in such a manner that they looked more like moving bundles of loose clothes than anything else.

I had, however, a good view of their heads, which were uncovered. Their complexion was a light brown; eyes black and slightly oblique; nose short, and almost straight, not prominent but well developed. Face, more round than oval, with well-proportioned mouth and chin, well-rounded cheeks, cheekbones protrusive but not prominently; broad, fairly high forehead, fully exposed. Lips, flattened. Their hair black – intensely black – rather coarse, long, rolled up (indescribably) and tied on the top of the head, fastened with bodkins or arrow-like hairpins about fifteen inches in length, apparently of wood inlaid with silver.

As if describing a breeze that filled his ship's canvas, MacDonald wrote that their general disposition had "a prevailing amiability." They had a graceful, modest dignity that seemed calculated to make a favourable impression. They were short, but not unshapely. He looked at the mass of stiff cotton that surrounded their slight figures and thought to himself that they seemed entirely bundled by expectation. This was, he decided, the only example of enforced modesty he'd ever seen.

He invited them closer, past the entrance of his cell.

"Welcome to the lion's den," he said, and they giggled, covering their mouths immediately. They slid into his cell, as if an incline had helped them to steer their robes. When they removed their hands from their faces MacDonald noticed that the Captain's wife had black teeth. The unmarried woman (her sister?) appeared to have painted her lips a brilliant red and her teeth were also tinged with this colour. The youngest, the Captain's daughter, had perfectly white teeth. If her face was pink, it was only the blush of youth that was written across her face.

He asked the women about their teeth and the Captain answered for them.

"This is an old custom," he said, "but only for married women. They make the black dye from warm water, a teacup of *sake*, powdered gallnuts, and hot iron filings."

Another application for the grog-yes, thought MacDonald.

"They paint their teeth with a feather brush."

"How many times?"

"I . . . don't know," said the Captain. He spoke quickly to his wife.

"Not so often," she said, hiding her smile.

From the Captain's wife, there is a new story MacDonald learns, about a child who lives in boxes. It is the tale of *Hako iri Musume*, the boxed daughter.

A long time ago, on the bear's plain in Saitama prefecture, there was an old couple who had no children. Masashi and Satomi had tried for many years to add more voices to their lives but their house was barren of joy and sound. One night, in desperation, they prayed to the moon for a child.

Of course, it was the night of the Milky Way when wishes are sometimes granted to young lovers, depending on the weather. The King of Heavens forbids lovers on opposite sides of the river to meet on any other day but Tanibata. The Milky

Way can mar this festival with clouds. And on those nights, if it is cloudy, the Princess Shyokujo cannot make her way across the river of stars. Kengyu may think that she is lazy, that she is afraid, or that she simply spent the night weaving instead of swimming. But rain makes the river too high. The clouds conspire against them and the night becomes too long and too far to swim. They may never meet.

But the moon was full on the night that Masashi and Satomi sent their prayers. They could see Heaven's River shining brightly through the stars. The moon was orange and quiet and (as they say) the Prince could wade across the river to meet his Princess without navigating through clouds.

Early the next day Masashi was out tending his fields. He saw the sun rise out of the bamboo shoots, against the skyline. A bamboo fork looked as if it was not so very far from the moon, and he could imagine the scrawled character *daybreak* played out across the world. Masashi was doubly fortunate that day: he was blessed a second time by actually becoming a character across the morning's page.

He could see the drawing in his own hands. He looked down, and saw the sickle that was written into the kanji for *father*. *Otosan*. He saw the knife cutting under a ricefield. The moment he imagined himself, imitating the word, a sickle in hand, he looked down to find a newborn baby girl. He'd been cutting bamboo, extending his own father's fields, slicing through stalks that were as thick as his wife's largest teapots. By chance he'd looked down into one of the stalks and there was the child, sitting in the bottom of her bamboo chamber.

The Heike say that bamboo grass grows by single rooms each year. The years hold us prisoner in these chambers, passing us from one year to the next. To look down is to see the future, a new year growing in height and width with each stubborn season. A past year's chamber can never be entered, once closed, capped on New Year's Day. Imperceptibly, each year grows toward closure.

Masashi found the girl in the first chamber, the lowest part of the bamboo. He brought the girl home, of course, and he and his wife raised the child as their own, never forgetting their debt to the moon who had left her for the day. She was so treasured by the couple that the baby grew up into a princess. And when she was twenty-one chambers old, they let her go, sent her back to the moon on the branches of the trees where she was born.

Hako iri Musume means *Boxed Girl* but the kanji that the Japanese use for the word *box* has two bamboo trees on top, another generic tree on the left and an eye to mark the changes of a year. A father will often describe his daughter as a "girl in a box," forever treasured in his arms and held as high as bamboo stalks against the morning's sky.

Conversely, the word for *shameful* comes from one very similar to *dirty*, and MacDonald writes it by placing dirty water beside the figure of a small child. He believes that the rationale for this pictograph is that it is shameful to leave a small child near such potential danger. The word reads (literally) *child drowning in dirty water*.

After the Captain's death, MacDonald was marched from Nootska to Tootoomari. If there were proper Japanese terms for these places, he did not know them. He heard the words and filed them away, shuffled onward, he thought, toward the city of Yes.

A pork moon hung above the stars. A moon that was not marbled but riddled with fat. MacDonald was hungry and gauged the world with his empty stomach. He was tired of rice, tired of the fermented beans and pickled oddities. Suddenly, he was nostalgic for sauerkraut – a seaman's staple that he'd vowed never to revisit.

He walked for several days and nights between prisons until he became wholly surprised by the changing landscape. One step jostled him farther along through a ricefield, or deeper into the woods, then another and another until it seemed he hadn't walked a level path in the whole of Japan. They rested and smoked at regular intervals. At some place by the sea they embarked on a junk and travelled south, toward Hakodate.

He was taken by *fune* from Western Yesso to Nagasaki. The trip would take six weeks to sail from Tootoomari, Rishiri Island, to Matsumae and – the wind being unwilling to bring them to Esashi – on to Eramachi and Nagasaki. MacDonald would see little of the day, being confined to a cargo room in the bottom of the ship.

A report at Nagasaki would follow. An interview with the prisoner would be brief and exclude any comment on the Captain's death. It was as if the guards hoped to save MacDonald from the truth or, at least, protect him from his own stories.

Ranarudo Makudonaruto, fisherman of Canada, aged twenty-four years, has been received in charge. He said that there was no god nor Buddha. He cultivated his heart and will and worshipped heaven in order to get clear understanding and enjoy happiness. He has nothing else to repeat.

But these Nagasaki notes were for later pages. He would meet the governor of Nagasaki, if that had been so ordered. The surprise would be his. Almost every new student who entered his cell would quickly say, *"Nihonjin!,"* and remark that MacDonald's dark skin, his black hair, and his short, stocky build resembled the Japanese. One student joked that MacDonald had spent enough time in Japan and that he had gained the language but lost his long Western nose. He was prepared for the same exclamation when he was called before the governor.

By sea he travelled in darkness. His only windows were painted portholes. He had walked a twin plank from quay to ship, looked at the black water under his feet, and he saw stained carnations where he had once imagined main-deck gun-ports. But the junk's red flowers did not shield a view or a cannon. These painted patterns were not even some grin of war, the false teeth of battle. At most, thought MacDonald, they were symbols or family crests. And like those mock forts that were erected on the coast of the Matsumae, these crests had deflected his eyes from the truth, and kept hundreds of American ships at bay.

The main deck held a crew of twelve men with six sculling oars, a captain, and seven others who hauled the wind on sails that were sometimes set, depending on the gate they followed. The crew sang and the scullers chanted in time with the junk's progress. They seemed to dip their oars into the beat of their song. The junk pulled on the waves and the men dragged her completely through the refrain. The oar blades were concave and angled downward to catch the water, so the song kept them in line, as much as the sea would allow. The sheer length and height of these oars and the downward haul of those curved blades gave them true sculling that mimicked a whaling ship's screw propeller. Their voices were fine and the ship moved quickly through the water.

Below, in the empty cargo room, MacDonald listened to their songs. His legs ached. His sleep was fitful. Mid-morning – the next day – the songs ended, the boat began to rock with the movement of the sea and several men came below. They offered him four black lacquered bowls and MacDonald unveiled boiled white fish, pickled radish, rice, and dried squid. He was thankful for the squid because it was so difficult to chew that it occupied most of his afternoon.

Fed and watered, MacDonald preferred to sleep under the waves in this small junk. Portside and stern, he could imagine water breaking over him as the ship ran before a gale, the lug sail above his bed, and the four other masts at his feet that made up the junk's spread of six woven sails. Plain sailing when the sea was calm, a porthole opened at night. The stars peeked at him from behind a grapnel anchor. Cross-staves measured the altitude of the stars. One cross-piece slid along a staff and graduated in degrees of altitude, until the top aligned with the river in the stars and its base with the horizon of Japan.

I quickly became tired of holding hands in darkened theatres and distant coffee shops and told her so. But Hiroko talked around the subject and did anything to avoid committing a plan, a belief, to stone. She didn't address sex; she suggested it, she circled, seemed to know and hint where we were moving without actually ensnaring herself in a promise.

The words "I want to make love with you" were never acknowledged.

The silence again.

"Do you want to make love?" was avoided at all cost. I realized that this question required a *yes* or a *no*. The question was not only impolite but embarrassing to refuse. For what was truly crude in Japan? Not love, certainly, but the words. The talking.

When pushed, she answered with brutal honesty: "No," she said. "We can't. Do you understand? You're leaving soon."

Another long pause.

"I once saw a man. He had a wife and a child. He took me places and when he left me he went back to his wife. And I wondered what he was doing with her. I don't want to feel that again, when you go back to Canada. We cannot. Do you understand?"

"Of course," I lied. "I understand perfectly. You only had to say so once." As if *she* was the one who had pushed *me* to respond.

We couldn't have sex and we couldn't talk about sex so I took consolation that her rejection was reflected in a simple difference of language. (Of course I rationalized her rebuke.) The subject of sex was banned? Fine. Only the suggestion of our attraction to each other would be audible. We relied on "stomach-talk," what the Japanese term a discussion which moves around an awkward subject, circumventing the obvious.

For me, Hiroko became a sentence – a long one – with a verb that I might never read. As with all sentences in Japan, subjects were left out, and the verb was left to the very end. The ultimate verb (*to love*, or, *to leave*) might be at end of this sentence, but sex was such a distant possibility that I knew we'd never speak about it (or around it) again.

I saw Hiroko a few days later, but she said no more about our "discussion," our argument, if you can call it that, except the phrase, *Fufu genka wa inu mo kuwanai.* "Even dogs won't chew on a marital spat."

If there was hope to be found inside that proverb, I'm sure I lost the flavour of it as I mulled over her intent, her meaning, in the days that followed.

Without the banned subjects of love and sex, we began to speak more and more Japanese with each other. Perhaps she knew that I liked to learn new phrases, or perhaps she thought I wouldn't dwell on our "relationship" when we spoke Japanese. Whatever her reasons, I realized that Hiroko could hide inside the language, while I could only fumble for a reference point.

When she took up painting, only the small blots of paint on her army boots betrayed her secret hobby. I noticed the colour magenta on the floor, one Wednesday night, and could imagine her walking a trail of blue and green to school. Without "weighty" subjects, our conversations seemed to brighten. I'd almost forgotten our differences, or separate worlds, until one day, when she asked, "*Kettsu eki gata wa, nani gata desu ka?*"

"I have no idea," I said.

This amazed her. "How can someone not know their own blood type? Blood is the secret to your character."

"How's that?"

"If you are A-*gata*, you are *majime*. This means that you are serious, punctual, methodical, and exact. If you are B-*gata*, you are like the radish, *daitan*: bold, happy then not happy, changeable and a little selfish. O-*gata* means you are co-operative. And AB-*gata*, you are double character."

"I'm probably B," I said. "What blood type do you have?"

"*Gata gata desu*," she laughed. "I have a rickety type." It took me weeks to learn the pun she gave me. The word for *type* in this case meant something *strange* or *unstable*.

And after this conversation, I began to notice other references to blood in Japan. Elementary students learned their blood types in school. Name badges listed both grade levels and blood types. She said that even sumo wrestlers honour the blood, by carving the hand-signalled calligraphy, *heart*, into the air after each glorious battle.

I thought that Hiroko's story only accented our differences, as if we were born adversaries in every realm: from elementary schools to wrestling gyms.

So my teaching continued, and the weeks toward summer vacation seemed to lengthen with the increasing heat and humidity. When I passed my fellow Santa – named June – in the hallway, even he seemed tired, and somehow beaten, under a veil of perspiration. His crooked smile wavered, then disappeared, when his nurse wiped his brow and mouth. Only Kazunori met me with his usual barrage of questions, and I let him rattle them off, one by one:

Can a tree bark? Can a zipper fly? Can a suit swim? Can a nylon cry? Can a face crumble?

Can a woman, I wondered, *what*?

Charlotte, too, was out of sorts. She was homesick – almost blind to the people and country around her. Some weeks she travelled to the U.S. army base and loaded herself with magazines, cheddar cheese, and Kraft Dinner. When she didn't have access to these exotic pleasures, she became an island all to herself. She said that she often dreamed that her father was dead or dying.

Once, in a stolen moment away from Enzo and the school secretaries, she told me that the previous night she'd woken up convinced that I'd slept with one of my students, the one named Hiroko. I was surprised by this news, that she'd noticed Hiroko and seen through my thoughts and somehow guessed our connection.

When Charlotte mentioned her dream I imagined Hiroko's small feet, speckled with a burnt landscape – the colour red – from that day's painting. Charlotte said she even knew our "positions" but would not tell me.

"It's my dream," she said, "not yours."

I pushed for more details and all she said was that she liked Hiroko, so she didn't want to talk about her like this. I said, "If you like her, why am I the one who is sleeping with her?"

"I don't know," she admitted. "But I'm trying to do my lesson planning and I can't get it done, because you're screwing around in my dreams."

"Was she wearing her army boots?"

"Please," she said.

And, like Hiroko, I smiled and let the matter drop.

That night, I noticed that Enzo's light was on, as usual, but I decided not to bother him. I did notice a flickering red glow in Charlotte's window, so I knocked on her door.

Wearing a chef's *happi*-coat and fuzzy pink slippers, she looked a little bleary-eyed. She was watching game shows, she said, and could use another *gaijin*'s point of view. The door swung wide.

One gladiatorial show involved three skinny contestants who wore black beanies and even smaller black bathing suits. In the first battle, these men fought sumo wrestlers for the chance to win the hand of a fair maiden. Whoever was thrown the greatest distance out of the ring – a ring with no ropes – was the winner. The men usually flew out of the arena and landed on a blue, gluey mat. Their cheeks stretched away from the floor like bugs from flypaper.

The second and final competition was both more complicated and more dangerous. The three skinny contestants were at the beach, sitting on small, kitchen-like chairs which faced the sea. They wore silver construction helmets, and fixed to the top of each helmet with electrical tape was a Libby's soup can. Heart-rate electrodes were taped to their chests and arms. Using electrocardiogram machines beside each contestant, a doctor would register the *blip* and *bleep* of each man's excitement level. Then, from the left, a large, heavyset man walked in front of the contestants and made his way down one side of the beach and back.

The doctors conferred amongst themselves: no changes.

Next, an old woman (with painful bunions, judging from how she walked) teetered down the beach, apparently oblivious to the three men who were sinking, unevenly, into the sand as they sat on their three chairs. Her face was wrinkled with age, but something about her must have interested the contestants because their heart rates jumped slightly. An inset camera monitored a pencil needle that twitched in excitement.

Then, a young woman walked in front of the contestants. Their heart rates leaped and the doctors watched their portable units intently. The young woman stopped, looked back at the men. She smiled.

One man's heart rate began to blink faster than the others. His eyes were fixed on the woman, but he suddenly realized his mistake and tried to turn his head and focus on a boat in the distance. The doctors pointed at their charts, and when the woman waved she seemed to trigger the fuse that dangled from the side of his head. The man jumped from the chair and started to run along the beach, screaming, "Danger, Danger!" He was halfway in the water before the firecracker shot from his head. The explosion pushed him to his knees. An underwater burst of bubbles signalled the end of his brief, perilous romance. If these programs were to be believed, love was essentially a battle with the heart, and the heart always lost.

I could relate to these programs – too well – but I found myself laughing with Charlotte at their dubious antics. Channel-surfing through Japanese game shows, we watched a man trying to cook an egg inside an airplane's antigravity room. The plane could dive for only two minutes at a time. But as the egg floated toward him, spattering the room with bits of yolk and shell, the cook swung his electric fry pan toward that buoyant matter, like God trying to fit a butterfly net around the Milky Way.

On the next channel, during a split-screen contest, a Hindu man threaded a live snake through one nostril and out his mouth faster than an Iranian newspaper boy could throw the daily news at a fourth-floor balcony. Two canoe teams crossed a frozen river, using paddles that scraped and skated across the ice. A woman took a bath in an eel pool while her husband rode a pole-climbing machine, without instructions.

Across the world, on a different channel, the Amazing Aiko Gitzo defined Mona Lisa's secret cravings and the reason for her smile. The contestants taped clumps of hair on a doll that looked suspiciously like the game show's balding host. And between these scenes, Western movie stars uttered their enigmatic phrases to peddle Japanese cars, mopeds, whisky, and a surveillance watch that took pictures of a man peeing against a tree. Sean Connery – too regal for words – sipped his Suntory whisky and raised an eyebrow at two Doberman pinschers. Michael J. Fox walked with a golden retriever, tripped over a rock and said, "Hello, come with me – glad it was you!" Then Columbo's Peter Falk, working as a bartender, sidled up to his patron (and the viewers) and said, "Ah, well, let me tell you about that. You see, I have a daughter, too."

Charlotte fell asleep midway through these programs so I let myself out without waking her. We'd never finished our conversation about Hiroko, about love, or sex, or about anything that personal. I suppose we both rebelled at the idea that the only two foreigners in the province should, necessarily, become "lovers."

When Hiroko finally agreed to come to my apartment for a cup of tea I think that I was more nervous than she was. I met her outside, near the parking lot, under a bulb that was swarming with insects. She followed me up the stairs, into the apartment, and she seemed to focus her attention on the hardwood floor, or the kitchen, or the tatami room – physical objects which did not seem to suggest *bedroom* or *sex*. We settled ourselves on the mats, in the tatami room, and I fumbled for a comfortable position.

I have no idea what we spoke about because I was absorbed in trying to play the good host, refilling her cup, navigating between radio stations, and changing the light to suit some mood I was bent on finding. Someone's radio voice, "Now you know The Rest of the Story," faded in and out of the evening.

When I leaned toward her, I chafed my elbow on the mat's whisk. I kissed her mouth, and felt it push back. I touched her arm and moved to unbutton her blouse. She stopped my approach. Her skin was soft and cool.

She smiled and winced – slightly – as if to remind me that I should behave myself, and that we'd been through this territory before. But I ploughed on. I kissed her cheek, her acrobatic chin, and watched her close her eyes. It seemed like a licence to go further. So I edged for the top button again, brushing my forearm across the mat, and was down to the third button before she had time to stop me. The hook of her bra was plainly visible and I leaned forward to stop her from putting her blouse back together.

Caught in the smell of her skin, I kissed her between her breasts, and ran my hand across her leg. I suddenly wanted to hear her speak or whisper something intimate, but she didn't give me that. It was as if to say something personal – and betray her thoughts – she might expose too much. But I think I actually wanted to hear her say "No" in that second.

Instead, her grandmother did that for us.

The telephone rang, shrill and sharp. My answering machine picked up the call and we both froze, listening to her voice, "Sex no, Hiroko, sex no, *dame desu*, sex no, sex no, sex no." *Click.* I watched Hiroko's face light up – her grandmother's words setting her chin to work, juggling her two lips into a full-fledged grin.

She kissed me then, and undid the rest of the buttons on her blouse.

Within seconds, the tatami mat was scraping all the skin from my elbows. I tried to roll over on my side, but Hiroko was on top of me suddenly and pressing her frame against mine. I felt a burning sensation across my lower back and realized that my shirt had crawled up, exposing more of my skin to the straw mat. The eight-mat room was so new that the tatami's bundled reeds were still sharp to the touch. My skin seemed to find each stalk's edge, like a tongue in search of a paper cut. At each mat's border, an indigo band of "monk tape" stopped my elbows from sliding further along floor. But between those borders my arms, back, legs, heels, almost every part of my skin seemed to sink, briefly, into the woven reeds.

We made love and I heard the distant sound of wheat being separated. I caught the dull smell of something burning, faintly, a long way away, but I didn't care. My body was seared with hundreds of thin incisions and I pulled her close, first wedging my face between her small breasts, then against her shoulder. I was half aware of something in the window, a moth, struggling for a vantage point of light.

Before Hiroko left, she asked me to poke my head out the door to see that Enzo and Charlotte were nowhere around. Then she ducked around the corridor and I heard her shoes patter down the stairs.

I closed the door and went back to the room. I found five strands of her hair on the tatami mat, one on my sleeve, and another by the stove where she'd made our tea. I told myself that I was collecting these remnants of her past so that Charlotte would not find them during a chance visit. This was true, or (as Enzo would say) true enough. But part of me enjoyed a second chance to touch her freely. I marvelled at her hairs' colour – an inkpot sheen. The strands were thick and coarse, almost as long as my arm. They broke with difficulty. I will admit that I smelled her again, vicariously, my nose filling with her perfume.

The moon in Nagasaki

Japan is an ellipse

MacDonald's whispering sea dogs

The moon was thin in Nagasaki. MacDonald looked through the hole of his open hearth and watched the moon rotate, ever so slightly, within a radiant fabric of stars and clouds that clothed the night. Less a sickle than a nail's quick, the moon drained into those stars and they pulsated effulgence, charging even MacDonald with wonder. A star, thirty degrees west, could be seen, then a band of clouds, then the rest of the Milky Way, and then night's blue dress that blurred and finally wove into the bamboo roof that framed his vision.

A man named K. Yamaguchi came for him that night.

MacDonald had been in Japan for almost one year. Yamaguchi, in the last twenty-four hours, had travelled all the way from Isahaya to Nagasaki on foot. He wanted to meet MacDonald at night, when they could both read the stars and measure the world in its proper suit.

Yamaguchi, he would learn, was someone who thought that history was a book of careful omissions, a way of cutting the tale so that it still read true. Between the severed years of 1847 and 1848, the small man had travelled across Ibaraki prefecture in search of an ellipsis. Finding none, Yamaguchi walked out of Ibaraki, through Gunma, Nagano, and eventually circled back toward the bear's plain: Saitama. At each resting place he had asked for directions to temples where he might find *sangaku*, the ancient tablets that used mathematical problems as offerings for the gods.

Made of wood, the oldest tablets were usually the size of his palm, but the longer theorems required more wood. The name and social rank of the mathematician were usually given, along with a general proposition – not self-evident, but demonstrable by chains of reasoning. The theorems could still be read and understood by mathematicians in the early 1800s.

A wandering teacher, Yamaguchi was regularly mistaken for a poet, a monk, a madman, or a beggar. His wife was used to his absences and admitted to her mother that her husband enjoyed all of these masks. He was a busy man, she said, and she rarely saw slippers on his feet between the Month of Teachers Running and the Month to Write Letters. Yamaguchi preferred to call himself a mathematician. He used the word humbly, without implying that there was some divinity in numbers – this belief he kept to himself.

He was a man who had small hands. Most people remarked as much, but they did not know that he also had poor circulation, and that he wore gloves when he wrote letters, with holes for his fingers to grip the brush.

An unlikely traveller, Yamaguchi and a handful of other scholars had vowed to spend part of each year mapping temple geometry in every corner of Japan. At the sound of a bell each December, the mathematicians would stand up from their *kotatsus*, leave their students, and spread out across the provinces in search of undiscovered tablets.

A circle, sphere, or some geometrical shape was usually moulded into the wood just above each written theorem. Whatever the inset wood – cherry, peach, a sliver of bush clover – Yamaguchi loved the mesh of clean shapes and the elegance of their designs. For him, collecting *sangaku* had became a crusade that went beyond the study of Euclidean geometry. He thought he could understand how his ancient colleagues had hoped to honour the gods with equations of divine symmetry.

Yamaguchi's only enemies were time, forgetfulness, and fire. His travel records, housed in two private collections in Saitama and Ibaraki, read like a race against the flames. His notes were scribbles, mostly in wild Japanese. Only when he found a particularly old theorem, already faded and obscure, did his gloved hand begin to slow. He painstakingly copied its design, in an effort to translate its original beauty.

Never is a theorem's proof given, not on the tablet, nor in Yamaguchi's notes. Nothing suggests to the gods (or to Yamaguchi's readers) that an earthly demonstration is needed. There are no descriptions of integers, no evidence to help establish a theorem's existence. At most there might be a vague reference to a proof, a geometric design that is meant to echo a theorem from yet another vantage point.

Usually, Yamaguchi travelled alone in search of these

treasures, and he avoided conversation altogether. But recently, he'd heard a rumour through the academic grapevine of scholars and translators. He'd learned there were several shipwrecked sailors being held at Nagasaki. And while this information seemed incongruous with his own vocation, he knew that Occidental sailors, with their gift for navigation, were notorious mathematicians. Their lives depended on an ability to read the heavens.

The sheer bravado of these sailors, with their sextants and quadrants, and the huge distances that they navigated, thrilled him. He knew that a sailor clings to the impossible belief that the earth is at the centre of the universe. Heavenly bodies circle round him. He maps where they rise and set. He measures all their declinations with a healthy disregard for the moon, who comes and goes too quickly to be called a reliable friend. The ability to look through an eyepiece, move the sextant's index arm, and "wheel" the sun into position is unthinkable for anyone but sailors, madmen, and gods. If Yamaguchi's wife included mathematicians in this list, then he was pleased with the company he kept.

So, in the month of August 1848, when K. Yamaguchi descended Japan on foot, drawing *sangaku* theorems into his notes, he travelled with the hope that he might be allowed to meet one of these Occidental mathematicians.

In Nagasaki, Yamaguchi dismissed the guards from MacDonald's anteroom, tucked his fingerless gloves into the side of his *happi*, then knelt on the floor outside the cell. He had never met an Outside Person before this night and he found himself strangely nervous at this prospect. His knees were unsteady. The tendon in one ankle twitched, as if his dreams – the unconscious – were sending some natural signal for his limbs to run away. He'd seen puppies make this same unconscious escape, while they twitched and ran from unlikely dream adversaries. He knew the phrase for that sleepless leg twitch, *binbōyusuri*: a poor man shaking.

But Yamaguchi pushed these thoughts away and convinced himself that he was simply tired from his long walk. He put his hand on the door to MacDonald's room and braced himself for the white face that would surely greet him.

"Excuse this interruption," said Yamaguchi, quickly, then he slid the door aside and bowed to the dark shape in the centre of the room. The man in front of him wheeled with multi-coloured shreds of cotton; he seemed to grow as his body turned and straightened from some task at the hearth. Some kind of scarf settled below his neck and he became a huge man who dwarfed his own shadow and made Yamaguchi yelp. The figure was so frightening that he managed to stifle the scream that rose in his throat.

MacDonald's face, torn quickly from the hearth, was black as cinder. "Good evening," he said. "My name is Ranald MacDonald." He smiled and extended a hand, as was his custom, then thought better of the moment and bowed to his visitor.

Yamaguchi bowed again then found the courage to introduce himself.

"My name," he said in Japanese, "is Yamaguchi Kazunori. I am from Ibaraki prefecture."

Yamaguchi had brought MacDonald toothpicks, a set of *kokeshi* toothpicks, that were narrow and pointed at the bottom. Each pick rose to form the semblance of a doll's head at the top.

Then he took an actual doll from his *happi*-coat and showed it to MacDonald.

"This is a family relic," he said. "A child's doll, of course, meant to appease the gods for some lost soul that did not reach adulthood. We keep it on our mantel, much like you keep your Bible."

They both glanced at the wall.

The room was dark so MacDonald lit a candle of seal wax and Yamaguchi quickly moved toward the flame.

"Can you see what it says, hidden in her hair?"

The weak light challenged MacDonald and he forced his eyes to read the doll's head. Made entirely of wood, the doll had no hair to part and MacDonald could find no writing between the dark lines that combed across her head. Finally, Yamaguchi pointed out a symbol that was etched near the back of her head. When he looked directly at the doll's face, the scar was hidden from view. Only when he turned the doll around, and ran his finger across that place where her dreams were hidden, did he realize what he had touched.

"A crucifix!" he said.

Yamaguchi smiled. "Yes," he said, "even we Japanese are rebellious people. I wanted you to see this before we begin."

In Nagasaki, in a partitioned prison, seven feet by nine, MacDonald constructed a city of language. He fashioned this imaginary place with outstretched hands, explaining new words and phrases to those students who entered his small room. The dimensions changed depending on their individual needs and where their conversations travelled.

Usually, his students came in twos; each man was supposed to oversee the other. Some days, spies hid within the rooms they fashioned. Silence was suddenly meaningful. MacDonald glanced at the floor, to his Bible and up to meet a student's eyes and thoughts. When he looked at the other student and saw downcast eyes MacDonald knew that he should avoid the sight of this forbidden book. These two particular students could not trust each other with a conversation on God's Word.

In English, one seldom uses collective nouns to describe "a wisdom of owls," "a faith of fathers," or "a simmering of sons." Yet MacDonald's students regularly used these Japanese counters for round, tubular, flat objects, for flowers, for people, and for those moments when they desired not to alert the listener about the truth of the matter. It was enough to say "five simmerings" or "two faiths" and both teacher and student would automatically agree that the subjects of these sentences were sons and fathers, or boiling rice pots and priests, or five seething things and two unspoken convictions. The subject was understood – though unspoken – and the tongue moved around these counters, like eyes that are drawn to view (and not view) a solar eclipse.

Other days, this moment of sight, downcast eyes, and soundless contract was absolutely readable. MacDonald could hear an intake of breath that followed some sentence he had just uttered. Much later, Yamaguchi would tell him that this pause, this quiet gasp, was both a warning and a mark of respect. An inward breath at the end of a thought was, he said, polite closure for the dangerous words that can fly from the mouth.

He told MacDonald that Japan is an ellipse. The foci of this ellipse are the samurai and their foot-soldiers, while the centre – the Emperor – appears as a pure abstraction.

It was an idea that Yamaguchi kept secret, something that he pondered but would not voice to any of his Japanese friends. He thought the theorem was political and potentially dangerous.

It was also theorem that could change Japan, he believed, and turn the country away from its illusory existence. By calling attention to the illusion the theorem plotted its weakness. By definition, if Japan was open to foreigners, the illusion and the ellipse would crumble.

It was MacDonald's turn to take an inward breath, not because he understood how dangerous the idea might be, but because the whole question was quite beyond him. He looked at Yamaguchi, took another inward breath, and mimicked Yamaguchi's favourite phrase, "That will do, that will do."

The exchange was brief – unnoticeable to the watchful eyes of the guard – so their lesson could resume. If the meaning of Yamaguchi's story was lost, at least his intent was clear. In this cell, some thoughts were best left unexamined and un-spoken. MacDonald decided that Yamaguchi was a scholarly man who did not fight with a blade but conversed his defence – his safe passage through this world – with nothing more than a sharp breath.

The joists between them lengthened, the room widened, and the sentences they spoke seemed to bend and stretch to accommodate the girth of MacDonald's mistakes. Yamaguchi was reluctant to make the same errors with English, as if desir-ing a clean page, or moveable typeface, to draft all his first efforts. After composing his thoughts, Yamaguchi spoke them carefully, cleanly, and MacDonald watched language pour fluent from his lips.

Yamaguchi became a regular student, the daily companion who had met him during his first week in Nagasaki. He had an open face, oval and smiling. His eyes were black, sharp and alight with their precision to jump from one language to another. He had a high forehead and a small bun on the top of his head that he fashioned out of his thin, black hair. He wore his two swords with dignity, but seemed to regard them as a necessary belt buckle and he reached for his ever-present Dutch dictionary with greater ease. His hands were small and scholar-soft.

The guards themselves did not so much listen as watch MacDonald's conversation unfold on scrolls. Calligraphy was the best training for catching the meaning of foreign words without actually translating them. As children, the guards had followed the movement of a brush, reading old, painted scrolls, and they learned how to occupy *the moment* of writing. Within a brushstroke, they grasped the mood by the curve in the word; they saw the cup of plum wine beside the page, the author's swaggering brush, and a moon that drained into some night or season. When they watched MacDonald speak a foreign language, they seemed to judge his words the same way: his manner, his breath, stance – everything but the words themselves – gave them some rudimentary sense of his thoughts. They read the moment by its shape, line, and colour on his face – another white page that seemed filled with written characters.

MacDonald tried his own hand at calligraphy but the pain in his knees and the pins in his ankles as he squatted "Japan-style" on a mat seemed to cramp all his thoughts. He couldn't move. His toes began to tingle, then his ankles and legs. Finally, when he felt nothing below his diaphragm, he could not reach the page without squinting. He rolled his hips to splay his legs out beneath him and found them useless appendages – too weak to carry him inside the character of a calligraphic word or to reach for a vessel of ink. A likewise exercise in futility: imagining what the guards were thinking as they watched his English lessons unfold.

Despite a roomful of ponderous conversations and the silence and hidden meaning of MacDonald's lessons, the room was quickly empty when the guards and his students left his prison. Usually, the hour was late and the evening itself seemed blank. MacDonald was suddenly alone in his cell and the room returned to its familiar dimensions.

Still, there were many English words that could not exist inside this prison and could find no place in his lessons. Just as there were buildings that could not take hold on ricefields, could not translate on sand or next to salt, there were many words that could find no strong foothold in Japanese. To find a phrase that could be aimed at the same thoughts, hearts, or ears in Dutch, Portuguese, Japanese, and English was like looking for a magnet that pointed in all four directions of the globe. Over the course of weeks, MacDonald opened his English–Portuguese dictionary, working his way from A to C, and tried to explain whole pages that had never found a home in Japan. He hoped to link those English words with the remnants of Portuguese phrases that had been left in Japan by traders and sailors.

"Above board, or fair play, and its opposite: a hidden crew kept below deck to surprise an enemy."

"Battle: the wing of a battle or he that is sent out before the battle to provoke the enemy, a battle between light-harnessed men, a battle where giants are prepared against gods, a battle between mice and frogs, the beginning of a battle, the onset of battle, a battle by the sea."

"Beard: a man with a double-edged beard . . ." (Yamaguchi, afraid of Leviticus 19:27, puffed again and MacDonald's definition ran dry.)

"Chin: a chin-cough, and the lower part of the chin, the chin of a man or beast, the chin of a fish, a chin that hath a chin longer than ordinary, to chin as the ground doth, a chin or cleft in the ground which a violent stream running down hill doth make."

MacDonald abandoned some of these words simply because he didn't want to explain them. He hoped to talk of other things besides battle. To survive their place on a tongue, dictionaries needed life – an utterance – or the push of words from one speaker to another. They lived only on the breath of conversation. Like him, some of these Portuguese words had washed ashore in Japan. After two hundred years of isolation they were smaller, perhaps, but they still clung to his toes and he tried to distance himself from this language, as if he could simply walk away from it and not speak of war. Vessels of understanding, these were worm-eaten thoughts that MacDonald left to rot.

Yamaguchi, for his part, began asking questions designed to compare MacDonald's English with other phrases that he had learned.

"*Shiver me timbers!*" he said. "What does this mean?"

MacDonald transcribed the phrase literally, then tried to construct meaning. A forest of confusion grew between the two men. MacDonald's metaphors sawed and hammered a wharf and wooden ship across the cell. He launched the vessel into the waters of one wall and Yamaguchi watched it hit rocks upon the other. The reverberation sent them both reeling, then ship and shoal evaporated. "My timbers," he repeated, "are shivering."

The next day, Yamaguchi asked him what was, *Enough to patch a Dutchman's breeches.*

"That is a patch of sky, a break in the storm," answered MacDonald, without telling him that Dutch sailors were also known for their frugality. Where Yamaguchi first learned these words, MacDonald didn't know. Each day he came with a new phrase, usually some ship-scarred, sea shanty that sailed perilously close to the equator, frustrated MacDonald into the doldrums, and sank their conversations to a resting place best left at the bottom of the sea, in Davy Jones' locker.

"What is a *Pea-nus?*" he asked, one morning. MacDonald blushed and walked around the subject until Yamaguchi guessed the meaning and told him that the Japanese equivalent was *little son.* Another day he asked about the *two-faced son of a sea cook* and MacDonald learned that, in Japan, a liar did not have two faces but two tongues.

He came to believe that Yamaguchi had heard these English words from some other shipwrecked sailor in Japan. But after more of these phrases, when both teacher and student were swamped in successive queries, MacDonald finally saw the truth in Yamaguchi's questions. There was another Western prisoner here, *in Nagasaki.* A sailor, certainly, and – judging from Yamaguchi's new vocabulary – he was American. He knew this because the *sake* they drank had turned from *grog* to *a Dutchman's courage.* Harmless words really, but they meant much to MacDonald because they told him (without telling him) that he was not the only prisoner in Japan.

He didn't ask Yamaguchi about the other American because he knew that his friend would only "save" him from this private, dangerous knowledge. A breath, a sigh, and a smile could erase both question and answer. So MacDonald let the moment sit, quietly, as if this question had grown into a person who made some strange comment every other day, and expected no retort, no answer, until the following lesson. Yamaguchi pretended that they were alone and MacDonald – mid-thought, mid-conviction – went on to other subjects.

An idea came to him, like a whisper, that he might be able to communicate with the other sailor by giving Yamaguchi a question to consider. The query would find its way to the other man and MacDonald would suddenly exist inside that sailor's prison, his thoughts suddenly fashioned with legs to travel and tongue to speak.

So he decided to give Yamaguchi something innocuous: the name of a specific body of water, a reference that would flow – if he was lucky – from some distant country toward the Columbia River. If the other sailor recognized the strangeness of that place, an odd river that had wound its way from some foreign shore, he might eventually find MacDonald's home, near Astoria.

That day, MacDonald went back to his lesson and Yamaguchi's questions, explaining English idioms, and hoped that the reference – as it came out of his mouth – would not unfurl their friendship with the slow passage of words.

"Meander," he said, "is a river in Turkey."

MacDonald traded stories one after another, and never voiced his wish to escape. He didn't want to betray his yearnings and infirmities to either friend or foe.

But one month after his meandering discussion with Yamaguchi, on April 26, 1849, Nagasaki harbour was lit by hundreds of paper lanterns. An American corvette – the *Preble* – had entered the harbour, with eighteen guns at the command of Captain James Glynn. The Japanese greeted him with cannon shots – a signal for the reserve samurai to come in from the interior.

MacDonald heard the shots from his cell, where he had been busy translating a monk's words from Japanese into English. The words had come from Mito, Yamaguchi had told him, and were written on a wall inside the castle:

Men of wisdom enjoy the water.
Men of virtue enjoy the mountains.

Men of wisdom move about.
Men of virtue keep still.
Men of wisdom enjoy themselves.
Men of virtue celebrate all others.

"A useful edict," said MacDonald, when Yamaguchi returned, "but how would you describe me?"

"I think you must enjoy water," said Yamaguchi, "or you wouldn't have left your captain's ship."

At that moment the cannons rang out and shook the monk's words from Yamaguchi's hand to the floor. He left MacDonald, then returned in the morning, with more people, guards, attendants, and the governor of Nagasaki himself. MacDonald's translations were quickly pushed aside. One of the guards held out a piece of paper and the governor took the page and gave it to MacDonald.

"There are 3,523 soldiers in Nagasaki," he said. "These are their names. They arrived last night."

MacDonald was silent. He looked for Yamaguchi among the soldiers but lost his friend's face in the crowd. The governor told him that more soldiers were coming. And that he was free to leave. Apparently, the captain of the *Preble* had asked after a group of American sailors who had washed ashore when MacDonald's name had surfaced.

Outside, the sun teemed daylight. His eyes couldn't focus. Yamaguchi touched his arm and someone else put his leather Bible in his hands. Then they walked him to the ship. It was his first "outside stroll" in seven months.

This is a peanut

Rita Hayworth in Hiroshima

A flight of stairs

Within my overworked foreigner's delirium, I was beginning to think of Japan as an affectionate prison. Well liked and well fed, I still couldn't shake the idea that I was a parrot who simply paraded language, bobbing my head, waving a peanut from one end of my cage to crack it in another.

"Peanut," I said. "This is a peanut."

And my students – the people on the outside of the cage – repeated en masse.

When I taught my adults, in *juku*-after-school classes, I was completely without supervision. Conversation seemed to flow better in these schools. And while none of us was tied to the dreaded Japanese texts that promised joyful English, I was tired of explaining acronyms, and the difference between Ltd., Corp., Co., M.B.A., B.A., and Ph.D. I seemed to be designing business cards instead of vocabularies.

I desperately needed a vacation, but I did not want to face the ordeal of applying for an interim exit visa or a ticket home for summer break. The airports were already too full of people who could afford the high cost of global travel, so I decided instead to travel within the country. Enzo wanted to take me north, toward his old home: Hokkaido.

He knew that I hadn't heard from Hiroko in a while – she had stopped answering my pointed questions, feigning new hobbies or new jobs. Whatever her excuse, I couldn't seem to keep her on the phone long enough for her to explain what was troubling her. She would say, "Nothing, nothing, I'm fine. I'll see you in class." Then another week or two would go by and I'd try to phone her once again. I knew she was avoiding me, and probably regretting what we'd done, but I had no idea how to speak to her using stomach-talk.

As for Charlotte, she had plans for Thailand.

I asked her if she had managed all the paperwork and exit visas by herself.

"No problema," she said.

Did she need another visa for entering Thailand?

"Nope. An American passport will get you into any decent country in the world."

I smiled at this bravado. "That's power," I said.

Gravely serious, waving one finger, she said, "Yes, it is."

I knew Japan was getting to her, too. I heard that a junior-high student had chalked the words KILL MISS CHARLOTTE on her blackboard. The principal and Charlotte made enough out of the message that the boy's parents came to apologize for the dreadful joke.

Enzo later told me that our Shacho was "playing this serious," too: if anything like it happened again he wouldn't be sending any more teachers to the school. And all I could think, on a more a positive note, was that the words were written in perfect English. Charlotte's students were learning some new verbs on their own.

I didn't realize how much I too needed a break until the image of Japan as a supple cage entered my thoughts. I wasn't desperate for *People* magazine, Slurpees, rhubarb pie, or English television; I just wanted to get away. Enzo's offer had come at the perfect time.

Enzo and I went first to Nagasaki, MacDonald's last prison before he returned to America. From there, we travelled coastal cities up to Hiroshima. There, Enzo wanted to visit Rita Hayworth, who was, he said, another of his drifting stories. He tossed me a cheap biography and I tried to figure out why she was included on our itinerary.

Rita Hayworth's real name was Margarita Carmen Cansino, but she was also known as the Hot Tamale, the Latin Lovely and the Flame-Haired Temptress. She acted in sixty-two films, including *Charlie Chan in Egypt, Under the Pampas Moon, Dante's Inferno, Human Cargo, Trouble in Texas, Hit the Saddle, Criminals of the Air, Only Angels Have Wings, Blondie on a Budget, Angels Over Broadway, The Strawberry Blonde, Down to Earth, The Lady from Shanghai, Champagne Safari, Affair in Trinidad, Fire Down Below, The Story on Page One, Circus World,*

The Naked Zoo, and *The Road to Salina*. (Enzo listed only the films that had something to do with places or flight.)

All her life Rita Hayworth seemed to gravitate toward men who would mistreat her. But she did not complain about this. One of her many biographers summed up her life by saying that she found herself in the eyes, arms, and cruelty of the men around her. After an unhappy life, searching for that cruelty, she died at age sixty-two, of Alzheimer's, speaking an unknown language. She died as her bed was being changed. She rolled over to one side, muttered some phrase, and died.

I knew Rita Hayworth for that one scene in *Gilda*, when someone (I don't remember who) asked her, "Are you decent?"

In a hundred different cities, across a hundred different screens, in a hundred different languages, she threw back her mop of red hair and asked, "Me?" or "*Moi?*" or "*Io?*" or – in Japan – "*Watashi?*" I read that her handprints are fixed in slab concrete outside a Chinese theatre in Hollywood. And underneath those hands, two pigeon-toed shoe impressions and a note to Sid, with thanks. I put the book down and finally asked Enzo what made her story drift.

"Rita Hayworth came to Japan," he said, "when someone taped her photo to the first atomic bomb."

Like Rita Hayworth, I was not prepared to meet living denizens of Hiroshima city – perhaps I'd expected a ghost town. I was unaccountably embarrassed and, as we stepped off the Shinkansen bullet-train, I half expected Hiroshima's citizens to turn toward me, stare and point at the American-looking traveller. My blazing bullet-train was suddenly quiet and the station's human movement – commuters, travellers, business-men, schoolchildren, Hiroshima's citizens – pulled me out, toward the station's marble lobby.

If I'd expected a wasteland of empty space, I was now dazed by the crowd's movement, and by the commercial bombardment of signs, posters, concession stands, Hiroshima postcard booths, key-ring gift shops, and souvenirs. I was conditioned to visit Hiroshima with guilty eyes, even though I wasn't a soldier, nor had any of my family died in battle. As a traveller, though, one visits an historically sad place and looks for meaning.

Through the haze of heat I thought I could see a festival; the decorated banners and flowers were beginning to line the city's streets. The streets were wider in Hiroshima than in other Japanese cities because the atomic bomb had levelled the city. Modern development afforded Hiroshima greater space, with large, open memorial parks and an uncomfortable sense of elbow room. It occurred to me that one could almost answer any question about Hiroshima with the ready response, "Because of the bomb."

We made our way to the Peace Park and walked around a series of sculptures dedicated to peace and the faint hope that peace might be contagious. The monuments were so colourful they glared. Sculptures were supposed to be lifeless, fashioned grey things – iron or concrete – but I found hundreds of colours, whole rainbows draped over the Peace Park sculptures. And when I moved closer, I saw that these colourful drapes were actually millions of origami birds.

Enzo said that the birds were dedicated to the memory of a

girl named Sadako Sasaki, who survived the atomic bomb. She'd outlived August 6, 1945, 8:15 a.m., by ten full years until she developed leukemia and was confined to bed. During that bedrest, Sadako's mother taught her how to make paper cranes – a symbol of health in Japan.

She said the prayer *sen pa tsuru* – "one thousand cranes" – believing that she could outlive the leukemia if she folded one thousand paper birds. At the time of her death, she'd finished more than six hundred origami cranes and, because of this tale, a paper aviary engulfs the Peace Park statuary each year.

Enzo told me that so many cranes are toted to Hiroshima and mailed by Japanese schools that the cranes hang in huge mops, becoming veritable *hills* of origami. I noticed that a recent rain shower had left most of the birds damp and blurred. Their colours were running. And because of those blurred colours, the cranes seemed silent and haunting.

Inside the Peace Park museum, I found other horrors: roof tiles that had melted into figurative art, charcoal watches, and hospital photographs that proved how a kimono pattern could be etched into skin. A building fragment still retained a man's shadow on a wall, as if he were still waiting outside a Hiroshima bank. It was the shadow of a man who was "erased" as the atom bomb echoed through his cells. The man was gone and yet his shadow did not move.

I had to run from that building. I told Enzo that I wanted to get some fresh air, just a few minutes and I'd be back, but I think he knew I wouldn't return. He met me outside, carrying a book from the gift shop. I didn't ask about his purchase, because the question seemed so innocuous, so banal, after all that we'd seen. Silent, we walked through the park, heading in a general direction back to the station.

When we reached the end of the grass, we were both surprised to find an Italian restaurant. Enzo nodded and I followed his lead. Minutes later, we were at a table covered by two dishes of linguine primavera, a bowl of calamari, two Caprese salads, one bottle of wine, and a heart-attack slab of tiramisù (for two).

I was surprised that Enzo wanted to talk about Rita Hayworth, but my mind was elsewhere, and seemed to swirl with incoherent thoughts and ridiculously simple epiphanies. It suddenly occurred to me that Hiroshima, this history, was in fact a city, filled with living people who also enjoyed fresh pasta. They went to the cinema. They watched Rita Hayworth and they disappeared into her image. They suspended their disbelief and pretended (for the course of the film, an hour and thirty-five minutes) that a city could forget its history.

I remembered a newspaper clipping, some years ago, which noted that Hiroshima city stood alone against Japan, protesting Japan's use of nuclear reactors and the shipboard movement of atomic products from France to ports seen and unseen.

The last thing I saw in Hiroshima, on our way back to the train station, was a floral tripod that blocked a large concrete building. Enzo pointed out the bits of black among the flowers – a symbol of death, which turned the signs from a store opening into a funeral announcement. There was a placard on the sign. A boy, a university student, had recently died of cancer. His name would soon be placed on the ever-growing list of bomb victims.

History was being played out before our eyes: a modern death from an ancient bomb. The city suddenly had a face, and a life. When I thought of the word *Hiroshima*, I could now envision something more of the man than his frozen shadow.

I saw his arm – his hand – reaching for a plate of linguine primavera. I watched him push back his chair, touch his stomach with a satisfying smile, then double back for keys he'd left on the table.

His sleep suffered for all the spices he'd eaten, so he woke early the next morning. The bank wouldn't open for perhaps another hour yet, but he could sit on the steps and watch the sun come up, across a skyline that seemed littered with possibilities.

The province of Hokkaido, to the north, promised cooler weather, so from Hiroshima we travelled west, then up the coast. We railed past Sado Island, one of the posting stations that MacDonald had traversed on his voyage from north to south, on foot and within the storage bin of a junk, while our own travel would jump from bullet-trains to ferries, from buses to karaoke taxis.

One hundred out of every twenty-three thousand commercial taxis were outfitted with karaoke boxes. Though some drivers had complained that their passengers were singing too loud, Japan's transportation ministry decided that Elvis Presley could not be held accountable for present-day accidents. We travelled when we could, within one of these mobile recording stations, and practised our renditions of "Michelle," riding shotgun with McCartney and a besieged taxi driver with hate in his eyes.

Only one driver actually complained – read: begged me to stop singing – but the irony of it, a *taxi driver* who was begging *us* to stop, propelled me through an entire rendition of Madonna's "Like a Virgin," in falsetto. When we were unceremoniously dropped off, Enzo consoled me on a street corner. He said that Japanese karaoke never attempts an *exact* translation of a song, only faithful renditions.

"Even in karaoke," he said, "the traveller's journey is in the footsteps of another."

From Nagasaki to Hiroshima, from Kyoto to Sado Island, we'd followed MacDonald's rough path to Hokkaido. He had descended Japan while Enzo and I walked up, as if we had all nodded to each other on a flight of stairs.

Enzo knew a university professor we could visit in Sapporo. He said that Professor Yoshida might even take us by car to Hakodate. So we had corresponded by fax, and I had read about Japan's ongoing feud with Russia for legal title to its northernmost territories. I learned that Hakodate's peninsula was actually a thin city built between two seas. I imagined the fish swimming through the streets at high tide, and lobsters walking like miniature bulldozers through gutters.

Enzo was anxious to revisit his birthplace and learn more about MacDonald. So we arranged to meet Professor Yoshida at the central train station in Sapporo. I saw him immediately: a small, well-dressed man who didn't wear plaid or elbow patches, but a business suit. This placed him firmly inside university administration, I decided. He was bowing frantically in our direction from the other side of an aluminum fence. In my rush to meet him I trapped myself – securely – between the batons of the station's turnstiles. I'd managed to wedge my exit ticket into a crease in the machine's metal casing, just above the slot, and jammed both the ticket and myself into the life of a poor train operator who had to rescue us both.

Professor Yoshida's first words to me were "Oh, you must be very skilful to put your ticket there." It was a backhanded compliment, but I liked him immediately.

Five minutes later I was free and Yoshida-san, Enzo, and I were driving through Sapporo in search of lunch. August was suddenly cool and fresh. Rain had recently washed the streets. And I became immediately nostalgic for Canada, having seen – for the first time in Japan – a sudden preponderance of birch trees. Traffic was minimal, the roads were wide, and the lamp-posts at most intersections seemed a decade too old for the computer age. The lamps were iron, ornamented with small forest animals, frogs, and birds. And – as if to justify the purpose of those metallic creatures – a ragged fox crossed in front of our car without a backward glance.

"A good sign," said Yoshida. "The fox is a very lucky spirit in Japan. Your trip is going well, I think?"

"Yes," I said, too distracted by the fox – this flash of nature – and Hokkaido's crisp, sweet air to answer him in more detail.

Three weeks ago the great outdoors had seemed to be embodied only in my bugs, Bob's fly kites, and the wild patch of bamboo that provided me with two clothesline poles. The nearby river, where Mr. Sato's tiger had been captured, was little more than a hollowed rock quarry. And I knew several manufacturing companies that did nothing more than polymerize spaghetti and lemon grass for restaurant windows. Even the trees were synthetic: Hiroko and I had laughed about the decorative plastic grass on every *sashimi* plate we'd ordered.

In Hokkaido, however, the taste of fresh air was bracing, so sharp in my lungs it felt crystalline. I mentioned the taste of this frozen moisture – I was struggling for an English approximation of what it conjured – and Yoshida told us that this kind of air was actually called *diamond dust* in Japanese.

He eventually took us to the Sapporo brewery for lunch. Inside, the restaurant was dark. The walls, brick. Long oak tables gave the open room a medieval quality, and I was delighted to learn that German sausages and beer were their specialty. A Western fix – with all the pleasures of European cuisine – was near.

During lunch, Enzo told Professor Yoshida about MacDonald. He didn't say that we were travelling in his footsteps. But the fact that we had travelled such a long distance likely betrayed our serious intent.

"Please forgive me," said Professor Yoshida, "but who was this MacDonald?"

This was a better question, I thought, than asking us about our reasons for looking for him. Hiroko would have asked me this – in the same apologetic way – by skirting around the real subject. Eventually the conversation would have edged toward something else: not why MacDonald had come, but why *I thought* he'd come. My theory – whatever that was – would give her my own biography.

"He had this idea," Enzo said, "that his mother's people – the Chinook – were somehow related to the Japanese."

Yoshida didn't reply. The silence lengthened while Enzo chewed the last of his sweet-potato fries.

Finally, I added, "I think he was looking for himself."

I didn't mean for my response to sound simple or pat, but Yoshida seemed to agree with this idea. He nodded his head, or perhaps he motioned for the bill. If he guessed that Enzo was dwelling on his own family memory, he didn't mention it. And from my answer he could only surmise that I was a simple explorer (in search of something even less concrete than family connections).

"I know someone," he said, "I think you should meet."

The president of Hokkaido University was a huge, multi-layered man who wore his tie, vest, suit, and overcoat like the sheets on an unmade bed. He had thick, white hair, and everyone who knew him said that he was a very busy man. Yoshida told us this news – again and again – that President Fugisawa was too busy to travel, that he was so burdened with university administration he didn't have time to pursue his chief passion: Inuit folk songs. In Japan, a man's worth might be judged by what he sacrifices, and Fugisawa, I learned, had sacrificed song.

In his youth, he had travelled to the North Pole, through the Northwest Territories and back through Siberia, and later published numerous accounts of his expeditions.

"Eskimo folk songs," he said, "are disappearing like cancer cures from rainforests."

"I'm not sure I follow you," I said.

He described his travels, and the process of recording Inuit singers. "Their songs," he said, "have a certain similarity – cadence, subject, even words – with some of the Ainu folk songs that you can hear in Hokkaido. I wanted to find out if the Ainu had gone to America from Japan, or if the Inuit had come here from your country. Both sets of footprints are gone. Their tools and bones are similar enough, but only through following language can we watch their passage."

"But how can you understand those songs?" I asked. "Or even compare them?"

"I listened to lullabies that had been passed from one crib to the next. One generation after another. I wrote them down and taped the singers before they died. I cannot think how we can follow the passage of the songs because they are like the Gypsies, I think, who have fallen out of a wagon and populated all of the corners of the world." He shrugged his shoulders. "Time," he said. "We don't have much time."

He also said that *Ainu* and *Inuit* became the same word when translated into English. Both mean *people* in their respective languages, as though there was only one people and the rest of the world was filled with spirits, inhuman creatures, and migrant ghosts. MacDonald's reasons for searching Japan for his mother's "people" suddenly seemed reasonable.

We spent rest of that evening in a bar, singing songs. Each of us pushed ourselves away from the low table and stood up to sing. I was drunk on *sake*, so the songs came easily. I managed to warble through a version of "O Canada," and a weak explanation that the words had changed, recently, because of the Queen, God, and the French. But as the night yodelled on, Enzo surprised me with renditions of old fishing songs from Yesso. I countered with Crowsnest mining ditties and all the songs I remembered my mother and father singing to each other in the kitchen, at maudlin moments and anniversaries: *Get off the table, Mabel, the money's for the beer* . . .

I was so pleased to have met Yoshida and Fugisawa, to have learned about Fugisawa's songs, that I wanted to give them something in return before I left Hokkaido. A bottle of rice wine seemed appropriate, so I presented one to each of them at the airport. Yoshida was embarrassed, but very pleased with the gift. He insisted I take his gold pen as a reminder of my trip. Fugisawa reached into his pockets and his hands came out empty, except for a pair of keys. An idea ran across his face and he then reached further into his clothing – it seemed – further along his pants and the back of his jacket, and finally pulled off his woven leather belt. The man was so large that his belt could wind completely around my waist *twice*, but he implored me to take this "small" gift.

I knew better than to argue with such adamant generosity. I'd once given my own students pins and key chains from Canada, and even the youngest elementary students felt this same need to reciprocate a gesture, no matter how small the gift. One young student was so overwhelmed with the Olympic pin I gave him that he reached into his pocket and gave me his Captain Jack pencil eraser – which had been used only twice, on his very best artwork.

His violinists were bell-insects. Each one played sforzando piano, a melodious "liin-liin-liin" that we could hear from across the street, as we studied. Grass larks, in his corner-most cages, sang in the key of G, exactly one octave higher than the highest G on our teacher's piano. Emma crickets played the longest, a trill in tremolo, and their songs were broken only by the staccato E, then F, of the nearby pine insects and bark beetles.

At the start of each June, hundreds of spliced bamboo cages lined the corner. His finest musicians were kept in polished cages that hung from an old umbrella. By September, when the other dealers were busy packing up their wares and their wooden carts, he walked away with an entire orchestra in the palm of his hand.

— Chosei Motoori, on the legendary insect-seller Hei Gaten

The beginning of term and my last few months in Japan went by so quickly I hardly noticed them pass. It was as if Enzo had taken a few pages out of his calendars and pocketed the months of September and October. After our trip, I saw Hiroko only a handful of times. She was avoiding me, I think, or pretending that I'd already left. As she'd predicted, my departure date seemed to loom over our lives, making us both miserable.

So I busied myself by organizing almost everything I owned. I wanted to avoid any excess-baggage fees so I boxed and surface-mailed all my books, gifts, and my own Aqua Fantasy machine. I also made the rounds to close my banking account and return my Alien Registration card.

And suddenly I didn't have that many days left. My trip was about to end and I had almost nothing to show for it. When I voiced this obvious fact to Enzo, he told me that *o-chi* is a kind of ending, "to fall down without the ending of a story."

"I don't quite understand," I said.

"The story moves on," he said, "like a man who forgets to bring the key to his mailbox, so his wife sends it to him. In a letter. This is *o-chi*."

I nodded.

"When you leave this place, our friendship will move on. Without an ending."

"Thanks, Enzo," I said, and meant it. I promised to write.

He said the word for *writer* in Japanese is *sakka*. The Japanese pictograph of the word combines *to make* and *home*, which seemed (to me) entirely appropriate for the writer who comes from one place and makes his home in another.

In foreign lands, said Enzo, stories change; they mutate with every telling, with every new translation. Santa Claus dies for our consumer sins next to an escalator. In a better world, Colonel Sanders gets his chance to play ball in the majors. But Western travellers, he said, who visit Japan will continue to find themselves translated, changed, *imagined* into something new, almost upon arrival. Absolutely.

I thought back to those strange, pencil-case slogans that I'd seen on my students' desks and told him that those words should be stamped PATAPATA into every foreigner's visa to Japan: One Year Visa. Valid for Single Entry. Necessaries of Your Changed Life. Sip Your Dreams by Drops. And remember: Flags Often Mark Important Spots Like Ice Cream Stands.

My last week, I waited for Enzo to leave for an appointment with his dentist, then I reached across my balcony and wedged Lolita's former container underneath his air conditioner. The eggs were intact. I didn't leave them there as a hopeful reminder

of the day we set the bugs free. I knew he would not forget me
– my sickle-cutters would remind him every summer, for generations to come.

The real reason I decided to leave him that sac of eggs was
that I thought Enzo might be more inclined to visit me in
Canada, if for no other reason than a polite, deserving revenge.

Just before I was due to leave, Kobashi-san met me at the school's
door.

"Come on," she said. "I want to buy you a traditional gift."

She drove me to a doll store and ordered me to pick one.
Hundreds of individual glass cases lined three aisles of dolls. On
each shelf they stood or squatted four dolls deep. Some of them
had large, oversized heads. They played flutes or waved hello.
Others wore masks and swung long swords or staffs at their
invisible enemies. I recognized some of them from the folk tales
I'd heard.

I saw Princess Shyokujo, wrapped in a blue kimono. Her
hands were up in the air and fumbling with a paper moon. On
the next aisle, Kengyu tried to swim across the Milky Way to
join her. Their river of stars was the space between their two
glass boxes.

In the second aisle, near the end, I found the one I wanted:
a blind monk who played the biwa, while (on a shelf lined with
ghosts and demons) a mob of samurai lunged, cut, sat, or
prayed.

Kobashi was pleased, I thought, but not overly happy with
my choice. She seemed quiet, almost resigned, and I had to ask
her if anything was wrong.

"I wanted to buy you a beautiful doll," she said.

I didn't think she wanted me to find some kimono-clad geisha who danced or drummed or sang to some distant tune, but she may have liked it if I'd chosen a character from a less violent folk story. Something less "extreme," perhaps, than Hoichi the Earless. But the decision was made. Hoichi's clear plastic case was boxed and the package was quickly delivered to my arms.

I had a gift for Kobashi, of course. Later that afternoon, I left it on her doorstop and I knew that she would recognize my rough calligraphy before she'd even opened the envelope. I'd found her an antique *soroban* in Tokyo. The abacus – what my student Kazunori called a "Japanese skateboard" – had five stacks of beads on the bottom and only two on the top. This was given as an appreciation of her regimental grammar, the *ka, ki, ku, ke* ... *KOH!* of her marching syllabus.

I finally saw Hiroko, but our meeting was brief, I thought, and circumspect.

She had agreed to meet me at a café in Kumagaya, a place called Class One Coffee. My bus bounced toward a district I'd never seen before, a small neighbourhood of vegetable merchants, mushroom guardians, and fishmongers, and I was dropped off two blocks from my destination. A long fountain – filled with mirror carp – split the sidewalk into two distinct lanes, so I walked next to it, enjoying the afternoon sun and the play of light on the water. Outside the café, I waited for several minutes and watched two young boys clap their hands for the fish to come to them.

Inside, the tables were small and partitioned with screens, giving each guest the illusion of privacy. The walls were bare, without shelves or windows to mar the room's respectable Zen decorum. I couldn't understand where the light came from, how it shot through a single doorway and lit the room. But the clutter of the outside world – and the fish that swam between the traffic – seemed very far away. When Hiroko arrived, ten minutes late, I noticed that two cedar pillars, black with age, framed my vision of her, and grounded her in her mien of relaxed maturity.

Her calm smile surprised me. She was not, I think, *happy* to see me; that isn't the right word. But she did seem sympathetic to the moment – our Last Official Meeting – as if she were coaxing me toward something pleasant.

"I thought you might not come," I said. It seemed like the right cliché to broach.

"Please." She paused to reach inside her purse, as if to look for the right words to finish her sentence. "Please don't think about that."

The hand came out of the purse, empty. Our waitress arrived and we ordered two cappuccinos from the plastic menu. I looked at the tabletop between us, and silently read the graffiti that had been carved into the wood. A few initials, pairs of names, hearts, arrows, and dates that reached back to 1984.

"I love this coffee house," I said, hoping to choke the silence that had come to our table, and pulled up a chair between us.

"I come here quite often," she said, brightening.

"I wish we'd come here sooner."

"You were leaving," she said. "Always."

I shrugged my shoulders, apologetically.

"It is my *own* place," she explained. "I didn't want to be reminded of you whenever I came here."

I must have winced.

"No," she said, "I don't mean badly. I have many places to go to think about you."

I suddenly felt selfish that I had wanted to fill her with nostalgia. At least for a while.

"But now," I said, "you have me in this place, too."

She smiled, as if to say that that was her intention. More likely, it was her last concession to me.

When the coffee arrived, she ordered a piece of chocolate cheesecake. I was half-aware of the meter that was running – the kitchen clock that gauged how much of a cover charge we would have to pay – and the other, larger meter, which was timing the end of our last date. I was thinking about her grandmother and I knew that my telephone was likely ringing, at that very moment, as we sat and drank our coffee. And when I looked at her, framed between the two cedar pillars, I was struck by how close she was to truly becoming a picture and, ultimately, a memory. She reached out of that frame, across the table, and her hand pushed past the graffiti. She touched my hand.

"I hope," she said, "that you have enjoyed your time here."

We had never spoken about love, but her one gesture – that public display of affection when she touched me – was sincere, and I realized that I already missed her. The waitress passed by our table and Hiroko held that second, leaning toward me, her hand on mine, while the woman breezed across the room, pretending not to see us.

Later, when I paid the bill, we walked outside to the busy street. For a quarter-hour, maybe longer, we sat on one side of the fountain while the carp jockeyed behind our backs for a place in the shade. Our shadows, an orange, black, and silver transit of life.

The next day, as my plane left the ground, I was surprised by the motley group of strangers suddenly seated around me. Compared with the smooth Japanese faces I'd known for just one year, these British, Russian, and Canadian faces suddenly seemed garish, even baroque. Their noses pointed in so many directions that I lost count of their angles and their fat, skinny, long, or flared distortions. Freckles, the cold, the sun, even liquor seemed to tinge each face toward the surreal. I could fully imagine a nose – my own nose! – and what MacDonald might have called a "grog-blossom."

And suddenly I realized what I must have looked like to a Japanese eye: Picasso features, nose askew, chin and cheekbones at brash angles, sharp edges everywhere.

Still, I greeted the Japanese stewardess – a woman with a smooth, delicate face – as if she were a long-lost friend. Hers was the first "friendly" face I'd seen here, at one thousand feet above sea-level. She offered me a set of headphones and I tried, from my sitting position, to give her a respectful bow.

She said, "You're welcome," in English, and quickly engaged another passenger with a smile and a thin blue blanket.

There was one vacant seat beside me, so I folded up the armrest and tried to jackknife my upper body across both chairs. I drifted off, listening to the engine's dull roar. I was finally following MacDonald toward the end of his travels.

Two-storey hotel

Postscript from Enzo

Ahazel line circled each iris and gave MacDonald's grey eyes an edge that other men seemed to notice. He was only fifty but in his halcyon days he'd begun to put on some weight, and he felt pains in his joints whenever the weather turned. He was still spry – a splendid hand with an axe – but he'd begun to imagine his body beginning to deteriorate, little by little. A summer ago he'd cracked two ribs and discovered a marvellous ability to rock himself out of bed each morning. This year, in 1874, partial deafness seemed to approach him. The absence of sound was like the sensation, under one's feet, of a distant train.

He had one lame horse – named Blacky – and two others that were getting smart and wouldn't come near him no matter what he called them. Bloated and partly spoiled, all three were getting fat on pea grass. Since he had no other animals, MacDonald felt safe to leave his shack – his place in Oregon – at least for a while. Of late, he'd been missing the wandering life, and he had heard about a Canadian expedition that was rumoured to pay explorers well.

The expedition's commander was a man named Robert Brown. A ship's surgeon, Brown was a self-taught medical man who had left his ship, the *Narwhal*, the year before. His certificate of discharge listed Dundee as the port of registry, ship number 221686, at an even four hundred and thirty-four tons, and noted that he had been whaling. But from the moment he stepped back on land, Brown was eager to get rid of the sea and rinse the salt from his skin. An inland expedition, he thought, was just the thing.

That August, Brown and MacDonald found employment in one of the first explorations of Vancouver Island. Their co-sponsor, the Oregon Botanical Association, had advertised for explorers and MacDonald had quickly applied for one of the posts. A total of four explorers would each receive forty dollars to map the interior and keep detailed journals, listing "all manner of trees and terrain" they encountered. Unofficially, Brown, MacDonald, John Butte, and an artist named Francis Whymper would also be searching for gold.

They met in Vancouver, decided on provisions, and reconvened at the dockyard four days later. Butte brought his dog, a fat mongrel named Besse, for protection. A ship carried them to Vancouver Island where they ventured inland, briefly, near Victoria, Lat. 48°25′22″N, Long. 123°23′02″W, and immediately lost all of their provisions to wild, ungodly animals.

"They were Cyclopean Smolenkos" wrote Butte, "one-eyed, jointless fiends who run along mountainsides swifter than black-tailed deer. Our dog was no match for these devils."

Brown's journal added: "Saakalitucks live, clad in beaver, seeking medicine by the banks of a nameless river, Gods of the woods and the roves of the waterfalls and of the running streams and they haunt the country out of sight of the saltwater – evidence incontrovertible!"

"Worse things still are the Masolemuchs," wrote the artist Whymper, "who fish on the great lake land and woe betide the wanderer when *they* become provoked! The ones who survive come back very thin and very woebegone, telling strange traveller's tales."

MacDonald knew that the Smolenkos, the Saakalitucks, and the man-eating Masolemuchs were actually thieving raccoons who had stolen their potatoes while they slept, but he didn't tell the others. The truth was too embarrassing. Instead, he looked up the word *potato* (*Solanum tuberosum*) in the Oregon Institute's guidebook and learned that it was a herbaceous flowering plant, perennial, and that it stays hidden from all who do not know where to find it.

This expedition, he thought, is certainly doomed.

The four survived by trading silver with the Natives and buying fish and fresh potatoes. Again, they left the smoking inlets – alive with traders and Native industries – and travelled inland, toward the wooded mountains in the mystical interior. They walked through waves of oak, alder, pine, and a bright shock of yellow maple.

Along the way they noted the plants, the rivers, and the glimmering bits of fool's gold they saw whenever the sun changed its angle. The mountains were igneous rock, thinly covered with vegetable deposit, but they found that some of the hills were scattered with grey syenite, sea-weary rocks that had drifted all the way from Alaska. Their guidebook also noted that syenite was a kind of feldspar and hornblende, a unique mixture that had originated in southern Egypt.

They pushed themselves through the woods, desperate to find the moist margin of a creek – any creek – where they could, for a time, glimpse the sun. They bivouacked in those gentle places, trying to avoid the thickets of prickly ash, or "the devil's walking stick." Remembering Japan, MacDonald thought that this long, leafless stem, surrounded by a crown of light green leaves, gave the plant a tropical appearance.

Brown was tired, mottled with hate, and less forgiving. His notebook scattered a bitter description at the plant as if he was throwing a handful of stones: "Covered with prickles, the stem enters the skin on the slightest touch, penetrating *even the back skin* with its pestilent quills. The plant deserves its not over-complimentary Latin name: *Pana horridum.*"

The four spent the rest of the afternoon picking the needles out of their pants and socks. The next day they found a creek and examined various species of berries, looked for mineral indications, and, in the afternoon, fried pancakes in bacon fat. By unanimous decision, on August 27, 1874, Commander Robert Brown – encouraged by the berries and the pancakes and a splash of sunlight – christened this good place, at 48°46′27″ N (at Meridian altitude), Slap Jack Creek.

Suddenly eager for adventure, they spent two full days walking through thick forest. They finally emerged on an open, beaten track, where they promptly met two hunters who were travelling to a central lake in search of deer. Brown was disgusted with meeting civilization so quickly, and urged the others to cross this worn path. The group went further into the bush, further into unplotted darkness, until they could just hear the sound of running water. From that point onward, the walk was easy.

"The river gladdened our hearts," wrote Brown, while MacDonald and the others stepped lightly on the wet rocks. MacDonald was comfortable walking on a wet deck, a ship's deck, and river walking was no different. He remembered the feel of the water running under his feet and the slosh of life that conspired to pitch him. He remembered walking through the water, and seeing the rake of clouds above him.

The four separated only once, so that MacDonald and Whymper could build a raft and descend the river together. They lashed two long boards together, tied the dog to the centremost plank, and let the rapids, chutes, and cataracts quickly distance them from the others. By the time Brown had caught up, MacDonald and Whymper had named half a dozen places. MacDonald founded Nagasaki Chute, Sumimasan Hill, and K. Yamaguchi Falls, but no one could pronounce those words, and Brown (the head and final editor of this expedition) followed them with raft and pencil and renamed everything in his wake.

They reached a ten-mile lake at 48°30'49" N, two hundred and fifty feet above the sea, and found that it was full of trout. A small stream flowed into the lake through a valley and at the left side of this outlet, said Brown, sat a prominent hill which he called Mount Brown. "This valley," wrote Brown, suddenly pleased with himself, "seems to contain *good* soil."

So they wandered through the haunted valley and found burnt timber, cedar, and silver pine. The woods were quickly silent. Wildlife disappeared. The deer hid from them, and even Brown came to admit that the landscape had become improbable and tedious. It became harder to put pen to paper and list the narrative of their daily wayfarings. The good soil gave way to "the same weary trudge over fallen timber, through lonely bush, over mountain streams, down rocky glens, footsore, tired, dispirited, carrying all our own baggage and now getting hungry." Having finished their last modicum of bread and bacon fat, the landscape positively disappeared from their journals, as if naming the island had depended on what they were eating. So they continued in a southerly direction (longitude, too, abandoned them) and struck out, through a forest of white pine, to look for the headwaters of Coffee Creek.

Happily, they did find a creek (though Brown was suspicious of its origin), and the group prepared to follow the water to its mouth. Before they tore down their tents, Butte's dog disappeared in the grass, and by the time they found her, she'd already given birth to eight golden puppies.

"This," exclaimed Brown, "is Delivery Creek!"

The men spent the night and let the dog rest, but they all made veiled jokes about eating the puppies if their expedition did not soon improve. In the morning, their stomachs growled and woke them early, so they divided up the puppies and carried them in the top of their packs. One croppy ridge after another, the mother ran ahead, suddenly light on her feet.

They slept beside Hungry Creek on September 3 and, having found nothing more to eat for three days, they waded through Starvation Creek on the fourth. On the fifth they began dropping luggage, extra clothes, and one tent on the north side of Deception Lake. The world turned into a sad, bitter place.

"It *looked* like the sea," said Whymper. "How can you tell from the top of that bluff?"

Bitterly disappointed, Brown wrote that "Deception Lake flows from the east, northeast, and forms a Delta of about 1000 acres which could easily be cleared for agriculture. At present, there are few berries with which to support life."

Butte added, "Here we caught five small trout and they were the most delicious morsels I ever ate. Staved off death for another day." The words were no sooner written in all three journals when, two lines later, Butte and Whymper took sick. From this quiet place to the end of their journey they made the "utmost efforts" to drag themselves through the bush. They followed a long seam of fine coal, then an old trail, and emerged, blinking in the new light, to find a Native Indian squatting in the riverbank.

The man disappeared and reappeared within minutes. He'd armed himself with a knife and rifle.

"He thought we were spirits," wrote Brown, "for no human being had ever come from the east. We soon conciliated him and convinced the old savage that we were men and brothers – very hungry and very faint."

The Indian brought the men down the river and gave them salmon and fish oil and MacDonald learned that they had followed a twenty-four-mile crack in the Alberni Canal.

When Brown's strength returned, he admitted that, "on this journey we discovered nothing of importance beyond what is enumerated, no gold except in the Nanaimo River, and though the country abounded with deer, bear, and elk, we were so unfortunate as to kill nothing from the time we left Fort Victoria. The map sufficiently shows the topographical names I applied to the objects of geographical interest."

The last camp – named only in MacDonald's journal – was called Yes. And from this "embryo town" with good trails and clean air, they made their way to the coast, to houses of entertainment and stores and civilization. On September 7, 1874, Brown, Butte, Whymper, and MacDonald used forks (instead of whittled pine) to eat a sumptuous dinner of roasted venison and sweet potatoes. They raised a sleepy glass of ale to the botanists and another toast to the government (who had paid for the expedition by taxing the miners on the river). And then they fell asleep in a two-storey hotel.

As soon as I returned to Canada I looked for MacDonald's name in several Calgary libraries, but there was little to be found. I searched further and discovered that some of MacDonald's papers, journals, and dictionaries could be examined in the Provincial Archives in Victoria. So I made the trip and arrived on a Thursday afternoon, happy to see that the archive was still open.

The room there was antiseptic and quiet. A window's dull light cut my table in two. Besides a security guard, two librarians, and me, there seemed to be only two other people in the building: Ranald MacDonald and his editor, Judge Malcolm Macleod. The "judge," I read, was actually a lawyer from Ottawa who relished the affectionate nickname, "Judge Macleod," that his friends had given him. He'd set about transcribing MacDonald's verbal wanderings and, acting as a jealous benefactor, Macleod had tried to insert his own view of Japan into MacDonald's.

From 1887, MacDonald had filled notebooks: Poppyland Scribbling Books, Dodd's Double-Covered Scribblers, Johnson's Progress Long Notebooks, Bicycle scribblers and pink Tourist Tables. The judge pillaged these travels and made them his own, politely pushing MacDonald aside to make way for the editor's true purpose: a fifteen-volume compendium called the *History of Japan, Old and New,* complete with an official translation of the constitution of Japan, and a monograph on dogs, with prefatory remarks.

The archive had filed MacDonald's papers under the name *Macleod*. But I thought that Enzo would be secretly pleased with his disappearing hero. It was as if the story of Ranald MacDonald was washing away before my eyes.

The notebooks were handwritten in black fountain pen, edited with a blunt pencil, on manuscript pages that were thick with glue, and pasted into Macleod's unlined notebooks. The title pages were rewritten to give MacDonald a cursory credit as a "Proto-pioneer in this, the hero of our story – wild as his act may seem, and of little consequence in the regard of the world in general."

I dropped the judge's tale, and looked for something concrete, something that had come from MacDonald's own hands. In one box I found MacDonald's Family Illustrated Bible, published in 1852 and willed to Macleod. The book contained one fern stem (brown and curved, holding all twenty-two fronds intact), and three silk bookmarks, which marked Paul's solemn charge to Timothy, Isaiah's triumph over Babylon, and a page describing the Character and Office of Christ. There were six purple flowers at Deuteronomy 4, along with a newspaper fragment that read, "WANTED: A Young Lad for an Office" and "The Stout Lady's Corset. SUPPORT NATIVE INDUSTRIES. BETTER VALUE THAN ANY IMPORTED. Crompton Manufacturing Co'y."

I carefully picked the flowers out of the Bible and asked a librarian if he recognized them. He shook his head and went back to the book he was reading.

"They're pansies!" said the security guard, from behind my shoulder. "And you can see more of them right outside the door. Shame to waste a nice day looking at archival flowers . . ."

He smiled. His name badge read WESTCOTT. He'd been a part-time gardener and a full-time prison guard. As a young man, he'd started at Williamshead Prison and whistled all the way to work. He knew it was time to quit, forty years later, when he heard himself whistling on his way home. "Spent a lifetime watching people," he said. "Just habit."

I nodded my thanks and gingerly returned to the Bible. Between the Old and New Testaments I found a list of deaths, births, and marriages for MacDonald's family. This list helped me compose a rudimentary logbook of MacDonald's life. The microfiche readers gave me the ending place for his drifting story. A journal, composed of several exploration reports, listed an "aide-de-camp, one R. MacDonald."

On my way out, Westcott gave me directions to the general area MacDonald had described in his journals: an embryo town, named Yes, with good trails and clear skies . . .

I rent a Jeep, in town, and travel north from Victoria. By super-imposing MacDonald's old map of the island onto a new one from Pinky's Boat and Auto, I drive the Trans-Canada Highway and parallel the explorers' route, north by northwest. Driving through Cobble Hill and Duncan, I completely miss Lake Cowichan, which – I think – corresponded in size and shape with Brown's "ten-mile lake, full of trout." I continue past the town of Ladysmith and turn west, just before Nanaimo, onto an unmarked road that faces the only duplicate landmark on both maps: Mount Whymper. Everything else has been renamed, all of Brown's creeks and gullies, every starved blemish, and every hungry brook. The gravel road drops off and finally becomes a dirt path, meant for trucks or campers.

At the end of that road, I find the town of Yes – if it can be called that. Little more than an RV park, there are row upon row of executive mobile homes. Each white unit is squeezed into a ten-foot driveway and there are television cables and water hookups for each and every port.

Partially logged, Mount Whymper stands, awkward and silent, in the distance. A large cloud hovers over the treed section, like a barber in search of a fresh approach. I meet the owner of the park and he waves a tired hand toward the moun-tain, as if to express its crumbling beauty with a single gesture.

Against the mountain, and to the east of the mobile homes, two metal industrial garbage bins block our view of the rising hillside. There are bear locks on the sides of these containers. A handful of dead crows lie, scorched and broken, beside a hole on the top of each bin.

"They're flying parasites," the owner explains. "I have the bins hooked up to a thousand-watt electrical current. Hit one switch and the crows burst into flames!"

I wince at the thought, but pretend to squint at his "ingenious" contraption.

"Sometimes they fall right inside," he beams.

I'd hoped to tell Enzo that MacDonald's city of Yes invoked some vague memory of Japan, but the truth was rather dismal and unsightly. The burnt crows, the garbage bins, the shaved mountain, the missing camp called Yes at the edge of MacDonald's Canadian wanderings: I wanted to leave all of these things out of my letters. Instead, I gave Enzo everything. I described MacDonald's gradual disappearance from the archive. I told him about the journals I'd found, and about the judge who had pushed MacDonald out of the way, eclipsing his story to make room for what he must have considered "proper" history. Finally, I gave him my account of the new city of Yes: an RV park at the edge of the Pacific Rim. I thought that he would be pleased with the notion of a drifting city – a city on wheels – and with the idea that a town might pack up and move south with the onslaught of winter.

In describing these things to him, I found that Von Siebold's map of Japan came into proper focus – at least for me. MacDonald's city of Yes, I came to believe, was something more than a journey's starting point, the dot on an old map, or the hollow place where two pages meet in the crease of a book. It wasn't even an ending place. I realized that if the city had drifted from MacDonald's hands into my own, it could just as quickly drift away, elsewhere. For myself, it has become a place where stories come and go, unfettered by date or proper names. It is a city that I've seen everywhere and nowhere: a place in MacDonald's imagination that I may or may not have glimpsed in my travels. As much as I'd wanted to discover some *thing*, or some place, I think I've given up on that grand illusion. These days, while I write this journal to Enzo, I'm more interested in the journey than the destination.

In Japan, the city of Yes remains undiscovered or simply abandoned. I've seen no other references to it, nothing beyond the old words of Hokkaido: *Yesso, Yezo,* and sometimes, *Ezo.* If one man's map or foreign dictionary can become another's guide, perhaps the city itself can shift and move, into one person's life, then out. With the proper imagining, perhaps the city can even return. I thought Enzo might agree with that idea, if only so that he could re-imagine his own past and find some of his father's lost memories.

Mid-October, five months before I had abandoned this book to the post office, I received a postcard from Enzo's present day. The back of the card read:

Thank you very much for your book. It was great fun to read the story about me. Not!

I am sorry I didn't write you immediately after I received your letter. I received it at the end of August. I was in Europe with my wife *in August.*

I got married to one of my adult students last June, whose name is Takae, thirty-two years old. She is nineteen years younger than me. Yes! *I am fifty-one now.* Shit! *But I could get married before my death coming. That was lucky, I think, maybe, I hope so, I am not sure . . .*

This is only a short note to tell you that I received your floating book and got married. I will enclose our wedding postcard. You will see the beauty and the beast. Not!

— Bowing twice, your friend,
Enzo

P.T.O. (please turn over)
I should have sent a note to you as soon as possible, I am sorry.

The postcard was actually their wedding-announcement photo. There was Enzo, grinning over a table of white carnations, half-empty beer glasses, wine, champagne, cucumber sashimi, and buns. He was shimmering in a blue tuxedo (with tails). A beautiful woman stood next to him, in front of a gold ceremonial screen. She too was wearing blue, but her gown and hair were alive with swirls and frills. She held five white lilies in one hand. With the other hand, she helped Enzo light a single candle with a long, electronic wand.

Epilogue: Walking Heaven's River

Near a graveyard, on the outskirts of Kumagaya in 1999, a burst of white blossoms lights three plum trees, and the wind gently waves the trees' branches. Just behind the trees there is a scattered forest of concrete telephone poles and several buildings that mark the edge of the city. The poles are unpainted, dull, and seem fixed to the sky. It is February and the sky is clear.

Two people, a man and a small girl, emerge from the concrete thicket and follow the bend in the road toward the swaying trees. There is a statue of a policeman at the corner; he has one hand outstretched to slow the imaginary cars and the frenzy of the next day's traffic. Past this statue and into the graveyard, the man walks, toe-to-heel, along a row of memorials. He is holding his daughter's hand. She is four and he has to lean, slightly, as they walk, so that her arm is not stretched too far from her body. His bottle thick glasses reflect the sun's light, and cast two small stars on the pavement.

They are talking about the day and about a funny man who smokes like a fish.

"Your grandfather," he says, "was a salaryman. From the salt."

Every now and then the girl jumps ahead, trying to step on the bits of light in front of her.

Some acknowledgements and a note on the title

I gave him a short account of some particulars, and made my story
as plausible and consistent as I could; but I thought it necessary to
disguise my country and call myself a Hollander; because my inten-
tions were for Japan . . .

– Jonathan Swift, *Gulliver's Travels*, 1726

This book is fiction. All of the characters are imaginary, except
for Ranald MacDonald and a few of his unsung cohorts. My
interpretation of MacDonald's year in Japan is a combination of
history, myth, and pure speculation.

B.C. Archives, in Victoria, helped me with MacDonald's
papers and correspondence. C.R. Boxer's *The Great Ship from
Amacon* (Lisboa, 1959) gave me some general ideas about the
trading patterns between Macao, Portugal, and Japan. The epigraph on page vii is from *Utz* by Bruce Chatwin (Penguin, 1988).

***

The Imperial decrees on pages 174–75, which effectively erased Japan from the world, were found in the *Encyclopaedia Britannica* (1911 edition). The passage about Com-Comly's skull, found on page 180, was taken from *The Chinook Indians: Traders of the Lower Columbia River* by Robert H. Ruby and John A. Brown (University of Oklahoma Press, 1976). The excerpt from James Dunn's *History of the Oregon Territory* (London, 1844) on pages 179–180, and the extract from *The Seaman's Friend* (1848) on pages 175–76, were found in *Ranald MacDonald: The Narrative of His Life, 1824–1894*, annotated and edited by William S. Lewis and Naojiro Murakami (Oregon Historical Society Press, 1990). Hei Gaten's insect orchestra, "quoted" on page 302, is loosely based on a description of insects found in a 1934 manual for hotel guests, entitled *We Japanese*.

The following copyrighted material is reprinted with permission:

The passage from MacDonald's dictionary on pages 245–46 is from *Japan* by Malcolm Macleod (call number Add. Mss. 1249). The quoted journal entries on pages 314–320 are from *The Journals of Robert Brown* (call number Add. Mss. 0794). These quotes reprinted by permission of the B.C. Archives.

The fragment from "Orchid Flight" on page vii is taken from the poem of the same name by John Minczeski. Copyright © 1983 by John Minczeski. Published in *Yellow Silk*, issue no. 8, 1983. Reprinted by permission of the author.

MacDonald's first vision, "*the bellies of wild geese*," on page 7, comes from a haiku by Kikaku (1661–1707), and is taken from *The Penguin Book of Zen Poetry*, edited and translated by Lucien Stryk and Takashi Ikemoto (London: Allen Lane/Penguin

Books Ltd., 1977). Copyright © 1977 by Lucien Stryk and the estate of Takashi Ikemoto. Reprinted by permission of Lucien Stryk and the estate of Takashi Ikemoto.

Noro Masashi's description of Hashimoto, found on page 97, was translated by Donald Keene in *Travelers of a Hundred Ages* (New York: Henry Holt & Company, 1989). Copyright © 1989 by Donald Keene. Reprinted by permission of the publisher.

The epigraph on page 203 is from *Geisha: The Life, the Voices, the Art* by Jodi Cobb (New York: Alfred A. Knopf, Inc., 1995). Copyright © 1995 by Jodi Cobb. Reprinted by permission of the author.

The translated extract from MacDonald's Nagasaki prison interview on page 251 is from *Ranald MacDonald: The Narrative of His Life, 1824–1894*, annotated and edited by William S. Lewis and Naojiro Murakami (Oregon Historical Society Press, 1990). Copyright © 1990 by Oregon Historical Society Press. Reprinted by permission of the publisher.

The excerpt from "The City of Yes and the City of No" on page 336 is taken from *The Collected Poems, 1952–1990*, edited by Albert C. Todd, with the author and James Ragan (New York: Henry Holt & Company, 1991). Copyright © 1991 by Yevgeny Yevtushenko. Reprinted by permission of the author.

Financial aid from the Alberta Foundation for the Arts is gratefully acknowledged. I would also like to thank the Markin–Flanagan Distinguished Writers Programme at the University of Calgary for giving me time to revise the final pages of this book.

My deep thanks to Ellen Seligman for her editorial prowess. To Jan Geddes for her voiceless cormorants. To Frank Oliva, Thomas Wharton, Richard Harrison, and Takahiro Sawagashira for some early advice and support. To Westwood Creative Artists and the gang at Pages, friends. To William Anselmi for the Napolatano-Fuji myth. To Harry Chase, Paul Cheetham, Aritha van Herk, and Alberto Manguel for too much to list.

And a separate line for Maria.

The title of this book comes from the old name for Hokkaido – *Yesso* – and from the beginning of a poem written by Yevgeny Yevtushenko:

> I am like a train
>   rushing for many years now
> between the city of Yes
>   and the city of No.

I was lucky to meet Yevtushenko during his book tour in Calgary. I'd just come back from Japan and he was en route to Moscow. Over lunch, at a restaurant that shall remain nameless, I asked him about the city of Yes, hoping to learn its mythic location. He answered, "Listen to me: this is true. You cannot even believe the labels that they glue to the outside of Italian bottles. I have many Italian friends. I can tell you: the Italian wine that you buy outside of Italy is from Albania!"

We settled on a bottle of Okanagan red.